C000254796

BURNT OFFERINGS

Danielle Devlin grew up surrounded by stories. After studying for a degree in English Literature and Creative Writing, she won a place on the Future Bookshelf mentoring programme with a story that would later become her debut novel, *Burnt Offerings*. Danielle was a founding member, and senior editor, of *Virtual Zine*, a publication that specialises in amplifying the voices of underrepresented writers. She now lives in County Durham with her daughter, Molly, and a host of four-legged family members.

BURNT OFFERINGS

DANIELLE DEVLIN

Polygon

First published in paperback in Great Britain in 2023 by
Polygon, an imprint of Birlinn Ltd

Birlinn Ltd
West Newington House
10 Newington Road
Edinburgh
EH9 1QS

www.polygonbooks.co.uk

9 8 7 6 5 4 3 2 1

Copyright © Danielle Devlin, 2023

The right of Danielle Devlin to be identified as the author of this work has been asserted in accordance with the Copyright, Designs and Patents Act 1988.

All rights reserved. No part of this publication may be reproduced, stored, or transmitted in any form, or by any means electronic, mechanical or photocopying, recording or otherwise, without the express written permission of the publisher.

ISBN 978 1 84697 616 2
eBook ISBN 978 1 78885 539 6

British Library Cataloguing-in-Publication Data
A catalogue record for this book is available on
request from the British Library.

Typeset in Dante 11.5/15pt by The Foundry, Edinburgh
Printed and bound in Great Britain by Clays Ltd, Elcograf S.p.A.

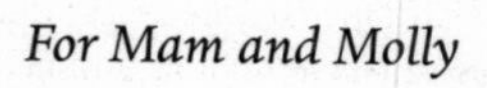

For Mam and Molly

OCTOBER 1589

'Beware; for I am fearless, and therefore powerful.'

MARY SHELLEY

PROLOGUE

The sea boiled.

It boiled and it raged until the rocks wept and the dawn cursed.

The women of North Berwick gathered to thunder against the ferocity of the storm. Shouts and screams drowned out by the furious crashing of waves. Their eyes fell upon the fleet trying to make harbour. The king's ships. Manned by town men. And all the while the sea was trying to swallow them whole.

Marion could think of nothing but her husband as the ships disappeared. Spinning. Turning. Sails cracking like thunder. She clung to her young daughter; all she had left of him. Both sodden with sea-spray and rain, barely able to hold their feet. She had begged him not to leave.

A widow in the blink of an eye.

'Ma' – she grasped at her mother's skirts – 'will Da be home soon?'

'Aye, before you know it.' Marion squeezed her tighter.

'Will he have the doll he promised?'

'He would never break a promise.' The words tripped on her tongue.

Marion tried to shake the image of her husband from her mind, but it stuck like hardened tallow, gripping her heart. She knew her words were true, but it was no longer his promise to keep; now it belonged to the sea.

All around her, mothers, sisters, daughters clutched at

each other, open mouths screaming at the sea. It would not help, for the storm was a wicked mistress who would not be beaten back by man nor beast.

They watched on as the king's ship *The Grace of God* pitched and rolled, battered by waves across deck, slamming into the men and knocking them from their feet. Maybe the men were screaming, shouts drowned out by the sounds of the storm.

* * *

'Lord, help us!' a man cried out on all fours, spewing seawater.

The ship heaved again.

'To yer feet!' the captain called, the weight of his shoulders smacking into the wheel. He snatched at the small doll that almost fell from his top pocket, pushed it further in. 'Get the ropes!'

To set sail on a Friday was ill-omened, the captain knew, but King James would not be dissuaded. His men had been mutinous but had agreed for fear of losing their heads. Who would trust him as captain now? If he survived, he would never captain another ship again. He had angered the sea with his folly.

'Captain, we'll be run aground!' The sea water choked the deck hand.

'On yer feet!' the captain bellowed again. 'This is for our king and queen.' He didn't believe his own words.

The deck hand tried to stand, but as slick as a seal he slipped across deck, and was thrown into the mast. Rendered as limp as a rabbit with a snapped neck.

'Get him below!' the captain roared over the sea. 'The rest of you, hold steady!'

The captain had been in Acheson's when the Dutch fleet had warned them about the reason why their crossing to Copenhagen had been so tempestuous. A half-truth, he'd thought, but the king would not listen. And now, as he was thrown about deck, the captain knew the truth of it. What would it take for the king to believe it? His men dead? His fleet at the bottom of the ocean?

The gulls were tossed paper, flashes of white as they tumbled against the gale.

The captain could see the pools of light flickering about the edge of the cliffs, like will-o'-the-wisps. Would it be his wife there watching? Waiting? With the rest of the women.

A gust of wind pounded the starboard side, sending the ship tipping and spinning off course.

The captain ground his hands to the helm. He had heard the Dutchmen's stories of the limbs they'd tied to dead cats, casting them into the sea to call upon a tempest. He hadn't believed them on his first crossing, but now . . . now there could be no other explanation.

'This is the work of witches.'

Husband of Mine

This is where my story began. Not in the bowels of the Tolbooth or the trial that followed, but here.

Everyone called me Besse, but my name was Elizabeth Craw. I was born a bastard to a dead mother. I never really belonged anywhere, but everyone in Tranent took me for Agnes Sampson's child.

It was a cold day. The last time the villagers had turned out in their droves like this, the sheep were dying. I had been no more than thirteen and Agnes was travelling. It was her that they'd needed, not me. What could I do? They needed a healer. What good was I? Agnes's blood didn't run through my veins. Those sheep died that winter.

On this day, Master Rivet had sent me out with a list of what he wanted from town. It was a small defiance, to sneak out when Rupert had forbidden it, but I'd rather risk his belt than disobey the man we worked for. I had everything I needed in my basket and was hurrying to get home when I stopped, and Jenny stopped beside me. I could already see what was there and it sent a shock to my heart. I put my hand out to block Jenny's view, but it was too late for that. Too late.

From where we stood, we could see nothing beyond

the pool of flickering light as they dragged her from the reeking pit, wide-eyed and smeared with blood.

Another flurry of snow blew against my craning neck. I could almost hear it sizzle as it touched my skin. Sweat trickled into my eyes as we pressed breast to back, vying for a better view. Pinned to the floor with no power over my own feet. I could not move. Like the others, we were drawn to the spectacle like moths to a flame. The smell of their overly ripe bodies clung to the back of my throat, choking me, like meat that had been left out to spoil.

Jenny peered through the ocean of backsides. I gripped her hand tighter and suppressed my gasp as they forced the poor creature through the crowd, towards the stake, its base littered with wood and tinder.

I should have carried on walking and spared Jenny, but what would be the point? There were few soft corners in our lives. Better the truth of what it was to be a woman, than a lie. Be forever on guard. Be forever weary.

The travelling Court Circuit had blown into Tranent like the wind from the Firth of Forth; in a squall of accusation and suspicion. The town's County Bailiff, Master David Rivet, met them at Dirleton Castle and escorted them here. Three days I had been made to witness the town turn on itself. Now, they circled like corvids around carrion, carving up the rest of her possessions.

Through the crowd, her baleful eyes met mine. Cold touched my cheek as the snow fell faster. I looked at her with no more than a passing glance, for fear they would mistake eye contact for familiarity. Suspicion bubbled beneath the surface, like a boil waiting to be lanced.

I knew the story well. We all knew what could happen. Two days before the cattle were to be brought down from their summer pastures, they had all been afflicted with murrain and almost all had died. That night, she had been working in the tavern when one of the Douglas brothers came in to drown his sorrows. She was comely and soft, a fine figure of a woman, not the poor, gaunt wretch that stood before us. His wandering hands had advanced with every ale she'd poured. Any ear within spitting distance had pricked when she'd told him sharply to stop with his lechery. The next morn, he awoke to a face full of pustules, riddled with pox. It almost made me laugh. Were they so stupid that they thought we had the power to summon such things but did not have the power to escape the fate it brought?

The men that had been in the tavern that night had all pointed their accusing fingers at her. It was all the evidence they needed. It was no wonder that the cows had come down with murrain. Did I not have to take care? Being one who understood the lore of herbs. Wasn't I the very one that might be standing there? Me with my witches mark, just below my right breast. She would be the first woman I watched burn.

Heavy ropes now snaked from her foot to her breast. She hung on the stake, as damned as Eve in the Garden of Eden. Above, the air was black with crows as they wheeled and flapped, cawing for their next meal.

A silence settled across the crowd as Master Rivet spoke. 'You have been found guilty of using sorcery, witchcraft and incantations, of invoking spirits of the Devil, of abusing the town of Tranent with the devilish craft of sorcery. You are to be executed today, the twenty-eighth day of October, in the year of our Lord 1589 by burning until death.'

She made no noise beneath the bridle that bound her tongue. Her soft eyes closed and her muscles became languid as the last of her fight ebbed away.

A thin blanket of snow had fallen onto the wood beneath her feet as the man's torch lit the kindling. I looked at Jenny, remembering her in her crib, the way her fingers played in mine, the way her cheek lay hot on my skin. I wished I had the power to give her safe passage through this life, but truth is, it would have taken a real witch to do that. As the fire took hold, it crept towards her chest, engulfing her. I prayed she would suffocate before she felt the flames.

I shrank back, pulling Jenny close. My eyeballs stung from the smoke that billowed skywards. The blaze swallowed her body, which writhed and twisted against the ropes. Her beautiful hand-stitched skirts were no more than ash. The cruelty of such a sight made me retch, forcing the contents of my stomach to the floor.

In the dying embers of the fire, she looked like a charcoal doll. Fragile, as though a gust of wind might cause her to crumble and be carried away on the wings of the crows.

'Did I give you permission to be here?'

Startled, I whipped around to face Rupert. Dressed in his travelling clothes and his black hair scraped neatly back. I should have been pleased at the sight of my husband, but that wasn't what I felt. Whatever we once had, had now turned into something else.

'Master Rivet sent me fir tallow candles and mutton. We just stop—'

'I ordered you tae stay home.'

'I'm sorry, Rupert. I thought Master Rivet had sent you up to Edinburgh. I wasn't expectin' you home fir a few days, so when he asked me to collect th—' I felt Jenny tense.

'He did, but I had more work tae do. I won't be leaving until tomorrow. Seems I've done mysel' a favour, seeing as though my wife is intendin' on whoring herself in my absence.' He pointed a finger towards the pyre. 'Is it him ye've come tae see?'

Shocked, I looked. Thomas Reed. I hadn't seen him in twelve years. Not since the final night of our handfast, when I sent him away.

'No, Rupert . . . No, I would never. It was you I married, please.' I placed a hand on his arm. 'I didn't even ken he was here.'

Thomas had his sleeves rolled up to the elbow, showing his forearms, and his fair hair tumbled loosely about his ears as he cleared away what was left of the burning. A year and a day we had been together. Part of me had been relieved to end it. To know that my heart would not be broken every time he left to fight in another war. My heart did break, but Rupert had been there to pick up those pieces, mending them into something that was never quite whole.

Thomas turned and caught me staring. His face creased into a smile.

'Home. Now. You'll wait fir me there.'

I dropped my head and turned, hiding my face, and

started walking. My heart hammered. Perhaps Rupert hadn't seen me glance at Thomas. I hurried through the crowd, dragging Jenny with me. It wouldn't pay to be late home – I was already in enough trouble.

* * *

I pushed open the door to the cot-house and closed it behind me, abandoning my basket on the table.

'Straight to yer room, Jenny, and don't come out until I say.' I kissed her on the top of the head.

She nodded and disappeared through the doorway.

I set about lighting the fire and was clearing away the clothes that I had left out to dry when I heard the click of the latch.

'What did you think you were doin', deliberately disobeying me?' Rupert growled, swinging his leather belt to and fro. 'Yer my wife – you'll do as yer told.'

'I'm sorry . . .' I said, backing away towards the hearth. 'You ken I only meant tae get what Master Rivet had sent me for. Look . . .' I pointed to the basket on the table between us. 'We only needed tallow candles and mutton, but it was so busy and Jenny wanted tae watch. I had no idea he would be there.' That's when I felt it, just below my belly button.

'So, my daughter thought it fit to disobey me as well? 'Tis a small comfort that she witnessed what comes of being a wayward, foul-mouthed bitch.' He watched me through narrowed eyes, circling me. 'You'll recall what I told you when I left this morning?'

I remembered every word.

'Aye, we weren't tae leave until you returned, but if I hadn't fetched Master Rivet what he'd asked fir, he would have had me flogged!'

'You're *my* wife. You belong to me. Not Rivet.' His face grew dark.

'I'm sorry, Rupert. I promise, I'll never do it again.' I moved, trying to keep the table between us. 'If Master Rivet asks me next time, I'll tell him he must ask you when you return from collecting his rents.'

'Yer right, you'll never do it again.' He edged further around the table. 'When did *he* decide tae make a reappearance?'

'Who?'

'You ken very well who . . . Thomas Reed!' he bellowed.

'I haven't seen him in twelve years. Not once, Rupert. I would never—'

'Disobey me? Oh, I think you proved you would. A good hiding might make you consider yer actions next time. Bring out my child. She can feel the strap first.'

'Rupert . . . Please, it wasnae the bairn's fault. I asked her to come.'

'She needs tae learn there are serious consequences when a daughter disobeys her father.' He flicked the strap. 'Ye've both done me wrong.'

'Please, Rupert, I forced her tae disobey you,' I quavered. 'You cannae blame a child fir her mother's transgressions.' I reached out to touch his hand, trying to make him see sense. 'It's me deserves 'em, not Jenny.'

He watched me closely, toying with what he might do next.

'Have it yer way,' he said finally. 'Kneel and lift yer skirts.'

* * *

Rupert's snores rattled through the rafters. I lay staring at the ceiling. I had brought it on myself. I should have known it would anger him. I should have known better.

He had changed in the year since Master Rivet had him travelling back and forth to France. He had become cold. Distant. Raised his fists more. War could be hard on men. I'd seen it so many times before, but we'd get back what we had. I was sure of it.

Rupert didn't cheat on me, and he didn't drink the way his father had. He liked to gamble, but what man didn't? I'd leave him if he ever went too far. He wasn't like Jonet Muir's husband, beating her half to death. Rupert was only being a good husband, after all, as my actions were a reflection on him. It was his duty to keep me in check.

Every movement made me wince. I was reluctant to get out of bed for fear of waking him.

I had been willing at first and did as I was asked. After the third crack of his belt, I could stand it no more. In the struggle, I kicked over a clay pot and sent a pan of milk skittering across the floor. I'd crawled to bed, too shocked to clean up the mess.

I tentatively manoeuvred myself to the edge of the bed, still wearing yesterday's dress. Hesitating as he stirred, I got to my feet and slipped unnoticed into the kitchen.

The smell of milk on the turn sent my stomach rolling. I tiptoed through shards of splintered clay and milky puddles on the floor to fetch the broom. I couldn't allow Jenny to see the devastation.

I busied myself on all fours picking up the biggest pieces. I hadn't spoken to Rupert since he'd allowed me to bed. Nor did I want to.

''Tis a bit of a mess, aye?'

I stiffened. I could feel him behind me like a wraith.

'It won't take me long to have it all cleaned up.' I gathered the last of the pot together.

'Come here.' He grabbed my hand and pulled me close to his chest, kissing my forehead. 'I'm sorry fir last night. You ken how much I love you and I don't like tae discipline you, but you will insist on disobeying me, forcing me tae take the strap t'you. I dinnae ken what I was so worried about – Thomas Reed wouldnae want a woman who cannae bare him a son.' He raised my chin with his hand and pressed his lips to mine.

He was always sorry. So was I. He never said the words, but I could tell by the look on his face that he knew he'd gone too far. There it was again. A fluttering in my stomach, so faint I almost missed it.

'I'm sorry,' I said. I should never have looked in Thomas's direction, but I faltered at saying the words *I love you*, after such a beating. 'I'll not give you cause tae do it again.' I flushed and turned away, clearing away what was left of the mess.

'No, I promise . . . That was the last time.' He grinned,

showing a glimpse of the man I'd fallen for. 'What do my two ladies have planned today? Chores fir Master Rivet, no doubt?'

I knew the way it could take hold of him. The way the beast rose inside. He tried his best to resist it, but it was a sickness. A sickness even my mother did not have a cure for. There would be no more outbursts now. We would be safe. At least for a while.

'Aye, I have my chores and then I have tae head into town tae meet with Agnes.' I needed to see my mother. I needed to know for sure. My heart couldn't take another bloodied chamber pot.

'I thought we'd agree ye'd have no more to do with yer mother's healing?'

'I promised I willnae help with any healing. I want nothing more to do wi' it, but I cannae deny my own mother.'

The atmosphere changed like the roll of a storm.

'I never asked you tae deny yer own mother. Surely you can see that it will do no good in these times to be associated with healing?' He didn't sound angry, but then, he never did.

'I'm sorry,' I said, knowing he would never believe me. 'I'm only visiting with her and helping with some of her chores.' I got to my feet.

Sometimes, if I looked away – if I carried on normally, kept walking – it would be enough to calm him. I tried to walk past him, but he grabbed me by the arm, nails digging into flesh.

'You think I'm a fool?'

'Rupert, please, you're hurting me.' I could hear the

pitch in my voice rise. 'Rupert, you ken I would never think that of you.'

His grip tightened and he pulled me closer, deciding what to do next.

'Please, you'll wake Jenny,' I said softly, pleadingly.

It was enough. His grip loosened and his arm fell by his side.

I stumbled back. What happened next would depend on me. I thought of the baby that might be growing inside me. I took a deep breath and picked up the pail. 'When is it you leave fir Edinburgh?' I swilled the floor of milk and watched from the corner of my eye as his muscles relaxed.

'As soon as I've finished breakfast. Master Rivet is allowing me to use one of his horses, instead of that old nag of ours.'

My husband never liked to look poor. He had recently taken to wearing the finest of clothes, French from the cut of them. He always said there was no point in a man looking poor and being poor, he needed to dress as the man he intended to be. It was a costume to him, like that of a jester but he knew of no acrobatics or juggling. My husband's greatest trick was to make women fall in love with him and the monster beneath the finery.

I stopped and hurried to the fire to put on some eggs. It wouldn't do to leave my husband hungry. He would be quick to anger again, so soon after the trouble I'd already caused. He came behind me and slipped a hand around my shoulders, his breath tickling my ear. 'Will you keep the bed warm fir my return?' He patted my behind.

I winced. 'Aye, I'll be waitin' fir you.'

'I'll make sure tae bring you a gift from Edinburgh?' He

slipped his fingers over mine, stroking them with a touch like a feather. 'A beautiful ring, fir my beautiful wife.'

Another trinket to go in the mausoleum of gifts that I'd never wear.

The last time we had gone through this whole to-do, almost a month ago, it had been over the nanny goat getting loose. Jenny had left the gate open. Rupert was right. I should have gone back and checked, but I was so tired from the chores. I had been so lazy.

'Almost cost us the goat. I dinnae have money tae be replacin' livestock,' he'd said.

It was funny, I thought, he always seemed to have money to gamble.

'No harm done. The nanny is back safe and sound,' I'd said as I cleared away supper. 'She's only a wee girl.'

'As her mother, it was yer duty tae make sure she'd done her chores.'

'As her father, you could have checked it on yer way home.'

Right there. Every time. I brought it on myself.

He never punched me. Nothing so crude as to leave bruises for my mother to see.

The next morning, I'd walked into the kitchen to find him whistling cheerfully and making breakfast. He glanced at me and smiled, as though everything was normal. Were we normal?

He always knew just what to say. Just like today.

I turned and kissed him.

Deadly Nightshade

I need to leave him.

Sometimes the thought came so suddenly, it felt like a jolt of lightening. I needed to take Jenny and get as far away from him as possible. One day, while he was away collecting rents. He would come home to find us gone.

But I had forsaken all others. To love, honour and obey, for better or worse, as long as we both shall live. My life was to be one of obedience and duty. It was not a woman's place to leave her husband.

Today the thought came as I cleared away the flour and scrubbed the table, to rid it of the smell of yeast. I'd left the day's bread cooling on the sill. I needed to finish my chores for Master Rivet and tend the goats and prepare for Rupert's return. He'd be home by supper.

'Come now, Jenny. I haven't got long,' I called. 'I have the pigs to tend to and I must go into town and fetch the apothecary fir Master Rivet; he's feeling under the weather.'

She trundled through like a goose, dragging her feet all the way.

'But, Ma, why do I have tae go?'

'You heard yer father; we mustn't disobey him or Master Rivet. Hurry now and get yer cloak on.'

I knew Jenny would have rather been out with Willy and the other boys, but if I allowed it and Rupert found out, neither of us would be able to sit in a saddle for a week. I picked up the basket and headed out of the door, letting the latch click behind us.

We walked into town, the long way, past bare, weed-filled patches and lazy oxen. Coming towards us were three women, each of their faces looking as worn as their dresses. The first carried spinning and mending, and the others trotted behind, all of them farm servants from the neighbouring cot-house.

'Good morning,' I said, as they passed.

The first woman scowled at us, and the other two turned aside, tittering.

We carried on walking past the small church and its empty graveyard. I touched a finger instinctively to the rosary hidden beneath my clothes, a crime that could see me banished from Scotland. Since the Reformation, the churches had become like mausoleums. Inside, they had taken all the paintings down, leaving sombre walls, visited only on a Sunday.

It came again. A tiny quiver, faint and soft as anything. Reminding me it was there. *I'm here, Mother*, it whispered.

We followed the weathered track as it twisted through thinning trees, emerging near the entrance to the apothecary. A small and very precise queue had formed. We fell in line and waited to be allowed inside.

There was a shift in the air, a murmur that rippled amongst us, causing all our heads to turn.

'Who is it?' Jenny asked.

'A young woman,' I whispered.

'Harlot,' hissed another.

The lady's presence sailed past us and was escorted over the threshold, missing the queue. A woman like that wouldn't need to go shopping, she could have sent a maid. Probably taking a walk to the apothecary to fill her time while her husband was out hunting. Rich women were allowed their whims; the poor simply had to humour them.

Jenny and I reached the doorway and were permitted inside.

'I'm here tae fetch the order fir the Rivet house, and he'd very much appreciate it if the apothecary could attend. Master Rivet is feelin' very much under the weather.' I handed over a small slip of paper to the woman with the pinched face, who regarded me coolly.

The corners of the lady's mouth cracked into a smirk as she glanced down at the shopping they were placing in her basket, enjoying every minute of their attentions.

I felt uneasy. Jealous, even. The apothecary was expensive, something I could ill afford. I felt around inside my pocket, gripping on to the only two shillings I had left.

'Ach, I'm sorry, Besse,' said the woman, passing judgement from behind her counter. 'We're goin' tae need Master Rivet tae settle the bill before I can let you take it.'

I felt my face flush.

'Rupert must have forgotten to pay it,' I flustered. 'How much did you say it was again?'

I could feel Jenny tugging at my dress.

'It's three shillings.' She tapped her fingers impatiently on the counter.

I felt around for my purse, to keep up the pretence.

'I only have a shilling with me.' I handed her the coin. 'I'll get Rupert to drop the rest in?'

'I cannae, Besse, I'm sorry.'

'We've been good customers all these years.' I tried to sound indignant, but I only managed to sound ashamed.

'I'll settle the bill,' the voice behind me said.

'No, please, I'll no' hear of it. I'll just run home and get the rest from Master Rivet.'

'Please, allow me.' Her voice was thick like velvet, with a hint of French about it. 'Three shillings, did you say?'

Now, as I looked at her, I could see how much she glowed. Pregnant, maybe six months. She slipped off her glove and counted out the coins. Married to a gentleman, no doubt. A man who wouldn't lay his hands on her; she'd see her baby grow. I placed my hand instinctively over my stomach.

'No, mistress, I couldn't accept it. My husband will be home this afternoon to settle the account.'

She took a hand in mine. 'I have more than I need. I'm only here a short while. My poor husband has been travelling between Scotland and our home in France for almost twelve months. This is my first and only visit to your beautiful country. My husband has the last of his affairs to settle and make arrangements for his young child, and then we return to France, as a family, permanently. Please, take it as a gift.'

I studied her. Mibbe her husband was a little like mine, after all? Absent most of the time. But a gentleman, at least, who would settle his affairs to be with her. To be with his family. Rupert had always been good at that, letting a woman know just what he thought she should hear. Just enough bait to snare her, to keep her on the hook wriggling and squirming until he showed her who he really was. Showed me who he really was. I handed back the parcel, wrapped in paper, to the woman behind the counter.

'No, I won't hear of it, but thank you all the same.'

I hurried outside, moving as fast as my thoughts; past the same queue, my mind turning as to what conjuration I could give Master Rivet, disguised as an apothecary remedy. As if in answer, out of the corner of my eye, I caught a movement.

'Besse.' A voice fluttered by my ear.

I whipped around to be met by Jonet Muir. A small, round woman of around fifty. Her neat, fair hair was covered by her cream shawl, but it couldn't disguise her sunken eyes and haggard expression.

'I've been trying to find Agnes, but I've been up to Leaplish and there's no sign of her.'

If my mother had been home, she would be found at the bottom of the garden, beneath the curves of the bare trees which coiled into the entrance to the forest. Never still, flitting around like the bees she tended and from spring she'd be tending her herbs, collecting plants and trimming stems to make curious tinctures. My mother had a certain ill fame among the people of Tranent. If she wasn't in her garden, then the only explanation was that she was travelling.

The faint tremble in my stomach reminded me of the urgency of needing to visit her.

'What is it that you were wantin', Jonet?' As if I wasn't

in enough trouble with Rupert: I promised him I'd have nothing to do with my mother's healing. 'She's travelling.'

A look of horror passed across her face.

'I . . . I . . .' she stuttered, unsure of how to go on. 'It was something fir my husband.'

As she said it, I knew. The whole village did. My mother could say what she liked about Rupert, but he'd never broken a bone. He didn't cheat. He didn't drink. Not in the way Jonet's husband did. Rupert was no monster. He could lose all our earnings on two flies climbing up a wall, but show me a man that didn't like to gamble?

'Is there something I can do?'

She pressed her lips into a thin line and shook her head.

'What is it you were after?' I said, careful of who was listening.

'He comes to me at night, his fists full of drunken rage. Yer mother said she'd help. She had something tae help him sleep. Something to stop him.'

I stiffened. There was only one herb that could do that. Belladonna. Just enough to make him sleep, before he got good and drunk. Something to take the edge off his fists. What had my mother gotten herself into?

'Jenny, will you just run back up to the apothecary.' I fished around inside my basket. 'I seem to have left my purse on the counter, hurry now.'

I watched as she disappeared into the thinning crowd.

'Are you sure that's what she said?' I hissed. 'Do you understand what it is yer askin'?'

She nodded, her eyes rimmed red. 'Today is his birthday, and he's been out drinking since sun-up.' She shook her head in desperation. 'I cannae . . .' Her shoulders sagged.

'I can get it, but not here.'

Not twelve hours had passed since I'd taken a beating for disobeying my husband, yet here I was again. Master Rivet was unwell, and I was meant to be finding someone to help. What did I think I was doing meddling in affairs I knew nothing about?

'I can pay you what I was going tae give yer mother?'

Jenny appeared at my side, like a lost lamb, tugging at my shirt sleeves. 'Ma, they—'

'Just a second, Jenny. Pay me only what you can, Jonet. I'll not see you without.'

'Ach, Besse, yer Agnes's daughter alright,' said Jonet.

If she gave me enough, I could pay what we owed at the apothecary.

'Aye, so they keep telling me.' At least Rupert wasn't in earshot. 'I have tae prepare dinner for Master Rivet before I can steal away. Meet me in the usual place. I'll fetch what you asked for.'

She disappeared into the crowd, and I turned to Jenny. 'What is it, lass?'

'Ma, the woman at the apothecary said you didnae leave yer coin purse there, said you must be mistaken.' She twisted her skirt between her fingers.

'I'm sorry, my wee one, I shouted after you, but you were already gone. It was in the bottom of my basket, after all. No harm done.'

Her face split into a twinkling smile. I placed a hand on hers. 'Come now' – I tugged at her small wrist – 'the mutton isn't going tae stew itself and you have mending that needs finishing.'

'Never mind the mutton,' came the voice of Allison

Balfour, standing with a group of women, like a coven. 'How is that lovely husband of yers? I haven't seen him around in a wee while.' Her nose turned up in the air.

'Aye, what's he up to these days?' said Isobel Gowdie, smooth as butter.

My neighbours had always taken to Rupert.

'Ach, he's just fine.' I waved a hand. 'He's out collecting again.'

'Oh, aye, always was a good boy, even when he was wee and the bailiff took him in,' said Marioun Lowrie her eye on Jenny. 'Isn't it about time you had another one, Besse? Add tae yer brood? I'm sure Master Rivet would enjoy havin' more children about the place, bein' as he has no granbairns of his own.'

The shock of her saying it hitched my breath. 'One day, mibbe, aye.' I forced the words out, the lie hanging thick on my tongue. Was I with child already? 'But, what with Rupert always away . . .'

'Speakin' o' that, have you seen Agnes? Only that husband of mine, well, he requires her services.'

As Jeane said it, I knew what kind of salve she was referring to – the whole town knew – and it was something far beyond my knowledge.

'Jonet, I dinnae want tae hear of yer husband's private parts again,' said Marioun. 'Every time you mention it, I feel my breakfast tryin' tae revisit me.'

'You ken my mother is a law unto herself,' I said. 'I cannae say fir definite but Rupert, I'm expecting him back this evening.'

Just the mention of Rupert being home would be

enough to discourage any unwanted knocks on my door in my mother's absence.

'Showering you with wonderful gifts, no doubt, when he returns,' Marioun said with a click of her tongue. 'I wish my husband thought as much of me.'

I smiled, casting my eyes to the ground before walking away.

* * *

For a moment, I had thought he might return early as a surprise, arms laden with gifts of sorrow, and put his arms around me and plant soft kisses on my cheek, promising that he will never raise his hands to me again.

He wouldn't. That was not my husband. He would bring a small trinket of his own choosing and I was to be eternally grateful. I had been born with no gifts, like my mother. The only gift I had been cursed with was to know my husband to the bone and be powerless to do anything about it.

Before I could steal away, I left him warm supper and a whisky. The last time I had been called away at such a late hour, I had left the table bare. I returned near dawn, tired and slick with rain. I hadn't seen him in the shadows. Waiting. I peeled off my wet things and warmed myself in the last glow of the fire beneath the hook cradling the pot that I'd been using to make candles.

I'd bent forward, picking at my skirts and shawl. As quick as a fox, he was on me. His hand coming up fast and connecting with my ribs. Before I could feel the pain, he had spun me by the elbow to face the fire. Streaks of red and orange flashed in my eyeline before the burning, throbbing pain across my ankles as they were struck with the pan from the hearth, spilling molten tallow over my stockings.

'That'll teach you to leave yer husband without a warm meal,' he'd said as calmly as though he were passing the time. 'Where's my supper?'

Tears had sprung from my eyes as I pulled together scratchings of cheese, piece of torn bread and the last of the gannet I'd salted. I'd tried to disguise my limp, but every time I moved my foot, I could feel the cloth tugging at my flesh.

His eyes passed over my offering.

'A good wife would never leave her husband without his supper.'

When I'd finally taken off my stockings, the top layer of skin had gone with them. Leaving an oozing redness that I'd spend weeks smearing with honey. The scars, though fading, were a constant reminder.

'Jenny,' I called as I covered my hair with my plaid. She trotted over obediently. 'I've left yer father's supper on the table. Now, he'll be tired from travelling, so you must stay well clear of him, you hear? And when he asks where I am, you tell him I've gone to tend Master Rivet in his sickness.'

She nodded and went back to the remains of the game she had been playing with the old farm cat, black as ink, who, more often than not, had become a master at avoiding her.

Letting the latch click behind me, I walked to the edge of our small patch of land. A candle burned brightly in Master Rivet's bedroom; he'd be pacing the floor, no doubt. I'd tend him in the morning. My shadow passed quickly beneath the sill and disappeared behind the tree-line. I had walked this journey a thousand times in the daylight, but tonight, knowing the lies I'd told, it seemed so much darker. It was strange how something so familiar could become so unknown in the darkness.

When the noise came drifting through the trees, it was as if the world had stopped. I could hear my own breath. In out. In out. A rhythm that shuddered against the cold, spiralling from my mouth like smoke, hanging in the air. Did I hear footsteps? I stopped and listened, holding my breath. Nothing.

The fear awoke something in me, so primal that my body felt as though it was about to burst from its skin. My heart beat in my ears. Thump. Thump. Thump. Then I heard it, behind me, leaves crunching beneath a heavy foot. I quickened my pace without looking around. It matched mine stride for stride.

The trees were sparse, but there was no way through. One way in. One way out. The watermill loomed before me, if I could only get behind it. I kept walking, faster now; feet and skirts catching on the undergrowth. I glanced over my shoulder, but the figure melted into the blackness. It was closer now, so close I could almost smell it.

Almost there. I could feel the sanctity of the watermill. Almost. But not quite. An ice-cold hand reached out and seized my shoulder. I stifled a scream as my breath was forced from my lungs.

'Besse,' a voice whispered. 'Have you got it?'

My body sagged at the relief of hearing Jonet's voice

and seeing her squat frame. The moonlight hinted at a smoky bruise above her eye socket, and fresh blood oozed from a cut to her cheekbone.

'You almost scairt me half tae death! Sneakin' up on people like that.' Beneath my hand I could feel my heart almost dancing from my chest.

'I didn't think.'

'I see he's been using you as his punching bag again.' Rupert never beat me like that.

'Do you have it, then?'

'Aye, I have it in my apron.' Her eyes darted to the gap she'd come through. 'It's all I have.' She crossed my palm with three shillings.

I had learned as a child, hiding in the darkness of Agnes's kitchen, that a desperate woman would pay any price. Once someone made the decision to come to her door, they were ready to do whatever she told them; to use tinctures made from ingredients she would never speak of. They would be happy to hand over trinkets that had been in their family for generations. And the ones that had been wronged . . . they would pay even more.

'Here it is.' I put my hand on hers. 'Now, you need to make sure that you dinnae put too much in.' I slipped the parcel into her hand. I had given her enough for a few nights, to tide her over until my mother returned. 'Just enough tae make him sleep.' I motioned an amount the size of a farthing in my palm.

I only hoped I had given her the right amount. Agnes had the knowledge from her mother, old knowledge that had been passed through their generations. Books required a woman to know how to read, and that wasn't a luxury most Sampson women had. So, she carried it around in her head. Agnes Sampson's face would be the first and the last thing you'd ever see.

'Will that be enough?' She stared at it, mouth agape. 'He's a big man.'

'It's a potent herb,' I said. Not utterly convinced.

'What shall I do with it?'

On those murky evenings, when I watched in the darkness, Agnes would make a brew, letting the belladonna boil.

'Hang it in a pot,' I said, with a confidence I didn't possess. 'Over the fire with just enough water to cover it. When it boils, let it cool and mix it in his whisky. You must be swift in getting him tae bed – he'll sleep like he's dead.'

'I'll be sure of it.' She squeezed my hand and turned, sailing away into the darkness.

I stood there a wee while, hiding behind the watermill, putting a good distance between me and Jonet. Being seen together would arouse too much suspicion.

It was here, on the edge of the wood, that I used to meet Thomas Reed. The memory caught and swarmed like my mother's bees, vibrating and humming as it came to life. I'd steal away at dusk, my red hair plaited down to my waist, still with a sprinkling of hay, and my bodice laced tight to accompany my best homespun skirt.

He used to tell me that I'd come from the forest; that the travellers had left me by the clootie well, where Agnes first found me, beneath a tangle of brambles and knots of cloth. He said that my milk-white skin and tawny eyes were the thing of fairies and, for the gift of that, Agnes must have paid a heavy price.

Whatever the truth of my beginning, I didn't want my ending to be behind this watermill, mistaken for some pedlar or, worse still, a harlot. I set off, wrapping my plaid around me and hugged my elbows. I couldn't wait around all night.

The snow had soon turned to rain, and now the fog was as thick as potage as I scrambled up the embankment, finally emerging from the trees scratched and dirty. Still, a fair trade to avoid the notice of Master Rivet. He wouldn't take kindly to his maid's gallivanting all over the countryside when there were chores to be done. Neither would my husband.

I pushed open the door quietly; the draught caused the candle to flicker. Jenny lay on her back in front of the dying fire, her hands folded across her stomach. I watched her a while, the soft rise and fall of her chest, black curls falling about her ears as she stirred.

She looked so much like her father. The same heart-shaped face. Same hazel eyes. When she was wee, I would spend hours just gazing at her, wondering. I was always so fearful that she would inherit her father's black humour, that she'd be quick to temper and slow to quiet. It would roll upon his face like a storm. But never hers.

Something didn't feel right. The air buzzed with a charge that made the hairs on the back of my neck stand on end. I could hear nothing over the throbbing of my pulse. It felt like an unpicked hem slowly unravelling, about to leave a gaping hole. I felt uneasy.

'Rupert?' I called softly, but there was no reply. His chair sat ominously empty, along with the bowl of supper I'd left.

I brushed the dead leaves from my skirts, held my breath and listened. Nothing. The silence seemed to echo around the rest of the house. It wasn't like him not to have returned. Where could he have gotten to at such a late hour?

'Jenny.' My gaze settled on her. Her eye lids flickered for only a moment and then closed again. 'I'm sleeping,' she muttered as she rolled over. She'd kicked off her shoes, which lay by the door. The old, inky black cat unfurled himself from her strewn stockings, mewing hungrily as he leapt to the tabletop, wanting to skim the cream from the goat's milk.

'You can only have a little.' I ladled a small amount onto a dish, which he lapped greedily. 'You ken you should leave this place' – I rubbed behind his ear – 'and find yerself a new home, Ratbag, before the next one comes along,' and patted my stomach.

I hung the rest of the milk on to boil. Taking a seat on the crackett I used for milking the goats, I began poking the fire, breaking apart the embers to encourage a flame. In what little light I had, with eyes that stung from the smoke and lids heavy with tiredness, I counted the stitches on the stockings I was knitting for Jenny. Mibbe it wouldn't be long before I'd be knitting for another wee one?

Eventually, as the shadows crawled across the stone and a thin crust flickered over the glowing ashes, I decided to make my way to bed. Rupert still hadn't returned. I finished the last of my milk, placed an arm beneath Jenny and scooped her tiny frame onto the pallet that sat at the side of our bed. The dampness weighed heavy against my legs, but I hadn't the energy to take off my skirts. As I lay down wearily beside her, the edge of her lip curled into a smile, just as it had when she was a wee bairn.

When the knock came, pounding, the sky was passing into sunrise. Rupert's side of the bed lay cold and untouched. I didn't stop to think. I grabbed Rupert's dirk from the top of the inglenook, sliding it onto the top of my skirts. I flung open the door to be greeted by Jonet Muir.

She was wrapped in what might have once been a cream shawl. Filthy and beaten. Her bare feet were pink with cold and covered in dirt. I hurried her in, sitting her on the crackett while I searched for my flint and tinderbox to light the fire.

'He's dead,' she said, putting her hands over her face.

'Who is?'

'Andrew,' she wailed.

'No, he cannae be. You must be mistaken.' I could feel my heart kicking in my chest. 'He'll just be sleeping. Did I no' warn you that he'd sleep deeply?'

'He's dead.' She sniffed, stifling a sob. 'He had a pallor the colour of my mother's when I went to wash and lay her out ready for burial.'

I stiffened. Her mother had been dead almost two days when they'd found her.

'Was he breathing?' I said, keeping my voice steady.

'No,' she moaned. 'I gave him it, just as you showed me, but he has an awful tremor and sent it spilling down his shirt. Asked me to fill it up again, so I did, like you showed me.'

'Again? Did you no' ken how much you were givin' him? I gave you enough tae fell a horse!'

'Will he haunt me, Besse?' Her shoulders shook with the force of her sobs. 'Am I going tae Hell?'

'No.' I wrapped an arm around her. 'No, he was a wicked man. He willnae haunt you. You just need tae call upon Father Cowper and have him tended tae.'

'He's lying in the garden.'

'The garden! Why was he no' in bed?'

'He . . . He just—'

'Shhh . . . shhh . . . He won't have felt a thing. But we cannae be leavin' him on the step like that.'

'Ma?'

Startled, I turned to find Jenny in the doorway rubbing her eyes.

'Ma? Why is Jonet here?'

I rushed over, ushering her back to bed. 'She got a bit of a fright, is all. Seeing such a terrible sight on her way into town. A snarling black dog appeared to her, blocking her path. Poor Jonet fled through the trees and saw our candle burning.'

Jenny edged around me, eyes wide with fear and fixed on the door.

'Did it follow her here, Ma?' she whispered.

'No, there isnae a beast alive brave enough to face Ratbag. It fled to the trees, tail between its legs.' Just as I said it, Ratbag meandered around the corner, head cocked, listening. 'I have to see Jonet home safe. While I'm gone, I think you should give him a wee smattering of milk, as thanks. What do you think?'

She nodded and the cat seemed agreeable, although he found her intolerable. He'd drink the dish dry and be out before sun-up, amongst the outhouses lusting after mice.

I glanced back at Jonet, who was quietly sobbing.

'Now, Da still isnae home, so you mustn't open the door until I return.'

Jenny nodded diligently, her attention on the cat as he coiled and rolled around the floor. She padded to the fire, with a stocking trailing behind her, and curled her bare feet beneath her.

'I'll be as quick as anything. You won't even miss me.'

I'd warned her not to go near her father if he was in one of his rages; I could only hope she'd heed my words. If he returned while I was gone, there would be no telling what he would do.

* * *

It was a short journey to Dunlollie. The house stood by itself, some distance from the road. Sparse, spindling trees lined the walkway, allowing only traces of sunlight to warm the frost.

Andrew Muir looked more peaceful in death than he had in life. He had fallen on his back in the frozen grass with an arm thrown over his eyes. Beneath the arm I could make out part of a clean-shaven jaw marked by skin yellowed and weathered from the sun. The shirt he wore had seen better days, hanging loosely over his massive chest and thick neck, tucked slovenly into his narrow breeches.

'You get his feet,' I said, pulling my skirts up around my knees and bending to the floor. 'We'll turn him over and try to get him into bed before you fetch Father Cowper.'

Somewhere in the distance a dog barked, a frantic,

guttural sound that drifted through the dawn. I slid my arms beneath his, bracing his weight against my chest. He was a great hulk of a man. Jonet began to shuffle backwards slowly, easing first one foot and then the other over the step and through the door. My arms burned as the weight became heavier and heavier, until I could stand it no longer. The bastard would have to stay in the hallway.

Jonet stumbled, jerking me forwards and causing his body to slip from my grasp, sending it flailing to the floor like a landed catch. A noise, like a rush of air was forced from his lungs. Jonet and I exchanged glances as her face drained to the colour of ash.

'Andrew? Andrew? Are you alright?' she said.

An incoherent groan came from the heaving mass on the floor.

'Mary, mother of God!' I hissed. 'I told you he wasnae dead! Did you no' check he was breathin'?'

'When you come upon yer husband sprawled on the floor in the dirt, when you ken very well yer the one that put him there, you dinnae wait around to ask questions,' she whispered. 'Look at the colour of him.'

She was right. He looked like a piece of battered tanners' leather, with eyes as cloudy as pearls. He began to move but wasn't fully in control. He reminded me of the foals on the farm; all legs and no sense.

'Get hold of him.' I slipped beneath his thrashing arm. 'We need to get him up the stairs.'

She fell in at the other side, taking half of the weight. The leaving of him would be worse than the carrying. He lolled between us, head swinging about his chest. By the time we reached the landing, we were sweating with the effort of keeping him upright.

'I dinnae want to go to gaol,' she said.

'Gaol will be the least of yer worries if this bastard wakes and realises what we did tae him.' I had to keep her in check; we needed to deal with the job in hand. 'Don't think about it,' I said, urgent and low. 'Think about nothing other than getting him into that bed of yers.'

'This way.' She guided us through the house, silent but for our shuffling as we carried our burden across the landing. She pushed open the door with her foot, revealing a room as dark as a cave, with no fire in its hearth. The dawn light dusted an outline around the bed, and we fumbled our way towards it, letting him sag against its softness.

'There' – I lifted his feet, swivelling his torso until he lay on his side, curled like a small child – 'let him sleep.'

We crept across the room, avoiding creaking floorboards and squeaking doors. Andrew Muir still slumbered on, snoring lightly. Our shadows passed down the stairs as we hurried into the hallway. Jonet lit a candle and opened the door to the parlour chamber. In the dim light of the candle, and with no hint of a fire in the grate, the low-hung ceiling made it feel even more dreary. The coldness of it chilled me to the bone. The furniture was sparse but included a sideboard – such a pretty thing, made of oak – and upon it, next to Muir's ledger, sat a decanter full of whisky and two pewter cups.

'Get one of these down you.' I poured a dram for mysel' and one for Jonet. 'When he wakes, you tell him that he came home drunk as a mule and fell in the garden, which is why he's covered in mud and smells of his own pish. You tell him that you helped him to bed, and you scold him about the mess of the sheets.'

Jonet silently agreed, blue eyes meeting mine over the rim of the cup.

'He must never know I was here, you understand? You must get rid of any deadly nightshade you have left, or it won't be gaol we'll have tae worry about, it'll be a stake.'

She watched me intently. Eyes rimmed with the red of tears and saddled with heavy flesh from lack of sleep. 'Then you'd best not be here when he wakes,' she said.

A Visit from My Mother

The sun rose softly, in blemishes of pinks and golds, filtered through a wall of pines. I waded my way through the soggy autumn undergrowth, my innards warm from drink. When I was wee, Agnes would take me to the edge of the wood, and we'd disappear for hours, getting lost in bare feet against thick moss, even on the coldest of days. Now, I could find my way home with my eyes shut and my feet bound. And I was still as surefooted as ever when I moved through the woods, picking up snails that hitched rides on the hem of my skirts.

Our cot-house sat between Master Rivet's house and the edge of the forest. Master Rivet was an old widower. He had made his money trading in cloth and wool, buying up land and other houses from Tranent and up as far as North Berwick and even Edinburgh.

We'd rented from him all our married life, a little space consisting of a kitchen, bedroom, pantry, hen house and use of a pigsty. It wasn't the most palatial of dwellings but convenient for what we needed, and Rupert could earn a tidy living while I worked as a maid in the household.

A raven edged sideways along the gable and, while fixing me with an inky stare, greeted me with a low, threatening rasp.

The house was in darkness when I pushed open the door. There was no welcoming fire, and the candlewick swam in a puddle of wax. Despite the kitchen's small size and low ceilings, we had wedged an enormous table in its centre, and Rupert's untouched supper still sat uneasily on it. My stomach rolled like a wave crashing. He still hadn't returned. But there, in his seat, sat Jenny, waiting to be fed.

'Ach, I see you're waiting tae have yer belly filled.' My eyes flickered around the room, and I got the fire going, put some water on to boil. 'No sign of yer da?' I said, trying my best not to sound worried but my heart felt heavy at the thought of what he might have stolen this time. My husband, the magpie.

I had never believed it possible to foretell futures, even when my mother told me of misfortunes to come, but today I was blanketed in a sense of dread that crept over me from my toes to my crown.

'No, Ma. It's just been me and Ratbag since you left,' she said, stroking the cat, who turned and gave me a yellow-eyed, malevolent stare and purred. 'I think he's starting to come around to me. He slept by my side all night.'

'I'd say it's more likely that you had some remnants of last night's stew on yer shirt.' I put the pot on the fire.

Jenny glanced down and, licking a thumb, rubbed at the dirty mark that stained her shirt. How could she not feel it? The hairs on my arms felt as though they were giving off tiny sparks, and there she was without a care in the world. Without so much as a warning, tears rolled down my cheeks and I felt a gnawing to be home at Leaplish with my mother.

'Willy says that he's found a tree we still havenae climbed.' Jenny beamed at me as I placed a bowl of potage in front of her. Ratbag looked up incredulously from his empty bowl.

'There cannae be a tree ye've missed in that orchard?'

Her forehead wrinkled. 'Aye, there is. He says it's an oak, up near Master Rivet's field where he keeps the sheep.'

'Yer taking up sheep worryin' now, aye? You ken how much trouble we'll be in if you get caught?'

She looked at me with anxious eyes and chewed at the corner of her mouth.

I bent forward and whispered in her ear. 'The secret is . . . Don't. Get. Caught.'

She fell about in knots, laughing, eyes glinting like a wee imp.

'While yer ducking from Master Rivet's gaze, I don't suppose ye'd see if there's any apples lyin' around fir the pigs?'

'Aye, I will, Ma.' She took a gulp of the potage and pulled off a heel of bread. 'There's bound tae still be some on the ground that isnae too rotten.'

'Only what you ca—'

Trouble always entered unannounced, and it usually followed my mother.

The door flung open. Agnes Sampson breezed in with an air of drama to rival no other, limping on her wooden crutch, resembling a clay pot that's been broken and mended badly. She was stalwart and sturdy, and seas parted when she arrived, as if she were the prow of a ship.

She had the kind of beauty that should only be admired from afar, because of her terrible squint and cheeks like the folds of a curtain.

Jenny stared, mouth agape, with the breakfast contents threatening to spill out.

'Jenny!'

Her mouth banged shut like a clam.

Her grandmother took up the seat closest to her, leaning her crutch up against the table and settling herself. Ratbag, always the happiest to see her, sidled up, purring expectantly in the hope she'd have remnants of breakfast kippers on her apron.

'Well now, hen,' she said, perching one cheek of her ample behind uncomfortably on the chair. 'What is it my granddaughter has planned today?'

Jenny stuffed her mouth with a piece of bread and extricated herself, skulking to the door before glancing over her shoulder and waving a hasty goodbye.

'You be careful!' I shouted after her. 'Make sure tae be home before it's too dark.'

'Oh aye, nice tae see you, Grandmother! We must do this again,' Agnes said.

'You ken she's been . . . uncomfortable around you since you lost yer leg.'

'Well, it's not as though I can stick the bugger back on. She's just going tae have to get used tae it.' She waited until Jenny was out of earshot and then a broad smile danced across her face. 'You'll never guess who's dead?'

'Who?' My stomach tightened.

'Andrew Muir!'

'What? Dead?' I said, trying to stop my fingers trembling.

The man had been very much alive as I'd hoisted him into his bed.

'As a doornail,' she carried on. 'They say he passed on the privy! Well, what a way tae go, yer breeches round yer ankles. It's terrible. Disgustin'.' She pulled a small piece of bread from the day-old loaf on the table.

He couldn't be dead. What would my mother say if she found out I'd given Jonet the belladonna. My heart kicked in my chest. 'What is? What's disgusting?' I fixed my gaze on the fire.

'Leavin' yer poor wife like that. She very old?'

'Sixty. I don't think he—'

'Fifty? There's old Master Grierson over in Humbie, he'd be a good 'un. She's going tae need someone tae take care of her now her husband's gone, she's not like you and me. That husband ay hers wouldnae let her work after they was wed.' She dipped her bread into Jenny's left-over potage. 'We makes a good livin' from helpin' folk.'

'I don't think th—'

'Did you tend him?'

'Not me.' I picked up a grimy cloth and put it in the pot of water already on the boil. 'Did someone take a sprig of rosemary up for Jonet?'

'Aye.'

'Did you see Jonet?'

'Aye, ah did. All snotters and tears, she was. It'll be hot in Hell, where that old bastard's going. If you're not goin tae eat those crusts, I'll 'ave 'em.'

'Master Rivet will hear you!'

'Am I no' allowed bread now?'

'Ach, no' the bread, I mean about Muir.'

'It's no secret that he used tae beat her more than that stallion of his.'

'Aye, that may be so, but you dinnae ken who'll be listening, and ye've got a mouth as big as the Tweed.'

'She always looks like she's been ridden tae Hell and back, that poor woman. She wasnae always that way.'

'Well, he cannae hurt her anymore,' I said.

'I'd like tae bet there's more than one woman glad tae see the back of him, ken?'

'Aye, tae be sure.' I stoked the fire.

'Any sign of that feckless husband o' yers?'

'Please, Ma, you know I dinnae like it when you call him that.'

'You should have married the other one; I liked him.' She poked around in the bottom of Jenny's bowl, chewing and clacking on the bread. 'I still dinnae understand why you insisted on marryin' that eejit.'

'You kent very well, he came from good kin and was well respected.'

'Aye, and look where you are now . . . A husband who beats you, and yer havin' tae make a living with me as a healer, the very job you wed him to avoid.'

'Don't tell such lies. He only lays his hands on me when I've caused him trouble. A good husband disciplines his wife. I may not always agree wi' it, but it is what it is.'

'Only tae discipline you, aye?' She snatched my arm and pulled up my sleeve, revealing the yellow wisps of faded fingermarks around my wrist. 'And what of these?'

'It was my own fault.' I pulled at the hem of my sleeve, covering my wrist back up. 'Somethin' and nothing. He won't do it again.'

'When will you see him fir what he is?'

We could make it right. Like it used to be. He just needed time.

'He is *my* husband and I will hear no more of it, under *my* roof.'

'You ken a woman can live freely without the want of a man.'

'And what kind of life did that bring us?'

She turned away. I should not have said it. She had always done what she could. I had never gone without. Silence stretched like a fiddle string between us, as though it would snap with the weight of the quiet. I should not have said it.

Agnes sighed and drew her shawl more tightly around her shoulders. 'It's getting dark in here, no?' she said grimly.

'Aye, 'tis a bit overcast this morning, but I've got a wee bit of candle left over from last night's supper.' I searched around for my tinder box and flint, grateful that my mother would say no more about it. Scratching them together to make tiny sparks, I watched the new flame dance momentarily inside my cupped hands before taking hold.

'Is that belladonna next to that wee candle?' she asked.

Shocked, I looked down at the table. Belladonna, I couldn't mistake it. Where had it come from? Surely I hadn't been so tired last night that I'd forgotten I'd put it there?

'Ach, no, the smoke off that fire must be messing with yer eyes. Them's bluebells our Jenny picked for me this morning.'

She knew, as did I, that there were no flourishes of bluebells at this time of year. I needed to get rid of it.

She threw me a sly glance. 'Ah, she's a good wee girl, that one. Nothin' like her father.'

Agnes was what you would call buxom, with a fair head of hair for a woman her age, although peppered with grey. Her eyes were prominent, the colour of seaweed. And, old as she was, she wouldn't allow herself to look it, swathing herself in layers of garments that put me in mind of an onion. She was sturdy and strong and had brought half of the village children into the world, Jenny included. All of them kicking and screaming with lungs on them like bagpipes. That's how she'd come by me.

When I was a bairn, she'd pull me on her lap, smoothing my riotous red curls, and tell me about my mother. *A woman she could not save in time.* They'd wept while they cleaned and combed her hair, cleaning the dirt from beneath her fingernails and dressing her in a white shift. Laying her out ready for the next world; all the while Agnes rocking me gently in the crook of her arm, promising that she would never leave me. She never did. It had always been me and Agnes.

'I've a wee favour to ask of you, Besse,' she said, rubbing the stump of her leg. 'John Ancroft's wife is due any day now and my hands is gettin' too old.'

In answer, flickering; like tiny wings, the beating in my stomach.

'You know I cannae. I promised Rupert I'd have no more to do with yer healing.'

'I know . . . I know . . .' She waved a hand dismissively. 'But you're a fine healer, Besse. My only daughter, who else can I pass all this on to? And I daresay you could do with the shillings? I heard what happened in the apothecary.'

I looked her square in the face and sighed. She was right. *Poor women don't argue.*

'I'll have tae see what's needed of me by Master Rivet first, you ken.'

'John Ancroft'll pay you handsomely, he isnae short on coin,' she said. 'I've already told Margret tae expect yer.'

'Well—' I barely got the words out before she interrupted again.

'And the way I sees it, that bairn will deliver itself. It's her third one, o' course.'

'Ma, I . . .' My tongue felt like a stone in my mouth.

'Spit it out, lass, what is it?' She threw me an impatient look.

I couldn't bring myself to say the words. Not again. Not out loud. I glanced down at my stomach, chewing on the corner of my lip like I had done as a child. If I told my mother, then he became real – and if, just if, he was real, than he could be taken away again.

'Besse?'

With a spin and a twist, I felt the quickening, and my hands shot instinctively to my stomach.

'Are you with child?' Agnes stepped forward, poking and prodding me like livestock. 'Have you felt a quickening?'

I nodded, gaze falling on my slightly swollen belly. My heart ached.

'Often?'

'Yes,' I breathed.

'Mibbe four months along by the feel of you.' Her

expression was troubled. 'You must promise me you'll be careful. Do you mean to tell Rupert?'

I motioned my head from left to right and right to left. No, it said.

Agnes blessed herself. 'You keep it that way, at least until your middle is so swollen you can no longer hide it. Promise me.'

'I promise.'

The Butcher's Boy

The morning had a crispness to it that signalled the start of winter. Jenny shuddered as she pulled the door closed and hurried towards the orchard. She couldn't help looking back, wondering if Agnes was following. It made her skin prickle just to think of her nan. She remembered the tales Willy had told her about the curse that had taken Agnes Sampson's leg. The ghouls she consorted with had come in the dead of night and taken it, leaving her with a hard, wooden stump.

The path to the orchard was narrow and slippery, the mud squelched beneath her feet. As she walked, her breath steamed in the dawn. She pulled up her skirts and bunched them around her waist. If only her mother would let her wear breeches, but they weren't for lassies. Laddies were allowed to do anything they wanted. They could climb trees. Go where they pleased, when they pleased. She was never going to be the property of a man. She'd decided that long ago.

She could always be found with Willy, one of the orphan boys abandoned at Mistress Cochran's, climbing the tallest trees they could find. Out in the orchard, Jenny was as brave as any boy. She had agreed to meet Willy after she had taken breakfast, and she hoped the bannock she stuffed in her pocket for him had survived – he was always so famished.

He was waiting when she arrived, shivering in threadbare clothes that had been worn by at least five orphaned boys before him, and the boots on his feet unlaced. He was tall and thin, like pieces of string held together with knees and elbows, and a head that she hoped he'd grow into. Curious to the eye, but she liked that about him. He was in his thirteenth year, which made him almost two years older. With his back to her, he was using a stick to try and shake an apple free from its branch.

'Willy!' she shouted.

He jumped, banging his head on the bough above, dislodging the rotten fruit. It landed with a soft thud. She picked it up, what was left of it, and hid it in the pocket she'd sewn into the lining of her skirt.

'I've brought you breakfast.' She tossed him a bannock. 'I told Ma about that great tree we still have tae climb. She says I've got tae see what apples I can bring back fir the pigs.'

'It's over near Master Rivet's, where he keeps his sheep,' he said.

'We cannae let Master Rivet see us or my mother. He'll see tae it that I'll no' be able tae sit down fir a week, and my da's run off with the rents again.'

'Again? Has yer da run off with them before?'

'Aye, my ma thinks I dinnae ken, but I hear things and I know things.' She tapped her nose. 'While he's away and the folks come callin' fir potions off my nan, I hear 'em whisperin'.'

'You shouldna be listenin' to folks's conversations,

not like that.' He shook the heel of bannock at her. 'The spirits will ken of it, and they'll no' be happy aboot it. Those folk come to yer grandmother when God has forsaken them, and not before. You'd be wise to stay well clear of it.'

She nodded sagely. She knew in her heart he was right, but she loved the thrill of hiding in the shadows when the neighbours came calling; it was almost as exciting as climbing trees and probably more dangerous. She loved the forest and to climb all the way to the highest branches. From there, Jenny could see smoking chimneys poking through the trees, thatched roofs clustered around the coastline and all the way to the church of St Andrew's, jutting out from atop its tiny island, waiting for ships to moor in the docks.

'Are you comin'? Or am I going tae have tae find this tree mysel'?' she said, walking away.

Willy stuffed the remainder of the food in his mouth and, with loose boots flapping, chased after her. They made their way through the field, over the ridges and furrows while Jenny whipped her stick through the cut wheat, making a noise like a *crack* and sending flocks of crows fluttering skywards.

'What is it they ask fir?' Willy said, scuttling behind her. 'Them that come to yer nan?'

'The women are the worst,' she said, biting at her lip. 'On their knees and begging at twilight. Swearing away all their worldly possessions; all for a potion of mandrake and henbane to bind the hearts of their lovers.' She balled her hands into fists. 'I never want to be like them. Not one of them.'

'No, me neither,' Willy snorted. 'I bet they could find them that's lost, as well?'

'Oh aye, ah've seen my ma and nan do that, when Janet Pigg misplaced her good-fir-nothin' husband – that's what my nan calls 'im. They found him three sheets tae the wind up at Acheson's Haven. More 'an three days he was gone.'

Willy glanced at Jenny, eyes wide with wonder. He had been all but four when his unwed mother abandoned him at Mistress Cochran's. He'd toured the countryside, begging and poaching. When word got back about his mischief, that was when the beatings started. They worsened when he tried to run away.

Jenny had never had any real friends, nor had she ever wanted for any, not until she happened upon Willy. She had been helping her mother when she heard noises through the wall of the pigsty. She found him cowering like a rat between the wet straw and the grain for the foraging sow. He smelled of rotten onions and scalded milk, and he'd cowered like a wild animal when she put a hand out to touch him.

When that hadn't worked, she'd called for her mother. She marched in and scooped the feral creature up in her arms, rubbing the dirt from his face with a lick of her thumb. The pair walked into the house, Jenny trotting behind them with interest, and settled by the fire. After giving him a decent meal and drying his clothes at the hearth, he was returned to the care of Mistress Cochran, on the understanding that she never raised a hand to him again – or face the wrath of Besse and Agnes.

Afterwards, Jenny appointed herself Willy's best friend and made sure he never went without a decent meal or company again.

As they approached the shallow burn, she heard Willy gasp. There, on the other embankment, was the fat butcher's boy, who always smelled of rancid meat. And there was the one they called Patrick, the baker's son, whose aroma of hops and yeast made him slightly more appealing. The rest of the horde scuttled behind.

She knew the butcher's boy was cruel and delighted in making Willy cry. She chewed her lip. If they carried on walking, they were sure to bump into them. But if they turned back now, they'd only follow them anyway. She made a decision and turned, pulling Willy by the elbow, but she was too late.

'Alright, freckle-face,' said the butcher's boy. He skipped across the mossy stone in the crook, towering over her. 'What you got there?'

He dropped the glassy-eyed carcass of a pheasant into the frosted grass and grabbed at the thick black rosary around her neck. It belonged to her mother; she'd taken it before she'd gotten home. She wasn't supposed to let anyone see it.

Jenny was just a child the first time her father went to France. That was the first time he'd gone missing. Soon after, Master Rivet had threatened to put them out of the cot-house.

Her mother had been forced to sell what little they had left, but she'd got their home back. The only thing she'd kept had been the rosary. 'No matter how we struggle, we must try to never sell this,' her mother would say. 'It's the only thing I have left of a very dear friend, and I want it to be yours when you're old enough.'

Not only had everyone seen it, but the butcher's boy had taken it.

'You give that back!'

'Look at her,' the butcher's boy said. 'You gonna cry?'

Patrick, with hair like straw, started braying like a donkey. The butcher's boy held the rosary high, just out of her reach.

'I'm warning ye!'

Patrick spat on the floor. He was greasy and covered in pox and reminded her of a sour loaf. 'I've heard yer mother's a witch,' he said. 'And yer grandmother's Black Agnes.'

'She is not!' Jenny growled. 'You shut yer mouth!'

'Only heretics use these.' The butcher's boy waved a chubby hand, causing the morning light to glint off the spinning rosary.

'They do not!' She stamped her foot. 'You give that back, you fat toad!'

He was almost two years older and three times her size. She was nimble and quick, but if she moved too soon, he would just pull the rosary further out of her reach. She held the stick by her side.

'Sh-she disnae mean nothin' by it,' Willy stammered. 'We was just leavin'.' He tugged at her arm.

The butcher's boy took a step closer, and Jenny lunged with her stick, right between his legs. He dropped to the ground like a stone, clutching himself. She wheeled around and cracked him across the back, forcing the air out of his lungs and his face into the mud. The rosary skidded across the burn, coming to rest in the reeds.

'You want some more?' She spun around to face the other boys. 'Any of you?'

She pointed the stick towards Patrick's gut, and he raised his arms in defeat. He and a boy with a wicked grin heaved the butcher's boy from the mud. The boys all stared at her, even Willy. She kept her stick pointed at them until they disappeared further up the embankment and back towards town. Her father might have only had a daughter, but he'd taught her how to fight.

When they were a safe distance away, Willy finally let out his breath. She gathered up her skirts and dipped her toes into the burn, which bubbled and gurgled like a new bairn, and retrieved her mother's rosary.

'Got it!' she shouted, balancing on one foot like a heron while Willy marvelled at her biblical temper.

'What are you doing with such a thing around yer neck? You'll see us both killed!'

'No one was supposed to see.' Jenny slipped the beaded noose around her neck. 'It's my mother's and, believe you me, I'm more scairt of her finding me with it than anyone else. My ma would kill me all over again.'

'What of the decree?'

'What, renounce our faith or leave Scotland forever?' She stifled a laugh as Willy helped her on to the bank. 'The king will never let it happen.'

He threw her a sharp glance. 'The king can, and he will. The whole of Scotland is aflame as he swarms the countryside looking fir *his* witches. Mark my words, you need to keep that hidd—' He stopped, looking at the iridescent, copper-coloured plumage of the bird that had been left on the grass. 'What in the name of—' he said, poking the bird with his foot. 'You cannae be lettin' a good pheasant like that go tae waste.' Willy checked behind him, still no sign of the butcher's boy.

'You were goin' tae say a rude word there, weren't ya?'

'Aye, but I didnae, so it disnae count.'

He'd grown up in Mistress Cochran's, like her ma would have if Agnes hadn't taken her in. Mistress Cochran didn't teach good manners like her ma did. She didn't like it when Willy used rude words.

'If I hear you, you'll owe me tuppence.'

She thought no more of the rosary around her neck. But the bird . . . her mother would like that, a fat pheasant for supper. Maybe it would stop her da being so angry. They'd like it better than apples for the pigs. They would like that very much. Now Jenny just needed to find a way to get the great lump of a bird home.

The Changeling

That afternoon, I woke groggily at the foot of the bed. The crisp air in my bedchamber signalled a dying fire. Agnes had taken her leave and flitted off, back up to see Jonet Muir, no doubt. I hadn't breathed a word of what had gone on and only prayed that Jonet would have the good sense to do the same.

The only thing moving in the cot-house were my thoughts. To my right, a gap on the bedclothes where my husband should have been. I wrapped my plaid around me and closed the shutters against the darkening sky.

I felt too sick to eat, so I wandered to the kitchen and found the cat curled on himself, as close to the red embers as he dared without setting his fur alight. I tiptoed around him and made a poor attempt at lighting a fire. Soon, the sparks fluttered towards the ceiling and I listening to the crackle of the burning wood. Ratbag unfurled, muscles twitching as he yawned, baring yellow teeth.

As I stared into the flames, images of Andrew Muir danced in their light, like a ghost wandering in the darkness. How had he died so suddenly? Just then, a fierce wind howled through the cot-house, rattling the pots and pans above my head, looping between the spindles of wood and causing the fire to sputter. Startled, I whipped around to find the door had blown open.

I held my breath, as jittery as a lie caught between my teeth, and stared into the blackness.

Jenny appeared at the threshold, like a wraith, scruffy and dragging the sorry carcass of a pheasant. I sagged with relief.

'Look, Ma, we found this up the field. Willy says it'll make an excellent supper.'

I assessed the feathered mass critically. 'Does he now? You know there's enough flesh on that bird tae feed a small army? And those pretty feathers would be good to soften our pillows.'

Twigs and leaves decorated Jenny's hair. I didn't care, I was just pleased to have her home. 'Sorry, Ma, I forgot about looking fir the apples, and I only found one.' She produced a sticky mess from the tear in her skirt. 'We climbed the tree and found a beaver. It was making a wee dam in the river; that's where we found the bird.' She rolled the carcass into the kitchen with her foot, to make enough room to shut the door. She pushed against it, but the wind was too strong.

'My goodness,' I said as I shoved the door with her, managing to close it. 'However did you make it home heaving such a heavy lump?'

'Willy helped me most of the way and I rolled it the rest.'

'Did you no' see yer father?'

'No, Ma. I never saw him.' Jenny hesitated. 'Was he tendin' Master Rivet's flock?'

I could tell by the grave look on her face that her and

Willy must have been causing a fuss with the sheep. If her father had caught them, there would have been hell to pay.

'Not that I know of, but you ken very well that when yer father is workin', he can turn up in all sorts of places.'

'We only saw some of the village boys.'

There was something she wasn't telling me. 'Which boys?'

'I didnae ken them. Willy said he'd seen them before up near the saddlers.'

'Were they in Master Rivet's fields?'

'Aye, but they just passed through,' she said with a shrug, her gaze drifting to the bird on the floor.

Clearly, I was going to get no more out of her. 'Help me get it to the table and we can prepare it.'

It would be a welcome distraction. Rupert had only gone to Edinburgh to fetch the rents, no more than a day's ride. That was two days ago. The feeling of uneasiness had dug itself in and taken root. Why had he not come home?

I turned my attention to the task at hand. Jenny watched me as I set the bird on the table, my sleeve falling back to reveal the blackened finger marks around my wrist. We began plucking it, until our fingers were sore and all its pink, mottled flesh was on show. All the while I could feel Jenny's eyes, silently studying me. I decanted the slimy entrails into a dish to be boiled later. Nothing would go to waste.

'Ma?' I flinched, hearing the question in her voice. 'Have you been bitten?'

I hastily pulled my sleeve down. 'No, no. I got it caught in the gate,' I said, a little more eagerly than I should have.

'You know, I think ye'd have made a better laddie.'

'No, Ma,' she said, pushing out her chest and making herself a little taller. 'Lassies can do anything laddies can, except better.'

'I think you might be right, but before the smell of you chases the rats off the grain, you need a wash.'

She kicked and yowled when I washed her, like some kind of a half-wild animal. It took almost an hour to clean her and pick the bits of twigs and leaves from her hair. When I'd finished, she was dressed for bed and there was still no sign of Rupert. The quickenings were coming closer together – soon I'd no longer be able to hide it. If he didn't return, where would I be? Homeless with two children, no doubt.

I placed a small pot of milk on the hook and threw some kindling on the fire. Just as I sat down on the crackett by the hearth, mind fuddled with tiredness, and began untangling the stitches I'd dropped in my knitting, Agnes breezed in. I'd clean forgot I'd agreed to attend the birth.

Agnes immediately began speculating about John Ancroft's child and whether it would be blessed with its mother's good looks or have the misfortune of resembling its father. 'The last three have all looked like their ma, even the wee one she lost.' She lowered her voice, to be mindful of Jenny. 'All girls, bonny wee things they are as well.' She folded the soft blanket she'd brought and put it over her shoulder. 'They dinnae want the bairn tae look like John – he has a face like a dog licking piss from a thistle.'

'They must be hoping fir a boy now, aye?'

'Oh aye, John will be, but I'm not sure about poor Margret.' She jerked her head towards the dusty light leaking in through the shutter. 'I told you, I need tae be away before sundown, no?'

'I know, but Rupert hasnae come home.' I could feel my face reddening.

'What do you mean, he's no' come home? Is that what all the trouble was at the apothecary?' she said.

I nodded. 'It looks as though he's made off wi' the rents, and now . . .' I walked over to the window, picking my words with care. 'Now, it's only a matter of time before Master Rivet comes tae realise that he's gone.'

'I'll always have work fir you. What's mine is yers, you ken that well enough. If you must, come back to Leaplish. I cannae see you without a pot tae piss in,' she said, her expression troubled.

'I'll be fine, I'm sure it's somethin' and nothin'.'

'Whatever John Ancroft pays, you take it and put it towards whatever debts is owed. Now, we must get gone before the last of the light dies.'

'Aye, aye. Jenny,' I called, 'make sure you mind tae light the candle and put a wee dish of milk out on the step fir the gruagach.'

'Aye, you must promise tae never forget tae leave an offering fir the fae,' said Agnes.

'I promise,' Jenny said as she skipped across the kitchen, wrapping her arms about my waist. 'Will you be gone a while?'

'Ach no, I'm just helping Agnes at the Ancrofts'. I willnae be long.' I kissed her on the forehead. 'Now get yerself tae bed and I'll be back before you know it.'

* * *

All Hallows' Eve was approaching and the crescent of the waning moon hung low on the horizon, touched with a lattice of white clouds. My missing husband wasn't far from my mind as we made our way towards the Ancrofts' house. The deep pink of the sunset sank behind the trees, bringing with it rolling mists.

Agnes pushed open the door to their cot-house. The flames from the candle danced in the sudden draft, illuminating the linenfold panelling. The figure of John Ancroft, his face rigid and grey, paced the hallway. As he turned, a nervous smile spread across his face.

'I've just sent one of the farm hands to fetch you.' He fidgeted with his shirt. 'Is he no' with you? The babe is on its way.'

Agnes moved through the house with an air of authority. Her thick-set shoulders and robust frame gave great confidence in her skills as a howdie, despite the absence of her leg. She took a pile of freshly pressed linen from Mrs Fitzpatrick, a woman who the Ancroft's seemed to inherit with the house and ordered John Ancroft to retire, before heading towards the bedroom.

'Besse, fetch some water,' she said firmly, disappearing upstairs.

After taking a bowl of water from Mrs Fitzpatrick, I ascended the wide staircase of polished wood. It was a thing of beauty, which opened out onto a modest landing. Soft murmurings came from the room where the door was ajar. The light from the fire flickered, casting shadows into the hall. I peered inside to find Agnes resting on her wooden crutch, confidently making examinations of Margret Ancroft, settled on the bed near the window.

'Willnae be long now,' Agnes breathed, rubbing Margret's leg. Then, to me: 'Don't be hoverin' at the door like some kind of wraith – fetch it here.'

I crossed the room and placed the bowl at the bedside. Margret's hair was soaked with sweat, and her red face contorted. She clenched her teeth and let out a noise like a wild animal, under the strain of the heavy contraction already upon her.

'Something's wrong,' Margret said over and over. 'I can feel it.'

My tongue felt heavy in my mouth. She was right. The baby was wayward and coming feet first. Just like the boy I'd lost. To say he was 'lost' sounded strange, as though I had placed him somewhere and forgotten about him. To say he was 'born still' seemed just as wrong. The river of blood between my legs. Agnes wrapping his limp form in linen. There was nothing still or calm about his birth.

Another contraction came, stronger this time. Margret bent double, bringing her knees up towards her chest with a deep groan. She fought against it. Blood soaked the sheets. Agnes moved quickly, throwing back Margret's nightgown. If she was worried, she didn't appear to show it.

'Right, Margret, this wee bairn is coming,' she said. 'Besse, can you come here?' She motioned me to the head of the bed. 'Help her tae lean back a wee bit.'

Margret writhed again, gripping the bed linen. She let out a pitiful scream as I tried to lean her back; her entire body was rigid with pain.

'Margret,' Agnes whispered, 'I need you tae drink this.' She held a small pewter cup against Margret's lips. 'It'll ease yer suffering.' The smell of the hemp and henbane festered in my nostrils.

'Ma! You mustn't.' I ran and closed the door to the chamber.

'Hush now, Besse,' she scolded. 'We've no time. There's a child's life at stake, not to mention its mother's. Can you have that on yer conscience?'

A conflict raged inside me. 'But if we're caught?' I shook my head. 'I cannae. If Rupert were tae find out . . .'

'We won't get caught. Isn't it that there are only three of us here? All in agreement?' She kept the cup at Margret's lips. 'Secrets have their place, Besse.' Her gaze fell to my swelling stomach.

'Mary, mother of God.' I let out a sigh. 'Fine, I'll help.'

Unable to keep from pushing, Margret's body took over. Agnes placed a hand over her belly and pushed. Her thin frame sagged as the contraction passed, her stomach relaxing under the nightgown, but still there was no sight of the bairn.

'Just one more,' Agnes said, working between Margret's legs.

'Agnes, this is no' like the rest of 'em,' Margret said breathlessly, but the next contraction started immediately, a force that rippled across her already exhausted body.

'Go on!' Agnes pushed in unison, forcing the baby down.

Margret gritted her teeth and pushed. She made a loud grunt and snorted as bloodied feet peeped through, then came a slimy body, followed by a head. The cord was wrapped around its leg, and a thin, filmy membrane covered its pink scalp. Agnes let out a gasp at the sight of the caul. I pulled at it and slipped it into my apron before Margret was any the wiser.

We welcomed John Robert Ancroft into the world almost a week past when he was due.

'All his fingers and toes,' said Agnes. 'Did I no' tell you there was nothing to worry about.' She wiped Margret's brow while she cooed over her first boy.

'Ma?' I pulled at her sleeve. 'Can I borrow ye?'

Agnes nodded. 'Margret, ye've done us all proud.'

We stood, the day all but lost, with our backs to Margret. I pulled apart the fold of my apron. Agnes gasped and blessed herself.

'Get rid of it,' she hissed.

'What is it, Agnes?' Margret pressed herself up. 'Is somethin' wrong?'

'Ach no, Margret. Besse thought the bairn had a caul, silly girl.' She turned and smiled at Margret. 'It wasnae anything of the sort. She's going soft in the head this one.'

We cleaned the wee man, and I disposed of the caul in the fire, along with the last of the liquid from the cup, before anyone could see it. She swaddled the boy, ready for visitors, and replaced the linen with a freshly starched sheet. The stillness of the room enticed an already fraught John Ancroft senior, who peered around the door and then entered, followed closely by Mrs Fitzpatrick and the three girls, like ducklings.

Margret's face had paled. The family gathered around the bed, with John taking the baby in his arms. As Mrs Fitzpatrick took the girls to the kitchen to fill their bellies, Agnes and I gave our congratulations and made our excuses to leave.

We made our way back in exhausted silence, almost eight hours after Agnes had first called at our cot-house.

'Between you and me,' Agnes said, pulling a swathe of fabric over her head, 'he's a wee changeling. You mark my words: they'll come fir him.'

'You cannae say that; the wee man is but a few hours old.'

'Did you no' ken that he made no noise when he came and was birthed with a caul? The Queen of Elphame will come fir him. It's only fae those that are born on this close to All Hallows' Eve wi' eyes the colour o' steel and hair as fair as that, you'll see.' She shuddered and pulled her shawl tighter.

'Are you tendin' with the good doctor this evening, Ma?'

'Aye, there's always the sick and infirm up at Auld Kirk Green. Will you join me, Besse?'

'I cannae tonight. I've hardly seen wee Jenny, and Master Rivet is wanting me tae milk the goats before dawn. You ken what Rupert's done: I daren't be late, aye?'

'Aye, I ken. But there's been a great consumption of the chest, half the town is riddled with it. Between me and Dr Fian, we can hardly manage.'

'Tomorrow then, aye? Come after sundown and I'll bring what few herbs I have. I dinnae like the thought of you on yer own.'

'How about in the morning, before you come up, we head to Acheson's Haven and see if we cannae find that feckless husband o' yers?'

'You'll be too tired. I couldnae ask you—'

'You weren't askin', I was tellin' you. Meet me at the

crossroads at dawn. See if Jonet won't have Jenny; it will only be a day or two. I'm sure she willnae mind.'

I nodded, knowing in my heart that, with her husband dead, Jonet was hardly going to welcome us with open arms but I could take her to Mistress Cochran.

'And thank you fir tonight.' Agnes rubbed a calloused hand against mine. 'Here . . .' She held out a fist and dropped the coins John Ancroft had given her into my palm. 'It's not much, but take it and promise me you'll be careful.'

'Aye, Ma. I promise. You dinnae have to worry.'

'But I do.' She kissed my cheek and gently touched my stomach before turning away, into the darkness.

A stillness seemed to envelop the woods. The only noise to be heard was the crunching of Agnes's wooden crutch as it pushed its way through the undergrowth towards Leaplish. The silence made me conscious of just how tired and hungry I had become. A strange emptiness washed over me as I stood alone in that clearing.

* * *

I could smell the stench of him when I arrived home. The bastard had been waiting for me.

'Where have you been until this ungodly hour?' Master Rivet glowered at me from the crackett at the hearth as he poked the dying embers.

'I was out helping birth John Ancroft's new bairn.' I pulled my plaid from my shoulders and shook out my hair, trying not to meet his eyes.

'You work fir me, lass, not John Ancroft.' His tone

was menacing, but no more than usual. 'I'll no' have you roaming around the countryside on my coin.' The fire hissed as he spat in the hearth.

'The chores were done before I left.' I folded my plaid and put it on the table. 'I kent you wanted the goats milking by dawn, and I dinnae think you pay me enough tae work through the night as well.' As I said it, I regretted it.

The weight of the poker struck me across the back of my thighs, throwing me to the floor.

'That mouth of yers. A good husband would have tanned yer arse. Looks like I'll have tae do it fir him.' His eyes narrowed. 'I've seen you leaving the house at all hours of the night. You been whoring yerself tae pay off yer husband's debt?'

He loomed over me, smelling strongly of whisky and dirt. I curled my knees to my stomach, trying to protect my unborn child.

'I'm sorry, I—' His huge, calloused hand struck my face. He was as handy with his fists as he was with the poker.

'"Sorry"? "Sorry" disnae bring back the mare he stole or the money I'm owed. I've seen you going out at all hours with old Goodwife Muir.'

'I'm earning now, an honest living.' I fumbled about in the pocket of my apron and placed my shillings on the table. 'It's all I have, but I can get more.'

'If I'd kent what he was, you would never have had none of it. And dinnae think Jonet Muir can give you work, a poor widow woman like her. Let me tell you this now: if you want tae keep this cot-house, yer going tae have tae do something fir me,' he growled, unfastening his breeches.

As small as he was, he was strong. He leaned down, grabbed me by my hair and twisted it hard. He'd lost all sense of reason. I struggled to get free; all the while he pushed himself down harder, hips against mine.

'How dare you! I'm no' some harlot!'

'Dinnae worry, lass, it'll be our little secret.' He grabbed at my skirts, lifting them higher, digging his nails into my thighs, pulling them apart. I wriggled again, but this time I got a slap across my face for good measure.

'Agnes Sampson's child, I always kent you'd be trouble.'

He raised his hand to hit me again but stopped dead, eyes focused on the table. 'Belladonna!' he cried, stumbling back. 'A witch under my very roof!'

Freed, I gathered myself and got to my feet. 'No, Master Rivet, no . . . It's just some bluebells that Jen—'

'Holy Mary, mother of God!' He pulled out a wooden cross, holding it to his face as he staggered for the door. 'Get back, foul creature!' He turned and fled the cot-house.

I hurried and locked the door behind him, then collapsed to my knees, making a noise somewhere between a groan and a sob.

'Ma?' Jenny stood in the doorway, rubbing her eyes.

I outstretched my arms and pulled her to me, choking back tears.

'Don't be sad,' she said.

'No, no. I'm not sad. 'Tis the smoke, is all.'

She clung to me. 'Are you cold, Ma?'

'Aye, ah think I am.'

Jenny jumped to her feet and brought me to the fire. There were still enough embers left for it to take when she threw on a couple of logs. Within minutes it was ablaze, crackling and spitting. We cradled each other until the first glimmers of light dripped into the parlour.

Jenny slept soundly on my lap. I shifted restlessly every time the door creaked, fearful of what was to come. I tried to settle myself, but the uneasiness lingered.

We couldn't stay any longer. I needed to find Rupert.

'Jenny' – I shook her gently awake – 'come now, you need tae be wrapped up nice and warm.' I hurried her along.

'But, Ma, won't Master Rivet wonder where we've gone?'

'Don't you be worrying about Master Rivet.'

I blew out the candle and threw the last of the belladonna on the fire. I stood for a moment, letting my eyes become accustomed to the dimness, and my heart to its emptiness. It ached for Rupert. I wrapped a parcel of cheese and bread and placed it in the leather pouch next to the tinderbox and flint.

'Layers, Jenny!'

Outside, the rain came down in sheets as I mounted the pony.

'Come now.' I lifted Jenny onto the saddle in front of me. I didn't have time to settle my skirts, but we'd be grateful of the warmth of each other. I pulled my plaid around us.

We moved off, with the pony breaking into a trot.

'Where are we going, Ma?'

'We'll find out when we get there.'

St Andrew's Auld Kirk

Agnes braced herself against the cold. It was a hard ride to reach Dr Fian up at St Andrew's Auld Kirk, and her pony was no more than a mule. She would have been grateful of company on such a chilly night, but it would have to wait until Besse could steal away.

Agnes thought of the drunken state Rupert would be in when they found him, no doubt hiding in an inn for the derelict and unlucky. The only place to find a good-for-nothing gambler who wasn't fit to lick Besse's shoes. She personally disliked Rupert. She disliked everything about him, from his impish mole face to the way he wandered about thinking he owned every woman in Tranent. She felt no one should be allowed to treat her daughter the way he did, and she often thought of cursing him.

Thomas, though . . . she'd always been fond of Thomas. He had been a strapping young lad and had grown on her like moss on a boulder. A gentle man. She had never understood why Besse had refused his offer of marriage.

With a soft click of her tongue, lost in her thoughts, she reined her pony to the east, slipping into an easy trot. Staying in the saddle had been hard when she had first lost her leg, but she was used to it now, and human and animal moved as one.

She had few herbs left to speak of, but no doubt Dr Fian would have arranged more supplies. There had been such a flux of people riddled with sickness. They had lost two in the last week, a mother and her child to the pox. Then, there had been the three men from Humbie who had diseases of the humours; at least, that was what the doctor had called it, but Agnes called it consumption. She doubted they'd survive the week.

The darkness of the trees thinned to reveal the grey hues of a chilly pre-dawn mist. As she left the forest behind, the narrow track took her past woods and orchards and fields filled with heather and up into low, rolling hills before disappearing behind cliffs.

In the salt-scented dawn, North Berwick seemed eerily quiet. She passed through the town square, which normally hummed with life but today was hushed with quiet. All that could be heard was the soft click of her gelding's hooves as they rattled across the cobbles. In the smoky fog, the heretics' post whispered, empty and waiting for its next guest.

As Agnes crossed the narrow causeway that connected the island to the mainland, the sea was as flat as a silver coin. The church of St Andrew's overlooked the ocean on all sides, with a small wooden harbour to its rear. Against the dawn, the light of the candles flickered in the sconces. Dr Fian was in residence.

She felt a bolt of terror as her eye turned up the lane leading towards home. All of the women in the village had become fearful after word of another witch hunt had travelled on the tongue of Goodwife Johnstone in the apothecary. They were being chased down like wolves. It was no longer safe.

She slid awkwardly from her pony, shifting her weight onto her leg while she lifted the crutch from the saddle. As she made her way to the doors, two men lay huddled against the stone.

'What are you boys doing out here? Are you tryin' tae have us all arrested?'

She hurried them inside, their pock-riddled faces illuminated by the candlelight. A heady gust of lavender and the musky smell of the doctor's poppy tincture filled her nostrils. She bustled through the narrow walkway with a click, click, click of her crutch.

'Dr Fian,' she called, 'I've found two more strays outside.' There was no answer.

She ushered the men into seats next to an old woman riddled with fever and went to find the doctor.

The walls inside St Andrew's were blistered with damp, and the pews stank of mould. It had been magnificent in its time, and now, in its dereliction, it allowed them to work surreptitiously under the very noses of those that stalked the healers.

'John?' Her voice echoed against the cold stone. 'Dr Fian?'

'Ah, Agnes, it's good tae have you back.'

He didn't look like a doctor. He had a tall man's stoop and strong features, like his father before him. His frame rose from the body that writhed on the floor.

'This poor wretch is mad with pain.' Dr Fian stepped towards Agnes, wiping his brow with the back of his hand. 'There's nothing else tae be done fir him.'

The face of the man on the floor was contorted, his belly swollen with purple ridges. Agnes took out a square of parchment from her apron and slipped it into the doctor's hand.

'Then the kindest thing tae do would be to give the man a painless sleep. The least we can do.'

Dr Fian took it and squeezed her hand. 'Thank you, Agnes. My supplies have been depleted. We must not leave him to suffer.' He took a cup and tipped in the powder.

'I found two more when I arrived. I saw tae it that they were brought inside.'

'I fear we are tae be found out if we keep growing in number.' He decanted the milk from the pot above the fire and made a paste.

'We're all at risk,' she told him. 'But we need tae be here – we cannae see these poor folk dying in the gutter like rats.' Agnes waved a feeble hand and swayed on her crutch, exhausted. 'None of us wants tae be here, least of all them.'

Looking across the refectory, their number had grown to almost twenty. The bodies of the sick lay festering on the pews and the floor. Soon there would be no space left. They tended two more churches through the week, and soon she'd have to travel to Edinburgh before her supplies ran out.

Dr Fian held the man's head, letting him drink. 'Just another sip.' He placed the cup to the man's lips again. 'Just one more.'

Soon, the liquid was gone. Dr Fian lowered the man's

head to the floor. The doctor stayed there a while, holding the man's hand. As the breathing slowed, his body began to relax, muscles no longer twitching and convulsing. His pain ebbed away.

'Agnes,' he said softly, moving on to inspect one of the young men. 'This man is riddled with disease; please bring me the leeches.'

Her fingers roamed through Dr Fian's supplies of apothecary jars. They were filled with mandrake, belladonna and all manner of herbs she didn't recognise. Her hand finally settled on the leeches, the creatures whipping and whirling behind the glass.

'Is it really necessary?' she said sourly, handing him the jar. 'All these wee beasties?'

'You've worked with me almost two summers; have I ever steered you wrong?'

At first it was only St Andrew's. The priest had allowed them the use of the church. It had provided ample enough space in the beginning. Then, the burnings began. Spreading through each village like a poison. Seeping into every rut and crevice and weeding out every heretic. It was becoming more dangerous for a woman to earn a living as a healer. The king saw to it that they were driven into the shadows. Agnes and the doctor had moved into the refectory to stay hidden. They were one man and a crippled woman with almost twenty sick and injured pilgrims, waiting for safe passage across the Firth of Forth. When the crowds were overcome with the bloodlust of a burning, however, neither law nor reason could stop them.

'No. No, you haven't, doctor. Ach, I'll have company

with me tomorrow's eve: Besse has agreed tae help. It will only be fir the one night, I fear it's getting too dangerous.'

'It will be wonderful to see her, Agnes. It's been a wee while since I last saw her. I trust she's well?' His gaze didn't falter as he busied himself with his leechcraft.

'Oh, aye, as well as she can be. That husband of hers is missing. I dinnae like tae speak ill of the man, she doesnae like it, but I hear stories of his gamblin' and all the women in Tranent seem to believe his lies, all wanting to bed him. He's nought but a bedswerver and a drunk.'

'Agnes, I know you've never liked the man, but he is yer daughter's husband, after all.'

'Aye, well, you're not having to go up to Acheson's Haven, trailing after him tae fetch him home, are ye?'

'A woman cannae go up there alone.'

'I willnae be alone, Besse is comin' with me,' she said, with an air of mastery that made him think twice before he answered.

'Can I offer you both some company?' he said cautiously.

Agnes pursed her lips. Travelling would be treacherous, so having the doctor with them could do nothing but help. 'Aye,' she said finally. 'We'd be glad of it.'

Acheson's Haven

The ride to Mill House was a slow one. The whole journey I hadn't felt so much as a flutter. When I arrived, I dismounted, lifting Jenny clear from the saddle. Mistress Cochran wavered on her doorstep, still in her nightgown.

'Besse,' she called, 'what are you doing here?'

I tethered the horse to the gate. Unsure of what to say. The rain beat down like a torrent. 'I'm sorry. I'm so sorry.'

'Come in, lass, you'll catch yer death. What is it?'

We followed, as did the dawn, banishing the darting shadows and illuminating the hallway. She hurried towards the kitchen. As we stood in the doorway, the water began to pool on the floor beneath our feet. We must have looked like wet hens.

'I'm sorry tae trouble you at such an ungodly hour but I need you tae look after Jenny fir a spell.' I spoke with urgency. I didn't have time for her to say no. 'She'll be no trouble, will you now?' Jenny shook her head as the torment spread across her face. 'And I trust there'll be no raisin' of yer hands tae my child when she's in yer care?'

Mistress Cochran's face didn't change. She stood before me, hair neatly scraped back and features like a weasel. She nodded. 'You have my word, Besse.' Then she turned to Jenny. 'Dinnae fash, wee one.' A smile curved at the corner of her lips. 'You can help me while yer ma is away, there's pigs tae be tended to and Auld Iain is no as sprightly as he used tae be, he could do with an extra pair of hands.'

Jenny's shoulders relaxed a little.

Mistress Cochran looked again at me. 'What is it that's got you in such a state?'

What could I say? My good fir nothing husband has stolen from the only man who would employ us and disappeared into the night in a whisp of smoke, leaving me to face his consequences, again. Instead I said. 'I've heard Rupert lost track of time up at Acheson's, Master Rivet needs him urgently fir some work back in France so I've been sent tae fetch him and yae ken Acheson's is no place fir a wee girl.'

'Have you told Agnes?'

'Aye. Well . . . some. She's coming to help me find Rupert.' I rubbed Jenny's shoulder. 'It willnae be fir long. Mistress Cochran will take good care of you, and I'll be back before you know it, with yer da.' I kissed the top of her head.

'Will you no stay fer a wee dram? You'll catch yer death.'

I shook my head, to frightened to speak for fear any resolve I had would be lost in the tears that were about to come. I had to find Rupert. My head was thick with worry, and for now I could only cling to the fact that Jenny would be safe, hidden at Mill House.

* * *

The track leading to the crossroads was edged with trees,

whose leaves hung like burgundy lace. The rain had abated, leaving behind it a blanket of sullen clouds. At the bend in the road, the shapes before me came into focus: Agnes's old nag and Dr Fian's fine beast, just down from a bare willow tree.

Just as I pushed the pony on, I felt it again, the unmistakable stirring in my belly. The tension in my body ebbed away. My baby was still alive.

'Ma' – I nodded my greeting – 'And you've brought Dr Fian?'

'I hope you don't mind, Besse, it was on my insistence. I couldn't see you go to such a place unaccompanied,' he said, his elegant, gloved fingers wrapped around the reins.

'Of course not, doctor. We'd be glad of yer company,' I said.

'Yer mother tells me that yer husband may be up at Acheson's Haven?'

'Yes,' I said shakily; how much had my mother told him? I needed to speak with her alone. My situation was more perilous than I could ever have imagined. 'It seems likely he was up there playin' a game of dice. Lost, no doubt. He was due home not three days since, and you ken I'm worried; it isn't like him not to come home.'

My mother muttered something under her breath.

'What?' I said.

Agnes cleared her throat. 'I said, I'd prefir it if the bastard did us all a favour and didnae return.'

'Agnes,' Dr Fian said, aghast. 'I don't think that now is the time nor the place to b—'

'I make no bones about how I feel about him,' she interrupted, straightening herself in her saddle. 'But he is my daughter's husband, and I will do everything in my power to bring him home.'

'I think we should leave now, to make the most of the daylight,' I said, reining the horse north towards the harbour. 'Mother, I need to speak with you.' She had to know the urgency of it.

She came without hesitating, drawing her mare alongside. On horseback, any attempt at privacy was almost useless. Dr Fian, curious but always a gentleman, hung back to allow us to move further off.

'What is it? Is it the baby?' she asked, voice tight with worry.

'No, the baby is fine. It's Master Rivet . . . he found the belladonna.'

I could see from the twitch of her jaw that the news was not welcome. 'Did he recognise it?'

'Aye, that he did, and he accused me of witchcraft before he fled,' I croaked, leaving out the fact that the bastard had tried to rape me; some things were best left unsaid and I knew only too well of Agnes's unholy temper.

I placed a hand on her arm and felt her body tense. I knew what she was thinking: that I'd be hunted as a witch. It was no more than I thought myself.

'Mary, mother of God! What on earth were you doin' with it on yer table? Were you givin' it to Rupert? Please say you aren't tryin' tae tell me he's dead?'

'It was an accident.' The words spilled out of me like a torrent. 'Jonet was desperate, and you were gone. I told her tae only give him a wee bit. Just enough tae make him sleep, before he would get too drunk and quick with his fists.' Tears pricked at my eyes. 'She'd used it nice and early, only he'd fallen, in her garden. I helped her get him up tae bed, left him snoring like a pig. Then you came over and told me he was dead, but he had been very much alive the last time I saw him.'

'You should have come to me, I could've told you how much tae give him,' she said, fists balled in temper. 'What were you thinkin'? What was Jonet thinkin', askin' ye?'

'She was desperate. You didnae see the state of her.' I reached out for her again. 'Ma, I dinnae want to go to gaol. I should never have helped her. Rupert was right, and now he's missing, and my children will be orphaned. We have tae find him.' I looked further up the track, cheeks chilled with tears. I was desperate to be away and moving. I just wanted my husband. He needed to speak to Master Rivet, to explain to him that I was no witch. He needed to pay back what he owed and make it right. Make it all right. I had more chance of seeing our sow fly, but Rupert was the only hope I had.

She set her hand on my arm. 'No daughter of mine is going tae gaol. We'll find him and we'll clear this mess up.'

'I would have been better goin' alone. It's too dangerous fir you and the doctor. It will arouse suspicion.'

She looked back towards the doctor, hunched in his saddle. 'It would arouse more suspicion if you went alone. I cannae see Mark Acheson welcomin' a woman who's been roaming the coast searchin' for her wayward husband, can you? Men are all fir an assertive woman, as long as she's doin' exactly what she's told and not interrupting their drinking. No, 'tis good that we have John's company, a good honest man. Someone those other men'll listen to.' She shrugged. 'And even if you say no,

I'm comin' anyway. Don't give me that look. You'd do the same.'

She was right. I couldn't deny it. We all knew it, even Dr Fian. We walked the horses along the ruts in the track, winding our way north. I had told her briefly about everything but neglected to mention I'd left Jenny with Willy at Mistress Cochran's. My heart ached at the thought of leaving her, but she would slow us down and, by now, there would be men out looking for us. It was the only safe place.

My skin crawled at the thought of what punishment Master Rivet would inflict on Jenny, if he found her. Every time I closed my eyes I could feel his touch on my skin, his whisky-soaked breath on my cheek. My mind's eye flashed back to his ghastly pallor as he stumbled back at the sight of the belladonna. But where had it come from?

I couldn't tell how long the journey would take, and the thought of it set my nerves on edge. The trees thickened as we walked on, green pines speckled between leaves of reds and golds.

As we ploughed on further towards the coast, the horror of my night seemed to ebb away like the tide, replaced with wavering joy at the thought of seeing my husband again. But sometimes he just didn't want to be found.

One time it had started when I'd walked into Master Rivet's unannounced. I should have known better. I'd caught sight of him through the window, sat large as life with a whisky in his hand, leaning smugly against the hearth. I'd seen hide nor hair of him in two days. Sick with worry, I pushed open the door, calling his name. That had been my first mistake. I should have known better.

He turned to me, smiling like a scythe. 'What is it, woman?'

Master Rivet carried on staring into the fire.

I remember wincing, hearing the fury in his voice. If I had just walked away when I'd noticed him in the window, all would have been fine. He would have come home worse for wear and slept it off.

'I would like my husband to come home, if it isnae too much trouble.'

Foolish. Foolish. Foolish. What on earth had I hoped to achieve?

His eyes shone glassy with rage as he crossed the room gracefully, coming to a stop in front of me. 'I'll be home when I'm good and ready, and not before,' he'd said it in a light-hearted manner, much too light-hearted for Rupert.

He ushered me away from the door and closed it behind me. He made sure to teach me a lesson, but not with his fists. For more than a week I waited, my eyes darting to the door at every groan, every click of the latch. He didn't return.

He was away so often, in the Borders or over in Edinburgh, that my life felt as though it carried on without him, but it had only ever been a day or two, never more. He finally appeared, almost three weeks later, like a phantom. That was the start of his trips to France. Weeks here. Weeks there. His outfits becoming more elaborate with every trip. As time passed I watched his gradual return to the man I had fallen in love with, but this time the ruse was not for me. I knew better than to ever question my husband. A husband who never wanted to be found.

* * *

The day was melting seamlessly into evening when we arrived. The boats that lined the harbour pitched and rolled, causing the light from the candles aboard decks to flicker. They were bright and steady enough to relieve some of the darkness. The air was filled with the smells from the cooperage, fish-meal and the stink from the butcher's pork as we entered Acheson's Tavern.

The noise was at shouting level. We managed to find ourselves a table, even though the place was packed. I looked around the room, filled to bursting with all manner of folk, from Shetlanders to Dutchmen. From whores to wives. Thick smoke spirals churned above. There was no sign of Rupert.

'Say what you like about Acheson's Tavern, but it's always full of men who should be home,' muttered Agnes, eyeing the man sat at the table in the corner and talking to a whore. She was dark-haired and fat, a face I thought I recognised from my visits to the apothecary. Was it Kitte? Or Janet? I couldn't recall.

'At least we're in the dry,' said Dr Fian, shaking the rain from his overcoat and sitting on the bench facing Agnes.

A man, standing in a crowd near the bar, threw his head back and laughed, spilling beer down his front. Another jeered, clapping a hand on the man's back.

'Ma, do you really think Rupert could be in a place like this?'

'Aye. Why don't we have a drink?' Agnes said brightly. 'We'll all feel better after a drink.'

'Oh no,' said Dr Fian. 'I shouldn't want to be drinking in a house of ill fame.' He looked vaguely around the crowded tavern.

'Surely, ye've got tae drink something?' I said. 'I ken I'm as thirsty as a parched field.'

'That settles it.' Agnes stood up and glanced at the crowded bar. 'I willnae be long.'

Dr Fian and I were left to our own private thoughts, with him staring fixedly at the table, his back as rigid as a stake. He was the most handsome man I had ever seen, alive or dead, even in his twilight years. A bachelor that attracted the attention of all the women as he entered a room, but the doctor had always much preferred the company of men. A secret that Agnes and I would take to our graves.

'There isnae a person in Tranent knows that we're here,' I said, as I eyed the door with uncertainty. Master Rivet was sure to be hunting me, with half the village. 'Once we find Rupert, we can be on our way, and no one will be any the wiser.'

We watched as the Orcadian took one final swig, lay back on the bench by the fire and fell asleep. There was a short silence from over near the bar and, a moment later, a great barrel of a man, with white sideburns that he seemed to be growing to distract from his baldness, towered over Agnes. I couldn't mistake Mark Acheson.

'I'd be grateful if we could be on our way sooner rather than later,' said Dr Fian, nervously.

'Thank you fir yer company, doctor. It's appreciated.'

He straightened himself a little. 'No need fir thanks. I didn't think that women should be coming to such a place, although I don't think the place is fit fir a refined man either.'

'Here we are,' Agnes said as she emerged from the swarm, carrying three cups. 'The only wine they have.' She sat down, glancing about her. 'I gave the man serving an extra coin fir information about Rupert. It seems he left two days since. He lost everything he had on a game of dice. Scuttled out of town, owin' a lot of money.' She took a sip from her cup. 'They say it was to privateers.'

I looked about at the throng. A man tried to kiss one of the women leaning on the bar; she rebuked him with a come-hither squeal. In that instant, I realised my husband was a complete stranger.

'He must be mistaken. *This* is where my husband has been spending his time?' As I said it, I felt the baby move.

Agnes nodded.

'I would like to speak with this landlord,' said Dr Fian, rising from his seat and disappearing into the crush.

I could tell from the way he walked that Dr Fian was as nervous as a hare being hunted. A man of his standing didn't keep the kind of company that frequented Acheson's. He preferred the company of men, refined men at that.

After being left unattended a wee while, the man locked his eyes on us and sauntered over to where we sat and slid his arms about our shoulders, like an adder.

'Let me buy you ladies another drink,' he said, in the hope of striking up some curiosity from either of us. A

Dutchman, by all accounts. 'My name is Coel Egbert. I ship at dawn, for Denmark on *The Grace of God.*'

'Laddie,' Agnes hissed, 'if those hands of yers touch me again, by the grace of God, you'll be bound fir the churchyard.'

'An old whore doesn't get to speak to me like that,' he growled from the corner of his mouth.

My heart sank to the depths of my shoes as Agnes stood up. It was no wonder Rupert wanted me to have nothing to do with her or her healing . . . she was a law unto herself. I took another sip of my wine and averted my gaze.

'Now, listen up, my lad' – she leaned deeper on to her crutch – 'I'm no' a whoor, and neither is my daughter. I'm auld enough tae be yer mother and a woman of good standin'. You'd do well tae remember it. You speak to any of the folk in here and ask about Agnes Sampson; you see what they say.'

'I hope yer not givin' Agnes any trouble?' Mark Acheson had wandered over, under the guise of collecting mugs from the table. 'I'd like you to leave these ladies alone.'

The Dutchman ignored him and shook his head, inclining himself close enough that I all I could smell was the stench of smoke, farts and spilled beer.

'You,' Mark said, towering over the Dutchman, 'I want you gone.'

Agnes leaned towards the Dutchman. 'Surely not before – Egbert, is it? – Egbert buys us that drink he kindly offered. We'll have two more wines.'

'Mother! Must ye?'

She let out a cackle. The Dutchman stepped forward; chin up, chest out, to let us know he wasn't afraid. Mark pointed him towards the door. If he didn't leave soon, he'd be gone by the seat of his breeches, the back of his shirt and a mouth full of dirt for his trouble.

'Devil's whores, the lot of them.' He spat on the floor. 'Stick it up yer arse.'

'Better a Devil's whoor than a tallow-catch!' Agnes called after him.

There was a short, hot silence ringing with her words as we watched him weave his way through the crowd and out through the door.

'He's one of the men that came over with the Dutch fleet, bringing the king's new bride. From what I hear it was a terrible crossing: a boiling tempest almost sank the fleet.' He cleared away the table. 'Same again, Agnes?'

'Aye, Mark,' she said, settling herself back into her seat.

'I'll put it on his tab.' He smiled down at me. 'And who is this ye've brought with ye?'

'This is Besse, my daughter.' She pointed in my direction and over-emphasised the next words. 'Rupert's wife.'

'My condolences, lassie' – he held out a hand, as if to apologise – 'fir putting up with such a man. I didnae ken a ruffian like Rupert had a hame tae go to.'

'Aye, that's my husband. I hear he's lost at a game of dice.' A look shot between Agnes and Mark, so quick I almost missed it.

'He did, aye, in a fashion. He got caught using loaded dice by the captain of *The Salamander of Leith*, Andrew Barton. Slipped out of town with his tail between his legs, two days ago. Haven't heard a word about him since.'

The more they talked about my husband, the more it

felt as though they were talking of some stranger, a half-truth that was laced with lies and fables.

Agnes cleared her throat. 'And what have you done with the good doctor?' she said, in an attempt to change the subject. There was something she wasn't telling me.

'Ach, some of the men have taken it upon themselves tae get the good doctor good and pished,' he said before disappearing to fetch our drinks.

We swivelled in our seats. Dr Fian, already three sheets to the wind, was swaying gently like a string of wheat. He was trying to prop himself against a fine-looking young gentleman who seemed to be reciprocating his amorous advances.

'John!' Agnes shouted. 'Dr Fian! It's time we were going.'

He waved a hand to beckon us over, one eye half-closed. 'Come now and meet this lovely gentleman,' he slurred. 'Says he knows yer Rupert.'

Agnes and I exchanged worried glances. The air buzzed as a fight brewed.

'We were tryin' tae be discreet,' I said in a low voice, trying not to attract Mark Acheson's attention. 'At this rate Master Rivet and half of Tranent will be here by dawn. Just look at him.'

We got over in time to see a fight break out. Shouting rose up over the din. There was a push and a shove, and then it was all over. Dr Fian lay sprawled on the floor, garbling drunken words. It sounded as though the whole tavern jeered.

'He needs tae go hame,' said the Orcadian. 'Afore he gets hurt.'

'You'll never guess . . .' Dr Fian forced the 's' sound through his teeth for much longer than he should have. 'He tells me their fleet escorted the king and his new bride.' He made a noise somewhere between a pig and a mule. 'But instead, the king spent his wedding night with a male whoor . . . Go on ask him, he'll tell ya.'

'Get him tae his feet,' Agnes barked.

I looked from Dr Fian to the door and back again, trying to work out how we were going to get him home to Tranent. He mumbled something incoherently as he tried to gather himself to his feet. He slid along the wall, his face bewildered at his legs' disobedience, before crashing back to the floor.

Someone must have sent for Mark, who took two hands and hoisted Dr Fian over his shoulder. 'Agnes, you ken you and yer kin are welcome anytime, but dinnae be bringin' me a man who cannae hold his ale,' he said, with Dr Fian lolling like a snapped neck rabbit on his shoulder as he carried him to our tethered horses.

'Aye, we'll be on our way.' Agnes swung herself onto the saddle and fastened Dr Fian's horse to hers. 'Lay the drunken bugger over here.' She indicated her lap. 'Might sober the fool up.'

Dr Fian was unceremoniously hung like a deer carcass over the withers of Agnes's pony. As we moved off, slowly and trying not to dislodge him, our drunken charge made an attempt at singing to lighten our moods, but he sounded more like a goose farting.

'What *are* you doing?' I asked.

'I'm a tryin' . . .' He paused, collecting his thoughts. 'Tryin' tae sing "The Witches Reel"'

'That's what yer callin' it?' said Agnes. 'How about you get some rest? You might sober by the time we reach St Andrew's.' She turned to me. 'Besse, you must fetch Jenny and meet me at St Andrew's. We can keep you hidden in the refectory until we can sort this mess with Master Rivet.'

Thankfully, it wasn't long before the doctor fell asleep, which put a stop to his incessant drunken singing. As the wine wore off, I felt my deep uneasiness return. *Where was Rupert?* Rushed as we were, I was no further in finding my missing husband. Fear gripped my heart. Now we were to return home, and I'd be forced to face Master Rivet alone.

Agnes and I carried on in comfortable silence. Whatever had been passed between her and Mark Acheson, my mother wouldn't tell me. She was right: the only place safe for us now would be St Andrew's.

From Wicked Men's Mouths

Towards dawn I'd left them back at the crossroads with Dr Fian now fully in control of his wayward limbs and his mount. The stars still lingered against the inky black of night as it fought against the sunrise.

I had been grateful for their company but beneath the silence of the tree bows my mind began to uncoil, stretching and flexing and allowing itself to think.

What if Rivet was already looking for me? The thought of it terrified me. At any moment our paths could cross. If I could just get to Jenny and get back to the refectory unseen, then we would be safe, at least for a while.

The rumours would spread like blistering damp. Already dripping from the lips of the washer women. *What happened when the bitter, twisted lies became truth?* St Andrew's refectory was no place to hide a child. I would give my mother three days. If she hadn't managed to find Rupert by then and put an end to the nonsense with Master Rivet, then we would have to leave, there would be nothing else for it. We'd have to flee like the Catholics.

Mistress Cochran wouldn't appreciate me arriving at such an ungodly hour. I squinted in the direction of

Mill House: not a flicker of light. I'd often wondered how she kept a house full of boys in line, but that was before we'd found Willy. Spare the rod and spoil the child, she'd barked, hands clasped in her lap when I'd burst in unannounced, Willy clinging to my waist. We came to a mutual understanding. She'd never raise a hand to him again, and I wouldn't call upon my mother.

My boy would never be afraid. Never. I'd make sure of it.

I carried on riding. Winding my way through the dawn and into mid morning. I had stared at the sky and I had raged against God. I had begged and I had pleaded. I had bargained and I had prayed but no matter what I did, I could not see a way to stop what was to come.

The pony heard the noise first, a great, low rumbling. I felt the muscles rippling beneath the saddle as he stiffened. My sweaty palms made it hard to hold onto the reins. He twisted suddenly, throwing me sideways as I struggled to hold him back. I stared wide-eyed into the oncoming sea of faces mad with blood fever and cries of the same.

The pony snorted and tossed its head, nostrils flaring before rearing full height and bolting. I tumbled to the earth in a flurry of limbs. I watched in horror as my only means of escape disappeared, almost taking Father Cowper with it. I stood and looked at the crowd. Most of Tranent were there, at least the ones that could be roused from their beds. Leading them was Gilbert Leith, a thick-set man with a scar that ran the length of his cheek, and his nephew, Iain.

Gilbert spoke first. 'Elizabeth Craw, you stand accused of the crime of witchcraft. What do you say?'

My voice died in my throat. The knot in my stomach tightened, until I was almost concave with despair. I instinctively reached for my belly, feeling for anything awry.

He carried on. 'The accused did cause the death of Master Andrew Muir by means of witchcraft.'

The crowd parted and the silhouette of Master Rivet filled the space. Dressed in his finest waistcoat and breeches, which only just fit where they touched. 'I've seen you leaving the house at all hours of the night,' he said. 'I ken she goes tae meet wi' her consort, the Devil.' The murmuring of the crowd quietened as they strained to hear. ''Tis right you call her a witch; she was the one who brought sickness upon my poor wife.'

I swallowed. There was an awed gasp as the crowd shuffled uneasily. Everyone in the village had known I'd tended Goodwife Rivet in her sickness, under the watchful eye of Agnes. I had treated her lameness and delirium, to no avail. Even as her condition worsened and the muscular tremors began, there was nothing more that could have been done.

''Tis nights she does her evil, grindin' her herbs and makin' her charms. She calls her coven tae meet at St Andrew's Auld Kirk.' Master Rivet spoke slowly and deliberately. 'I've seen it with my very eyes.' The excitement of the expectant crowd grew.

'Yer a liar, David Rivet!'

The ranks of the crowd surged forward. My heart felt as though it was trying to escape from my mouth. I was shoved and jostled as clumps of hair were torn from my head. Thrown face-first to the ground, they bound my hands behind my back with leather fastenings. I pulled against them, but they wouldn't give.

'You'll be brought before the witch pricker,' Gilbert Leith said, holding me tightly.

'No!' I thrashed and shrieked, but with a Leith on each arm it made no difference. I turned to face the crowd. 'Rivet tried tae rape me! This is his doing!'

The hysteria was palpable. Hands tore at my clothes, and fingers clawed at my flesh. I was dragged through the crowd, and the two beasts steering me paid me no mind.

The rain was coming down harder now, laced with hail. My skin stung from the force of it. I looked down at my belly. Was I to lose another baby, like this? Did God think so little of me? I knew I was being taken to the Session House, where I'd be held until the Privy Council was called. Just like the first woman I watched burn.

'Gilbert,' I croaked, 'please, you ken very well I had nothing tae dee wi' it. I've healed yer wife and birthed yer second child.'

'Silence, witch. I dinnae want tae hear yer poison.'

My stockings had fallen around my ankles and, with no shoes to cover them, they were slipping over my feet, causing me to stumble. I paid them no mind. Thoughts of Jenny swirled like a storm. What possessed me not to tell my mother where I'd hidden her? Now, all I could do was to hope and pray that Mistress Cochran would keep her hidden, keep her safe.

As we walked on, the air became salty and sharp, with the rasps of the crows being drowned out by the gulls. I followed them like a cow being led to market, down a narrow track which took me through a meadow filled with heather. A white building loomed on the horizon.

The dark shapes of ravens lined the roof, cawing skywards. Pushed roughly through the door, I landed on the stone floor with a thump. As my eyes adjusted to the gloom, I could see the room itself was small, with a table holding a jug of filthy water and some stale bread. Finally, with my hands unbound, the room fell silent with the slam of the door.

After being in childbed twice, modesty wasn't an affliction I had suffered with, but walking through the crowd had left my clothes in shreds and my pride in tatters. What little clothing I had left was soaked through and I had nothing to light a fire. I rubbed at my wrists. The skin was beginning to bruise in purple ridges. Wrapping myself in a blanket and hugging my knees, I must have resembled a dog that had been swilled with a pail.

Somewhere between fear and frostbite, I lay listening to the roar of the sea and prayed that Jenny was undiscovered. She would be terrified I hadn't returned, and Agnes would be frantic. If she could only find Rupert, he could put a stop to it. Master Rivet would listen to him – hopefully.

Later – I don't know when – I was roused by the sound of hoofbeats on cobblestones. I sat up stiffly and assessed the bread that had been left; it would have made a better weapon than breakfast. I submerged it in the jug of water to soften it. My stomach ached, but it would have to go on doing so.

When they came for me, I was bound again. This time they made sure to silence me. Tears trickled from my eyes as they forced the scold's bridle over my face, filling my mouth with the taste of metal when the spikes pressed against my tongue and the soft flesh of my cheeks.

I was marched through a crowd that parted like bees from a smoking hive. I searched their faces, each of them refusing to meet my eyes. Faces I'd known all my life and now like strangers, every last one of them. Then my eyes happened upon Mistress Cochran hiding behind the kirk. I was grateful for her presence but, fearful of recrimination, I didn't rest my gaze on her for long. Was she looking for Agnes?

My legs grew heavy with dread as I was herded through the village square. Three members of the kirk looked at me, each one seeing a Devil's whore. The first, a man I didn't recognise, was stout and balding on top. The second was a man of about my age, sharp and wicked. The hatred rose from the pit of my stomach like bile.

I glanced at the last man. I was done for.

The County Bailiff, David Rivet, was sat in the third seat. His hair was neatly combed and atop his head was the blue bonnet that he made me wash for him to attend church every Sunday. The glint in his eye told me I was about to be paid back for every mortal sin he had committed.

'Elizabeth Craw, you have been charged under the Scottish Witchcraft Act of 1563. Anyone who should use, practise or exercise witchcraft, enchantment, charm or sorcery, whereby any person is killed or destroyed, shall be put tae death without benefit of clergy.' He lifted his face to the crowd. 'You'll be winched until you confess yer accomplices. Leith, bring out the ropes.'

In that brief moment, my soul broke. What accomplices? My only crime had been to give Jonet something to help her husband sleep. Was I to give him the names of my kin, my mother? Dr Fian? What of my husband? Should he not be made to pay for his transgressions? After all, it was Rupert who had stolen the rents. I could hear the collective murmuring of the crowd as the wind whipped my tear-stained face. 'Witch!' they shouted.

The Leiths wound the rope around my temples, being careful not to touch my skin, leaving several feet hanging loosely at each side. Neither man raised his eyes to look at me; their fear was palpable.

A man on each rope, they both stepped two paces backwards at the command of the kirk. The rope slid across my forehead, searing my skin. I could taste my hot tears. The leather of the bridle darkened as it filled with liquid, chaffing the skin on my cheeks. I gasped as it slackened, falling to the floor in a tangle of shredded cloth and jeers from the crowd.

'Bring her tae her feet.' I felt rough hands upon me as I was dragged from the floor. 'Take off the scold's bridle.'

As they peeled it away, I tentatively moved my jaw, which ached terribly. My tongue was beginning to crust from the whipping winds, and I could still taste the blood from where one of the spikes had penetrated the flesh.

'Two nights ago, when you left the croft, where did you meet wi' yer Devil?' I couldn't mistake the voice of Master Rivet.

'I was out birthin' John Ancroft's bairn,' I rasped.

This was met with audible gasps and jeers. 'The bairn's dead!' 'A changeling!' 'Burn her!' Agnes had been right; he must have survived nought but a day. It was hopeless.

'None more harmful than a woman curing without

having studied. Tie her tae the whipping post,' commanded Rivet. 'Strip her naked. I've no doubt her garments are charmed with the skin of the Ancrofts' unbaptised child. They say she took the caul.'

Excitement rippled through the crowd. I was at their mercy.

Iain Leith took me by the elbow and dragged me to the heretics' post. He looped a length of rope around my wrists, tying it tight and hoisting my hands high above my head, fastening me to the post. I pressed my forehead hard against the damp wood, tightly shut my eyes and waited.

Hoofbeats thundered over the silence of the crowd. Through the crook of my arm, I angled my face towards the direction of the sound. A gentleman in ceremonial plaid dismounted a stallion and walked briskly over to the members of the kirk.

'Cannae ask why you think it necessary tae interrupt this meetin' o' the kirk, dispensing justice in the name of the Almighty?' said Rivet, clearly angered.

The man pulled out a slip of paper from the inside of his coat and handed it over without a word. It was passed along the line until it reached David Rivet, who simply blinked once or twice.

'Cut her down,' he said.

The crowd seemed stunned. Never had I been so grateful for whatever pardon had been on that parchment. Finally, the truth. Gilbert Leith pushed through the crowd and sliced through the rope. As the tension gave way, my aching body sagged and I stumbled before collapsing to my knees.

'By order of James VI of Scotland, you are tae be moved

tae the Tolbooth prison in Edinburgh, where you are tae be further examined by the witch prickers,' said Rivet as I felt the familiar hands of the Leiths at my elbows, lifting me to my feet. 'You have relied upon the charity of Master Rivet and that of this village since yer husband disappeared. Any property you have will now be sold and the debt repaid.'

'No.' I planted my bare feet firmly in the cold, sodden earth. 'You cannae take me. NO!' I thrashed and kicked and pulled against them. 'No! Get off me, you bastards! No!' This time when I kicked out, my foot connected with Iain Leith's knee, sending him face-down into the mud. We were quickly lost in the surging crowd, in a sea of crude taunts. I soon felt cold hands upon me once more, and I was shoved back towards my rectangular prison. There, I was again thrown to the stone floor with a bone-shuddering thump and shut inside like an animal.

I crawled to the door on all fours and began beating it with my fists. 'Let me out of here!' I screamed, pulling myself up and kicking the door, blow after blow until I collapsed with exhaustion.

The room rang with silence. It smelled fetid, and the stale bread was gone, along with the filthy water. Had they hoped I wouldn't return?

I wanted Rupert. I wanted my mother. But most of all I wanted Jenny. I touched a hand to my stomach. He was still there, I could feel it. He hadn't left me. Crawling numbly under the blanket, once more my dreams turned to Jenny as I drifted in and out of consciousness and waited for the darkness to consume me.

A Boy

Even in winter, Mistress Cochran's garden was filled with the scents of flowers. Jenny idled amongst them, scuffing the ground with her foot. She felt like she had waited an eternity for her mother to return; she knew it would be one day, maybe two at the most, but she was bored. Boredom was the affliction of all children when left alone longer than five minutes.

The new day was glorious with its bright skies and sharp breeze. Her belly was full from the rough bread and goat's milk the kitchen maid had given her at breakfast. She wandered to the edge of the neatly tended lawn and climbed the fence. Looking down the track, she could see smoking chimneys poking through the trees and the narrow stream that weaved its way all the way to the shore, where her and Willy had bumped into the butcher's boy.

Someone's there. Mistress Cochran had left hours ago to head to town, and since then the place had been empty, apart from Ian, the stable hand who was away tending the horses. She held her breath and bit her lip and listened to the soft crack of branches behind the tree-line. She wished Willy was here.

When Jenny finally summoned the nerve, she squeaked open the gate and edged her way down the track, keeping close to the hedgerows. A few times she glimpsed motion, but it was too far off to see clearly. She crouched down in the furrow hidden in the long grass and listened to the crunch of the dried leaves and the crack of every branch echoing in the stillness where the trees thinned.

When the grey mare thundered up the track, kicking up mud and slurry, Jenny's heart raced. Mistress Cochran dismounted and, holding the reins, she hurried towards the door.

'Ian!' Mistress Cochran shouted. 'Ian!'

A slender man with a face pointed like a rat's bolted from somewhere near the back of the house. His hair was pulled taught and fastened, so that it hung down his back with wisps of grey, which matched his eyes.

'Aye, mistress.'

'Please, take my mare,' she said, handing him the reins.

Jenny watched from her hiding place, far enough away not to be seen but close enough to listen.

'Ian, have you seen the wee lassie that is staying with us?' she said with a pained expression.

He stared blankly and shook his head before leaving with the mare plodding behind him. Jenny scrambled over the dirt and ran back through the gate.

'There you are. Quickly now, lass, get inside.' She hurried Jenny over the threshold and closed the door firmly behind them. 'Listen now, I want you tae go straight up to yer room and close the door. Make sure tae lock it and dinnae open it unless it's me that knocks.' She pushed her towards the stairs. 'Hurry now.'

Jenny hitched up her skirts and took the stairs two at a time. The polished floorboards groaned underfoot as she made her way down the gallery to the second door on the east side of the house. The empty bedchamber resembled a dark cave. The fireplace alone was almost as big as the bedroom she shared with her mother. She slid inside and locked the door behind her and hid beneath the bed.

She had heard the stories from Willy, and Mistress Cochran terrified her. Jenny had felt safe knowing that the threat of her mother and grandmother would be enough to make sure Mistress Cochran would not lay a finger on her. Now, she wasn't so sure.

A short while later a gentle rapping came at the chamber door. Jenny held her breath and waited.

'It's okay, it's me,' said Mistress Cochran through the door.

Jenny crept from her hiding place and reached up to turn the key. Mistress Cochran slid through the door and locked it just as quickly as she had opened it. Every line of her body sang with nerves. Clutched to her breast she had a pair of breeches and a small set of shears.

She steered Jenny to the bed. 'Sit down, lass.'

'What is it? Why do I have tae hide?'

'When I went tae fetch beans and herbs this morning, I saw a great procession heading fir the whipping post, you ken?' She folded the breeches neatly and laid the shears on top.

'Aye, Ma says it's the one they use fir heretics.'

'That's the one.' The old woman took Jenny's hand in hers and sat down on the bed. 'They had another witch, so I was told. I took a peek from outside the old butcher's and there, tied to the post, was yer mother.'

A noise somewhere between shock and fear burst free

from Jenny's lips. She held her hand across her mouth. 'Do they intend to burn her?' she whispered.

'That I cannae say, but what I ken very well is that they will be lookin' fir a witch's child.'

'But my mother isn't a witch.'

'No, she's no' a witch, but that willnae stop them from looking fir you.' She squeezed her hand gently. 'I promised yer mother that I'd keep you safe, and that's exactly what I intend tae do.'

She picked up the shears in her thumb and forefinger and gathered Jenny's hair. Mistress Cochran worked in silence, and Jenny's curls tumbled onto the bed covers. After a short while, Jenny stood before her with the hair shorn close to her head. She handed her the breeches and a starched linen shirt that she had taken from the stable boy. Willy would never recognise her.

'Take off yer things.' She helped Jenny out of her skirt and blouse and into the breeches and shirt. 'Now, if anyone asks, you are my nephew, Robert, visiting from Edinburgh. I shall have you work in the stable; you seem tae have a knack with horses.'

Jenny turned the name over in her head. It sounded like her father's. Maybe it would make it easy to remember. Rob. Robert. She couldn't tell if it was fear or excitement or somewhere in between but she had always wanted to wear breeches, to rough and tumble and play in the mud. She could climb trees, swim burns – and no one would utter a word.

She picked up the pewter dish, gently blowing the hair away. The reflection that stared back at her was no longer her own. The round, freckled face of a boy blinked back at her. Grubby and indistinct. She doubted her own mother would recognise her.

For the first time in her life, she looked like her father.

Something Wicked This Way Comes

Agnes and Dr Fian had ridden in silence all the way to St Andrew's, with the doctor wincing with every jolt. Acheson's Tavern had offered more questions than answers. Somehow, Rupert had managed to disappear and, with talk of another woman on his arm, Agnes was keen to know the truth of it.

'I've asked that Besse fetch Jenny and I'm goin' tae have them stay inside the refectory,' Agnes said it as more of a statement than a question. She didn't need the doctor's permission to hide her daughter and granddaughter, although she would need to tell him something. 'Master Rivet isnae happy that Rupert has stolen the rents and he's threatened to throw them from the cot-house.' She decided he didn't need to know about the threat of the witch hunt.

'Agnes, you must report him.' Dr Fian was seething.

'To who? He is the County Bailiff, is he not? Who would believe me? It is his land to do with it as he sees fit.' She paused, weighing up how much to reveal to the doctor. 'It appears that my son-in-law has himself another woman.'

'How can you be so sure?' the doctor said, clutching at his pounding head.

Agnes had no sympathy for the drunken oaf. 'He's been lying low since he was caught tryin' tae fleece the Dutchmen with a set of rigged dice, but Mark Acheson tells me that Rupert often goes there with another woman on his arm, a French one at that. Besse has every right to know.'

'Agnes,' he said carefully, 'do you think you should be taking up the matter with Besse? It occurs to me that when other women are concerned, it's often best that a wife remains oblivious.'

Of course, it would be better. Agnes knew of her daughter's fragile condition. That was exactly why she hadn't told her and sworn Mark Acheson to secrecy, but Agnes needed time to think, without the doctor's interference, before Besse returned with Jenny. It seemed to her that everyone seemed to be hiding something, Rupert more than most.

As they neared the refectory, she pulled up her mare, dismounted with an air of good riddance and ventured inside, leaving Dr Fian to fend for himself. The place looked more mouldering than usual, with no candlelight in the sconces. Muffled voices and mutterings from the infirm filtered from the pews as the click of her crutch and the dim glow from her candle roused them from their sick beds.

Dr Fian, although sore of head and regretful of his exploits, came in and got straight on with his work. Agnes busied herself in the vestry, alone with her thoughts and watched over by the stone angels and their folded wings.

Later, the hammering noise shattered the silence. Cries from across the causeway pierced the air as Agnes pulled open the door to be greeted by Jean Gray, breathless and slick with rain. Her eyes darted between Agnes and Dr Fian.

'Agnes!' She heaved air into her lungs as her voice rose and fell. 'They've taken Besse!'

'Come in, come in, lass,' Agnes said, ushering her inside. 'Tell me.'

'They . . . they arrested her for witchcraft . . .' Jean breathed.

'Who did?'

'Master Rivet and the kirk.'

Agnes's eyes flicked momentarily to Dr Fian, before she said, 'What of Jenny? Did you see my grandchild?'

Before Jean could answer, the noise from the crowd on the causeway grew, as they got closer. For a moment, it seemed as though the whole church was holding its breath.

'Quick,' whispered Agnes, 'over here.' She blew out the last of the candles and they waited.

The approaching horde swarmed across the walkway, baying for witches' blood. Dr Fian crouched between pews, knees pushed against the stone. He cradled a baby to his chest, swaddled in an old rag.

Now, only the holy doors separated them from the mob.

'We've no way out.' Agnes stood with her back pressed against the font.

'We could leave through the north door and escape through the kirkyard,' Dr Fian said.

The roar of men echoed as they rained blow after blow against the door, sending splinters into the darkness. Agnes could remember the church before its desecration, before the papists were converted. Now, so little remained, and it all belonged to the kirk.

'What of the rest of them?'

The refectory was littered with the sick and infirm. On such a bitterly cold night, to have them face the freezing sleet and attempt such a dangerous crossing would almost certainly mean death.

'You must take the child and flee,' Agnes said. 'I'll stay here; that door won't hold much longer.'

'And leave you here? I cannae poss—'

'You can and you must. Someone needs tae find Jenny.'

Agnes took him by the elbow and ushered him, with Jean, towards the north door. She placed her ear against the wood and listened. Stillness. She fumbled in the darkness until her hands clasped the key, it turned. Air rushed into the chamber with a hiss. Agnes took off her plaid and wrapped it around Dr Fian and the baby, securing it with a silver stag's head brooch edged with thistle.

The shouts and crashes from the doors were coming faster. Dr Fian hovered, unwilling to leave her.

'There's no more time,' she said briskly. 'I'll be alright, they'll no' think I'm anything more than a cripple. Now, go.'

He turned and headed for the trees that lined the north of the kirkyard, Jean not far behind. Agnes watched in silence as they disappeared into the woods and, with a final glance, closed the door.

The light from torches seeped through the cracks and

fissures in the door, casting strings of orange against the pale stone.

'JOHN FIAN! You are wanted on charges of witchcraft and sodomy. Open these doors!'

Frightened eyes darted back and forth in the darkness of the refectory. Those that were able huddled together. Agnes turned towards the noise.

The doors blew open. Feet thundered into the stillness of the church; hands tore at flesh as they searched amongst the bodies, calling the doctor's name.

'Agnes Sampson?' she heard them ask a man, who raised a tired hand and pointed in her direction.

Agnes faltered and fell to her knees. Tears rolled down her cheeks. The doctor had managed to escape. There was nothing more to be done.

'What of the rest of yer coven? Where is Fian?' Gilbert Leith barked.

'I've seen no doctor.' She cast her eyes to the floor. 'I'm just a cripple helping the sick.'

'I ken very well that yer more than a cripple.' He yanked her by the arm and pulled her awkwardly to her feet. 'You'll be joinin' yer kin in the Tolbooth.'

Beneath the Trees

The birds woke before I did. I stirred groggily under the blanket. Specks of dust drifted in the crisp November sunlight, guided by the drafts that blew through the fissures in the wall. I sat up slowly; my head felt like a sack of rocks.

I closed my eyes and she was with me, Jenny. Her freckled face and brown eyes as she giggled and plucked the pheasant on the table. The smell of the fire and the candlelight flickering while her warm hands brushed the hair from my face. I breathed her in and held her there until she dissolved.

My throat still ached from the force of my screams and my eyes were still heavy from the noises I had heard through the night; I was sharing my cramped quarters with rats wearing horseshoes. Between that and the sound of the screeching gulls over breaking waves, I didn't think my head would ever recover.

Apart from a square table and a chamber pot that was overflowing, it was about as spacious as my mother's pantry at Leaplish. Agnes would be frantic, and poor Dr Fian . . . *what must he think of me?*

I pulled the blanket tighter around my shoulders, barely covering my nakedness. There was no way of disguising my swollen face. I touched a finger to the skin of my cheekbone, still raw from where the scold's bridle had dug into my flesh.

I shuddered. Soon I'd be taken to the Tolbooth. It would be more than a day's ride to Edinburgh, and that was with a sturdy mount and one rider. Before Jenny was born, I often travelled with Rupert collecting the rents for Master Rivet. I had been such a fool. Everything he said was right: I should never have gotten involved with my mother's healing. It had only brought me heartache.

I was startled from my thoughts by the hum of the cart and the rattle of hoofbeats. Muffled male voices seeped through the stone as the door groaned open to reveal Gilbert Leith. Unable to hide the disgust on his face, he covered his nose with his hand.

Waiting in the pre-dawn light was a man I recognised immediately. He looked me over, with arms folded and eyebrows knitted together, troubled.

'Witchcraft, you say?' He stared at me blankly.

'Aye,' said Gilbert Leith. 'She denied it, but proceedings in the matter were brought to a halt when it was ordered that she was tae be taken tae the Tolbooth.'

Thomas Reed looked me over, taking in every line of my tattered dress and blanket. I glanced up at him, close enough that I could almost touch him. It had been twelve years. He wasn't the skinny young boy I remembered. Now he was broad and muscular, a strapping man grown. *Did he recognise me?*

'Have you no' something tae cover her modesty?' he said, looking away from me. 'I've got a cart full o' thieves and rapists.'

What little hope I had of him recognising me had been extinguished. I was alone.

'Accused of being a witch, sneaking about at night, doing all manner of evil deed – it's the rapists that wants tae be scairt of her,' Leith said.

'That might as be, but I will no abide rape,' Thomas said. 'Bind her hands if you must, and she can ride wi' me in the front of the cart.'

Without protest, I held out my hands and watched as they bound them, this time in irons. Then Leith brought out the scold's bridle.

'She isnae goin' tae bite. I hardly think that necessary.'

'Your funeral, Reed.' Leith shrugged his thick shoulders and cast the bridle aside. He held me fiercely by the elbow. "Tis you who will have tae listen to her dripping her wicked poison.'

'Wicked poison, is it?' I snarled. 'The same wicked poison that old rapist is dripping?'

'That's nought to do wi' you, witch,' said Leith as he herded me towards the door.

'Nought to do wi' me, but that bastard can spread whatever lies he sees fit!'

He hit me then, in the stomach, with such force that it knocked every wisp of breath from my lungs. As I struggled to inhale, I was thrust towards Reed.

I blinked like an owl against the light. Had he not held me by the arm, I would have let the ground take me. He steered me towards a carthorse pulling a prison wagon, with barred windows covered in filthy, white-knuckled hands.

The icy wind whipped against my bared breasts as

I tried in vain to cover myself. The cart was filled with thieves, rapists and the like, so wicked that they scared even Thomas, who had them fettered hand to foot in the back of the wagon. The fat face of a man with blackened teeth and weeping sores peered through the bars. I shuddered.

I was hoisted awkwardly into the front of the cart. The irons on my wrists were so heavy I couldn't have swatted away a fly. Thomas climbed in next to me, taking the reins softly in his hands. It took a while for the horses to get the cart moving.

'You 'll be safe up here, dinnae fret, Besse.'

'Is it you, Thomas Reed?'

'Aye, it is.' He laughed deeply. 'It's been a wee while, has it not?'

'Almost twelve years. I have a wee lassie now, almost grown.'

Twelve years. Before I could stop it, the memory I had tried so hard to forget appeared as though it was yesterday: Thomas creeping into my bedchamber at Agnes's, the night before my wedding, begging me not to marry Rupert. But I couldn't have married Thomas. What kind of life could he have provided? Yet, I still had the onyx rosary he'd given me, the last gift from his mother.

The man I was meant to marry.

'Twelve years, aye.' He pushed the horse on. 'How is it that ye've got yerself caught up in this mess?'

'I dinnae ken . . . I . . . I think it was Master Rivet.' My eyes pricked. 'He tried tae force himself upon me . . . Thomas, I . . .' The tears rolled, hot and wet.

'Hush now,' he said in a voice I was sure he'd use

to soothe a horse. 'Dinna cry, Besse. I'm sure it'll be something and nothing.'

My muscles ached. Behind me, shouts of protest could be heard from the occupants of the wagon as they rattled over each bump in the road. We soon picked up speed and, as the village fell further away into the distance, I inclined my head and attempted a sideways glance at Thomas. His broad-shouldered frame filled the space amply. He must have been over six feet; I was dwarfed in comparison. My eyes traced the line of his jaw, slightly speckled with whiskers, and a shock of thick flaxen hair, like a haystack after a storm. He wore a simple linen shirt, dark breeches and a leather overcoat. Not the wee boy I remembered.

We rattled on, in tense silence, through the forest. The frost still marked the shadows of the pines across the grass, which showed up what the morning light couldn't see. Thomas guided the carthorse easily with a squeeze of the reins and the soft sounds of encouragement.

Jenny would be safe for a time with Mistress Cochran, but for how long I couldn't be sure. By now, word would have filtered through to my mother. With any luck, Jenny would make her way to Leaplish.

After a while, we stopped at a crossing. At the pace we were moving we wouldn't get to Edinburgh before nightfall, so we would have to make camp. Rupert had always taken us out into the woods to hunt, and I knew every rut, crevice and berry bush: all I needed was an opportunity.

As we waited, a black-bearded man approached on a stallion. The glassy-eyed carcasses of a half a dozen rabbits lolled from the waistband of his breeches.

'What's with the lass?' he said.

Thomas shrugged. 'I couldnae put the lass in wi' those animals. It wouldnae be right. 'Tis not fir me to decide her guilt.'

He frowned. 'You dinnae ken who or what she is, and yet here you are letting her sit next tae you, large as life.' He shook his head. 'Yer goin' soft.'

'Aye, well, she's just a wee slip of a thing.'

'We've a good distance tae go yet. Any problems, you cut her throat, you understand?' He nudged his horse into a trot and disappeared amongst the trees.

I swallowed hard as I watched the hilt of the dirk that hung at Thomas's side.

'Thank you,' I said, and I meant it.

The tracks through the woods were carpeted in swathes of burnt orange which rustled as the hooves pushed through. Jenny would have been in her element picking through the hawthorn and rowan that lined either side. As fierce as a salmon, the movement in my stomach whipped and whirled; I pressed my hand closer to my secret child.

We carried on in silence for what felt like hours, with no more between us than the faint whip of the reins. Everything I had seen in the last couple of days had left me empty. I couldn't bring myself to talk to Thomas, even if he wanted to listen. Jenny may as well have been in the London for all the chance I had of getting back to her.

The forest grew dark as clouds rolled in, sweeping in circles from the east. A deep rumble rattled through the trees. The noise of the first of the rain startled me as it bounced off the cart, making a noise like coins in a tinderbox.

Then the cart came to a stop as the forest thinned into a clearing enclosed on one side by a rocky outcrop.

'We'll camp here tonight,' Thomas said, lifting me to the floor. He felt surprisingly warm. I might have taken comfort in it, had I not been trussed up in irons. I thought about slipping away into the trees. The muscles in my legs twitched with indecision as I inched my feet through the damp grass.

A hand grabbed me tightly by the elbow. 'Why don't you sit down, lass.'

I was manhandled towards a pile of boulders. He untied the horse from the cart, whispering to it softly before he allowed it to graze on a patch of grass. The black-bearded man approached through the trees. He didn't dismount but simply let the stallion stretch its neck as it grazed while he spoke to Reed.

There was something about the smell of the storm. It slipped across my skin, heavy and thick as a blanket. A sign of trouble to come. The oppressive feeling hung in the air, and a flash of lightning sparked across the sky, burning blue and white hot. Thunder grumbled from the east, causing the ponies to dance uneasily.

A pile of freshly collected branches began to accumulate in the clearing, and Thomas got a fire going. Smoke spiralled from the damp tinder, almost too wet to catch a spark.

I looked at the sprawling blackness through the trees, each one looking exactly like the last. I wouldn't be going anywhere in this light. I'd have to wait for sunrise. They were sure to gorge themselves on whisky and meat. While they slept it off, I'd edge my way through the woods and find my way back to Mill House.

Stepping towards the fire, a tiny flame danced in the tinder nest, making the damp wood hiss. I stretched out my hands against the warmth. They were stiff with the cold and swollen from where the ropes had chafed.

'Warm yerself through.' Thomas fell in by my side, as a warning. 'Now, I trust you, but you cannae be lettin' on tae Broch that we ken each other, you understand?' He nodded towards the rustling trees. 'Brian Macfeaghuis. We call him Broch on account of him coming from Faithlie.'

Broch's darkness reminded me of Rupert's. A wicked black humour beneath his smile.

As Thomas finished, Broch approached and tossed the rabbits over; Thomas took one and hid the rest in the cleft of a rocky outcrop. It didn't take long before it was skinned and trussed up on a makeshift spit.

* * *

Sometime near midnight the storm eased. The clouds parted to reveal the shard of the moon. Flames danced, casting shadows against the overhead crag. I looked away from the fire, towards the wagon. The prisoners were still, apart from one who had a ghastly cough.

''Tis an awful chest he's got,' I said, almost in a whisper.

Thomas gave a laugh. 'That's no concern of yers.'

'I saw some horehound back there. It would ease his sufferin'.'

'I dinnae think we should be easin' the suffering of a

charlatan and a murderer, do you?' Broch said, taking a swig from his flask and passing it to Thomas. 'Guilty until proven innocent. I dinnae see fifteen good men protesting his innocence, do you?'

'I dinnae see fifteen good men protesting mine either,' I said, over the growing rattles, as the poor man heaved to catch his breath. 'He's still a man, after all.'

I pulled the blanket around my shoulders awkwardly and tucked my bare feet inside my skirts. My breath hung in the air like a cloud of smoke. Coughing as he was, he'd be half dead by the time we'd reach Edinburgh.

'If yer that taken wi' him, lass, you could always travel in the back wi' the rest of them. After all, you are a witch.'

'I'm no' a witch. I'm a healer. A fine one at that.' I got up, hugging myself irritably.

'That would depend on yer perspective. Witch. Healer. Is it no' all the same?' The grease on his beard glistened in the firelight as he sucked on another rabbit bone. Thomas's eyes didn't flicker as he carried on whittling a piece of wood.

'No, it's no' the same. Witches are a faerie tale told by men with private parts the size o' maggots.' The words came out more bitterly than I intended. 'A feeble excuse tae punish a woman every time she cannot be bent tae a man's will. Healers cure yer ills and deliver yer children. I hardly think they're the same.'

Now that the rain had stopped and the noise from the wagon abated to a rasp, I could hear the sounds of the stream as it pooled beneath the rocks.

'You must be famished. Will you no eat wi' us?' Thomas

motioned towards the rabbit. 'Get this down ye,' he said with a ghost of a smile.

I was ravenous. I could have eaten anything that he'd put in front of me, potatoes, cheese or buttered bread. I took the piece of rabbit and slowly began to chew. It landed in my stomach like a stone, causing a ripple of sickness.

'Are you no' hungry?' said Thomas.

'I cannae eat.' I kicked dirt into the fire.

'I'd at least gi' it a try. There willnae be much by the way of food in the Tolbooth,' he said as he sucked the last of the meat from a tiny bone, discarding it into the fire.

We all shifted uneasily, each one eyeing the other.

The silence shattered like a clay pot in a fire. The shrieks of the men came thick and fast. I followed Thomas and Broch to the cart.

The noise had faded by the time we reached the door. The poor soul lay prone on the floor, shackled to an avalanche of a man. By the blue of his skin, he had no air in his lungs.

'You have tae help him,' I said.

'Leave the bastard tae die. One less tae worry about,' said Broch.

'You cannae leave a man to die!'

'You know so much about it, you do it, healer.'

'I cannae do anything in these chains!'

Thomas walked over, taking the keys from his belt and reaching for my wrists. I recoiled, but he managed to grab me and held me firmly.

'Now, if I remove these irons, you're not going tae make a run fir it, are ye?'

I shook my head. The irons dropped to the ground with a soft *clink*.

'Get him up!' I pulled his body into a seated position. 'Give him a drink!' I took the flask from Thomas's outstretched hand. I held the flask in one hand and the man's chin in the other. He pursed his lips like a baby bird. The liquid passed over his lips easily but rather than swallowing it, he choked, bringing on another fit of coughing.

'Have you nothin' else?' I said.

'Only what's in the flask.'

I worked swiftly, trying to tip his head back. He searched again for the flask. 'He wouldn't be in this state if you had let me fetch the horehound! It willnae do you any good returning tae the Tolbooth with a cart full of dead prisoners.'

'Then you need tae make sure he lives another day,' said Broch.

'Then you had better bring him tae the fire. Can you take off his chains?'

Broch removed the irons.

'Do yer duty, healer. Fetch yer horehound.'

'Now, dinnae make me regret taking off those irons, lass.' Thomas gave me a stern look. 'Straight back, I dinnae want tae have tae be chasing you around the countryside.'

'I'll go with her,' said Broch. 'Get on wi' it.'

He gave me a short shove and hustled me towards the line of trees. The moonlight broke through the trails of fog and spindling branches.

The noises from camp had faded by the time I reached the horehound. It sat at the foot of an oak tree, wrapped in brambles and nettles. I pushed my fingers through, pulling a handful of the plant and stuffing it into the top of my skirts.

Broch gave me an impatient glare. 'Are you done, healer?'

'Aye, this should be enough.'

As we neared the rocky outcrop, I stopped, licking the deep scratches on my hand. Even in the blackness, the gentle bubble of the water made me pause to listen. I looked up at the night sky to try and gauge my position, but it was obscured by the trees. I could carry on walking through the stream and up between the trunks of the pines. That would take me back to Mill House and to Jenny.

'Keep movin'.' Broch pressed me forwards, gripping my arm, then froze. The noise of a skirmish burst through the trees. There were shouts and cursing, and he placed a finger to his lips and urged me to hunker down behind a nearby bush. Squinting through the web of branches, I watched as he sprinted off, vanishing into the darkness.

I crept forward, the brambles scratching my ankles.

A thrill of panic ran down my spine. The shape of a thief bent over Thomas. I watched in terrified silence as his arm raised high above his head before he brought his fist crashing down. Thomas went limp.

The door to the wagon hung open. Empty.

As I drew nearer, the air was filled with a heady mix of spent gunpowder and woodsmoke. My heart beat as though it were trying to escape from my chest. I glanced towards the outcrop where Thomas was but could see no movement. I held my breath and listened. Not even the horses seemed to be breathing. The eerie sound of the frozen leaves being crushed underfoot made gooseflesh prickle on the back of my neck.

As I turned to run a hand grabbed my arm. I stiffened and stifled a scream.

'I'm here tae thank you.' A gigantic shape stepped out of the darkness. 'I couldnae have done it without you.'

My heart sank. I had begged to have their irons removed. Instinctively, my hands flew to my belly. The avalanche loomed over me, as large as life and with a mouth filled with blackened teeth.

'No need fir thanks.' I smiled vaguely, trying to wriggle free but the hand around my arm twisted.

He looked more than double the size he had on the wagon, with broad shoulders stretched between two arms like the trunks of trees. His crooked nose and missing teeth showed he was no stranger to a fight. A gold band hung loosely from a chain around his neck. I'd have known Rupert's wedding ring anywhere.

'Yer coming wi' us, lass.' His face contorted into a sort of twisted grin. 'A mile or so back, where we passed the crossroads, we need tae follow the edge of the stream and it will take us out tae sea.' He pulled out a small drawstring bag. 'I have these jewels as payment, half of what I've buried. We can leave tae safety; you'll be free.'

'Pirates?' I whispered.

'Of a sort.'

Flee. We could dissolve into the inky blackness, like coins into the depths of a well. Like we were never there. I could be free. Free to raise my boy. But what kind of mother would I be if I left my daughter behind? No. I had to get back to her, and the only way I was going to do that was to find Rupert. Master Rivet had always thought of Rupert as a son, the only person who would have any hope of making Master Rivet see sense and drop the charges was my husband. I cast an eye back to the man's neck and the wedding band that rested neatly against his collarbone.

'How did you come by that ring around yer neck?' I said, a little louder.

'I won it' – he rolled it nimbly between thumb and forefinger – 'in a game of dice.' The metal glinted in the moonlight.

'And what of the man that lost it?'

'A dullard and a drunk,' he spat. 'Waiting to board our ship.'

'*Your* ship?'

'Aye, *The Salamander of Leith*, meant fir France. Looking to sail end of May on the spring tide, his wife disnae do well on rough seas.' He reached out a hand, crusted in filth. I took it begrudgingly. 'Privateer Andrew Barton,' he said. 'I ken yer the bonny witch I've heard so much about.'

Andrew Barton. The man I'd heard about at Acheson's Tavern. Something wasn't right. What would Rupert want with France? He went all the time for Master Rivet, he had no need of finding passage on a ship belonging to a privateer, unless he didn't want to get caught. My heart drummed in my ears. He was leaving us for France. He had no idea I was in childbed; would he be so eager to leave if he knew? I had to get word to him. I knew he had a cousin who sold wine in France, so maybe he'd been offered work; or worse, forced against his will to work for Andrew Barton. My head reeled.

I wriggled against him with one arm, but he still held me tightly. 'Why don't you take yer leave, I'll no' hinder you,' I said.

'I cannae leave a pretty wee thing like you fir the gallows. It would be such a waste.' The stench of his reeking, rancid breath stung my nostrils, but it was probably no worse than my own.

'I must thank you, Master Barton.' I tried to balance my feet on the uneven ground. 'But I'll have tae decline yer kind offer.'

The corners of his mouth twitched. 'It wasn't an offer.'

He grabbed me by the waist and flung me over his shoulder like a rag. I could feel his lean muscles flexing beneath his shirt as I kicked and thrashed. Although he was much larger, he was slow and cumbersome. I beat him furiously with fists and feet, but he merely laughed.

I shifted my weight to try and unsteady him. He caught me as I moved but he tripped on a rock. We tumbled together to the earth. I got to my feet and started to run but my foot got caught in the undergrowth, sending me spinning to the ground like a stone. In an instant he bore down on me. He was the weight of two men, forcing the air from my lungs. My hands scrabbled and slipped around in the mud, searching for something to pull myself free.

The weight of him shifted, allowing me just enough room to wriggle out. I scrambled on my belly and made for a gap between two fallen rocks. I didn't dare look back. I forced myself into the dark crevice. The sound of my heart filled my ears like a crashing sea.

I peered from my hiding place but lost his form in the shadows. I could still hear him. Still smell him. That beast had taken my husband. What was I going to do? Batter him with my skirts? Barton had the strength of ten men and was twice my size. My legs twitched with the urge to run.

In the silence, hands slipped across the rocks. My breath hitched. Nearer now. Heavy feet slipped through the undergrowth. Fabric tore against invisible branches.

When the shouts came, they were distant and unknown. Barton kept his back to me as the others raced into the clearing. It must have been Broch or Reed, or both. They circled like a pack of dogs, each eyeing the other. Barton was surrounded.

'I'll no' let you take me alive.'

I caught the flash of a short sword in Thomas's hand. 'That can be arranged.'

Barton made an unexpected lunge and caught Thomas by surprise, knocking the sword from his grasp. It skidded across the ground and came to rest at my feet.

The writhing mass rolled across the floor. Broch side-stepped them as Thomas shouted something I couldn't quite make out. Broch glanced back at the wagon for enough time to see something moving in the shadows and bolted, leaving Thomas in the clash on the floor.

Backwards and forwards they rolled. As the fight moved closer, I could see their faces. Thomas's back to the ground, he held up his arms weakly to guard his face, but blood seeped across his teeth and his left eye was all but closed. The man-mountain Barton sat across his chest. I could hear the crack of each blow as he pounded his flesh. Thomas was exhausted and Broch had fled.

Having a husband with a fierce temper like Rupert, I

had seen my fair share of brawls and knew how to handle a sword. I stretched out my leg, feeling my way through the grass with my toes and almost cutting my foot on the blade before I found the hilt. I inched it closer and bent to pick it up. I coiled my fingers around it, testing their grip, and edged out from my hiding place.

I skirted around the men, unnoticed in the shadows, keeping close to the rock face. I was directly behind them now, with Barton's back facing me. I took a deep breath and steadied myself.

'Barton.'

He took his eyes off Thomas for a second and glanced at me. That was all I needed. I thrust the sword into his shoulder, skewering him. He grabbed at the wound, bewildered. Thomas jumped to his feet, grabbing Barton and choking him. Barton grasped at the arm around his neck, but I pointed the bloodied tip of the sword towards his throat.

'I . . . I've got jewels. Let me go and I—'

Thomas tightened his grip. 'You'll no' be needing those where you're going,' he said.

Broch let out a murderous scream and burst through the undergrowth brandishing Thomas's flintlock pistol.

'Did you bring the irons?' Thomas grunted.

'Aye . . . What in God's name happened here?' The flintlock swayed wildly between me and Barton.

'The irons?' Thomas pushed the words through gritted teeth as he wrestled with Barton.

Between them, the men managed to manoeuvre Barton's hands behind his back and secure them in the irons.

'Are you alright?' said Thomas to me.

My hands shook. He moved close enough for me to see him: his wounds wept blood and sweat, smearing his shirt. He turned away and was sick behind a rock before swilling his mouth with whisky.

'Did he hurt ye?' he asked.

My body trembled. I couldn't speak. He placed a hand on my arm and rubbed it gently.

'Does it hurt?' I said, gathering myself.

'Aye, a bit. I need you to tend him. Can you do it?'

Barton was sitting on a rock near the fire. The look he gave terrified me. I steadied my shaking hands. He was just a man, after all. I tore a piece of cloth from my underskirts to tie around his arm.

'I could have made you rich,' he whispered as I drew close. 'We could have been away from here.'

I ignored him. 'How is it you come to know my husband?'

'Who might yer husband be?'

'Rupert . . . Rupert Craw. The man whose ring you wear.' I slipped my fingers around the cool metal. 'Where is he?'

He turned his chin up to look me in the face. 'Lookin' at those bruises, I'm guessing you didn't win then?'

I shook my head. 'Not this time.'

'Tell me that the other one is worse off?' He glanced over at Thomas.

I ignored his taunts. 'What have you done with my husband?' I whispered.

'I've never heard of him.'

Anger flared inside me. He knew by husband. He knew him better than I did.

'Do you ken what these men will do tae ye?' I said, nodding at Thomas and Broch. 'They'll slit you from yer arsehole tae yer mouth and delight in doing it. I just have tae tell them of our conversation in the woods.'

He thought of it. His eyes darted from me to the men and back again.

'The man you speak of . . . I gave him a good hiding too,' he said. 'On account of his rigged dice.'

'What of him after that?'

'He took it with good grace. Had he not, you might not have had a chance of finding him alive.' He sucked the air in over his teeth as my fingers roved over the wound. 'He wouldnae leave, followed me tae my ship, begging me fir passage tae France. He tried tae pay wi' this.' He showed me the ring again. 'It didn't even cover his debt, but a man who is willing tae give up his wedding ring is a man down on his luck. I took pity on him and said if he could come up wi' the rest, then there'd be a place on my ship, but not before.'

I shook my head in despair. My husband was leaving. Leaving me. Leaving us. I had to find him, to plead with him to stay. We could pay off his debt to Master Rivet. Make it right. No good would come of him leaving.

'Get on wi' it, woman,' Broch said impatiently. 'We need to leave, now.'

'Hold still,' I said, fumbling with the ends of the torn fabric as I tried to stem the bleeding.

With the bandages tied, he gave a quiet grunt of pain as they got him to his feet. I took a step back and stumbled over what I thought were rocks. I glanced down and could barely tear my gaze away. At my feet lay the consumptive man who I had been treating. Dead.

Secrets and Lies

Jenny had been woken just before dawn, along with the rest of the farm hands. Now, she sat across the table from them, breaking fast as they ate greedily from bowls filled with bread and cheese, like pigs at a trough.

'Wha's yer name?' one of them said as he mopped at the last of his slops with a piece of bread.

Jenny froze mid-chew. The same piece of dry bread tumbled around inside her mouth. She wished Willy was with her, but he would have been as nervous as a papist at a meeting of the kirk. She swallowed hard. 'Robert.' She studied their faces but didn't say another word.

'Rob, you say?' Grey eyes flickered up from a mop of peppered hair that belonged to a wiry old man. 'You have a knack wi' horses, Mistress Cochran tells me.'

'So my da used tae say.' She took a sip from a cup, but no more than she needed; pissing would be the hardest part.

'I have use of a stable lad.'

'Come now, boys,' the cook said, hustling them from the table and towards the door. 'You as well, Robert, you must go wi' Ian.'

She missed Willy. She'd hardly seen him since her

arrival. The other boys had taken their leave and headed to search for acorns for the pigs. One of the farm hands – Alex, they'd called him – had been there no more than a week.

As they crossed the yard, Jenny couldn't help looking over her shoulder and wondering when the witchfinders were going to catch up with her. But they were looking for a girl with black hair and long, hand-spun dresses, not a waif of a stable lad working his aunt's farm. Even so, she had spent the night waking in the darkness, frightened, listening to the crackle of the fire until the sun came up.

It didn't feel right, watching the sunrise from somewhere that wasn't home. She hugged herself. Two days ago, she would have given anything to wear breeches. Now, she fidgeted everywhere she went, the breeches itched between her legs.

'So, yer Mistress Cochran's nephew?'

'Aye,' she said, hurrying to keep up.

Ian was tall and his skin was dark and leathered, like an old saddle.

'Get a move on, laddie. The rest of 'em was plucked from over Humbie with promise of shoes on their feet and food in their bellies, and there isnae one of them that wouldn't break yer leg fir a chance tae work in the stable. So, I suggest you work hard or you'll be picking acorns wi' Alex, nephew or no'.'

Jenny nodded.

'You'll break at noon, not a moment sooner.'

The paddock he led her to was right by the stables, in a meadow bare with winter grass and lined with woods. Two ponies grazed lazily, side by side at the fence line.

'First, you'll fetch the water. Then you can help me mend this wall.'

She left Ian to his work and headed back in the direction from which they had come, in search of two buckets and Willy. The yard seemed to be never still: herds being driven to new pastures; the cook hanging freshly made tallow candles; fetching, carrying and mending. She tried to slip past unnoticed, but she caught the attention of Alex with a barrow of acorns, who eyed her like a sparrowhawk hunting.

'Auld Ian had you over near them woods?'

'Aye.' She kept her eyes firmly on the ground.

'There's wolves in them woods, growin' bolder by the day, big enough tae kill a man.'

'There is not!'

'I heard it from my cousin. One walked into the market, bold as anything, and plucked a sheep from under the farmer's nose. Sheep, cows, a *boy* – makes no matter, they'll kill what they like.'

'Yer cousin shouldn't tell stories.'

'You callin' me a liar?' he said, giving her a hard shove towards the side door to the stables. 'What would you know?'

'My grandmother told me plenty about wolves,' she muttered, pushing the side of a pail with her foot. 'They dinnae sneak about in markets stealing sheep.'

'What are you playin' at?' Ian stalked past her, stiff with fury. 'I didnae think they'd moved the stream last time I checked?'

Jenny scuffed the floor with her shoe and followed reluctantly after Ian in the direction of the stream, empty pails skimming the ground.

'Pass those here.'

She lowered them down to the old man, ankle-deep in the water. 'One task I gave you, one, and you couldnae even do that.'

'I'm sorry, I—'

'I dinnae want tae hear another word. Here' – he thrust the full pails in her direction – 'go and water the horses. If I catch you stoppin', yer wee arse will feel the back of my hand.'

Jenny didn't utter another word, sloshing and spilling all the way to the meadow with Ian marching behind. Jenny rolled under the fence and sidled past the bay mare, who eyed her with suspicion as she emptied the pails.

'Let me see what I've let myself in fir. Go on, laddie, tether that mare.'

Ian rested himself against the wall with arms folded and waited.

Even though she was an accomplished rider, her father had never taken the time to school her with horses. She could barely tell the tail from the teeth. Holding her breath, she reached out towards the mare's muzzle. It flicked its tail and snorted but didn't move. Slowly, she reached towards its withers, gradually resting a hand on the animal's back.

'Well, you haven't sent her skitterin', but you havenae tethered her either. You seem to ken a little and have at least a thimble o' sense.'

'Aye, some.'

'Well, I suppose you'll do fir now, laddie. You've a lot to learn, but I'm happy tae teach you, as long as yer willin' tae work. This old mare's hopping lame; we need a mixture of mugwort and comfrey boiled with some sheep suet. We'll see if the cook will let us in the kitchen – let's see if she'll let us away with a bit of sage from her wee garden as well.'

Ian was just reaching down to inspect the injured hoof when the mare caught sight of Willy approaching with a basket. The horse pulled away, rearing and twisting to face the threat, sending Ian clattering into the fence in a hail of swearing and muttering.

'Blasted animal,' he said, turning to face what had caused the trouble.

His face softened when he saw Willy with a basket sent by cook. He took it gratefully and sat himself against the mended wall, offering the food to Jenny. 'Working wi' horses is hungry work, aye?' he said, as she took the bread he offered and ate it hungrily, all the while smiling at Willy. 'Will you be here long?' Ian asked.

Jenny hadn't really thought about it. She wished she could find her father. He would know what to do. Her mother had said only a day, two at most. Now, she wasn't so sure. 'As long as my auntie will have me,' she said vaguely. 'Do you mind if Willy sits wi' us?'

'Ach no, get yer arse down, lad.' Ian took another bite. 'Was yer da a horsemen?'

'No, Da . . . Well, Da . . . he didnae ken much about horses. The only one we owned was a mare he won in a game of dice. Have you always worked fir my auntie?'

From the corner of her eye, she could see Willy shifting uncomfortably at the lies she she spun.

'Oh aye, yer aunt and uncle were always kind tae me, and I've been wi' them almost thirty years. Strange, yer uncle never mentioned you, God rest his soul.'

She watched as he polished off the last of the cheese and bread. Willy had barely touched a thing.

'My uncle wasnae very fond of my mother. My auntie sent fir me after he passed.'

He nodded, satisfied with her answer. 'Now, we best get back to work,' he said, scrambling to his feet. 'The horses willnae wait around all day.'

Willy turned and began walking back to the house.

'Willy,' she hissed. 'I need tae stay disguised. I cannae have them find me.'

'I know, I know. But I hardly recognised you . . .'

'You ken it won't be fir long. Do you have any word of my mother?' She was careful not to let Ian hear.

'Nothin'. Last anyone heard they were takin yer mother tae the Tolbooth. And I heard the butcher's boy sayin' somethin' about Black Agnes, but I wasnae sure of what I heard so I willnae repeat it.'

'We havenae got all day!' shouted Ian.

'I'll have tae get back. Meet me after.'

* * *

Jenny hadn't seen Willy the rest of the day. Once she and Ian finished mending the wall, they headed back to the stables to clean the stalls, ready for the horses to come in. The smell reminded her of a nest of weasels.

'Go and empty that barrow,' he said.

She wrinkled her nose but thought it was better to hold her tongue and not complain. She picked up the handles and began navigating it across the cobbled yard. It bounced and jiggled, threatening to send the contents all over the floor, which she was sure would get her another scolding from Ian.

As she passed, Alex leaned lazily against the corner of the stable wall, his head cocked to one side. 'I see yer only good enough fir shovellin',' he snorted and spat a shiny globule of spit that landed just ahead of her.

Jenny had met boys like him before. Boys that were much worse. If the butcher's boy couldn't make her cry, Alex certainly wouldn't.

'Much better than you at it,' she smirked. 'That's why yer only trusted wi' collecting acorns fir the pigs.' She carried on walking.

What she didn't see was Alex stick his foot out. She tripped, sending the contents of the barrow skittering across the floor. She turned to glare at him.

He cackled like a chittering crow, pointing and whooping. 'I'll ask Mistress Cochran if you can be trusted tae help me wi' the acorns!'

Jenny scowled, kicked dirt at him and stalked off into the trees. She bit her lip sullenly and glanced back at the stable block. She wasn't going to go crying to the old man for help.

By the time she clamoured through dense thickets and the last of the brambles, the skin on her arms was scratched and bloody and she couldn't feel the chill. As the forest thinned, a cleft in the earth made way for a trickle of a stream. At the water's edge she fumbled around in the pocket of her breeches to find the black rosary her mother had given her. She dropped to her knees, wishing she could saddle one of the horses and ride it all the way home.

Her ears pricked. The voices drifted softly like rustling leaves. It had to be Alex and the rest of the boys come to taunt her. This time she didn't need to summon any courage. She crept as quietly as she could back up the embankment to the thin wall of trees and crawled back through the small gap. He wasn't going to get the better of her this time. She kept herself quiet as a fox and pressed her back against a tree and listened.

Their pitch was thick and low, like the men she'd heard in the inn over in Humbie when her mother had become desperate to find her da when he hadn't come home. Drunkards, her mother had called them. It wasn't the boys, but she couldn't quite make them out. They were too far away; their words melded with the sounds of the woods.

Jenny slipped further into the trees. Finding a foothold in the small burr of an ash tree and reaching for the boughs above, which were encased in frost, she climbed and shimmied out along a limb until she could see just above the edge of the stream.

She was closer now. They didn't seem to smell like the men at the inn. The smell was rancid, like the butcher's boy in summer. She could hear the sloshing of their feet against the stones. She would have opened her mouth to breathe, but she didn't dare. A thick-set man idled with his back to her while his companion was obscured by an oak.

'Two shillings fir the rope,' he insisted. She couldn't make out the figure, so she edged closer, teetering over the edge of the embankment.

'I was promised four shillings! There is a lot of work goes into a good winching, I even brought out the scold's bridle.'

'Extortion!' His voice shrilled through the trees. 'I was promised that you would rid me of my wife and yet she still lives and breathes to ruin my new life. I'll give you three.'

'Do you take me fir some kind of eejit? Four and not a penny less.' He folded his arms across his chest. Now, as the sunlight illuminated his skin, she could see the scar that ran the length of his face.

'If the bonnet fits.'

He took hold of the outstretched hand and shook it.

Her breath quickened. Gilbert Leith. She craned her neck, straining to hear.

'They took her this morning.'

'You saw it fir yerself?' said the other man.

'Aye, handed her over mysel' to some gaoler from the Tolbooth,' said Leith.

'Any sign of the girl?'

'Nothing yet.' Leith picked at something in his teeth. 'She can't hide forever, someone will have sight of her afore long.'

Her feet betrayed her, sending pieces of crumbling bark fluttering below.

'What was that?'

Jenny sucked the air in over her teeth. She edged nimbly backwards. Inch by inch, she slid her feet. First the left and then the right, like she was dancing a reel.

'Nothing more 'an a damned pigeon.' Leith looked skywards, squinting.

'I don't want tae hear from you again until you have my daughter.' He turned on his heel to leave. She couldn't make out the colour of his eyes, but she couldn't mistake that walk – the slight limp – and the broad stretch of his chest. Rupert William Craw, her father.

Tolbooth Prison

The rest of the journey towards the Tolbooth was uneventful. I had stood uneasily holding a torch while they dug a grave for the man that died in the woods. It felt ghoulish to bury him in unconsecrated ground, but it was better than if he'd died in the Tolbooth and been harvested for the dissecting table or left for the crows.

As we headed towards Edinburgh, we watched the dawn rise in streaks of pink and blue. Morning mists still lingered, obscuring the view of the valley. It had been years since I had last travelled this way with Rupert.

The thought of Rupert disarmed me. My husband's past behaviour did not endear him to my mother – too quick with his fists and even more reckless with the earnings of others – but to abandon his family, I could not . . . no, would not, believe it.

We arrived finally, with all but one prisoner. It was a small consolation to be accompanied by a man who had known me before. A man who didn't see a witch. Every flicker in my belly made me sick. I had never known fear like it. What would they do if they found me with child? Would they cut him from me, leaving me an empty husk to die at the stake? Or, worse, cut him from me and allow me to live?

I kept my thoughts to myself as we passed through the entrance of the city wall. The great fortress and its impressive turrets overlooked Edinburgh from its craggy summit. The rest of the town grew slowly down the tail from Castle Rock. I was grateful to come from the west, to miss the Nor' Loch and its douking stool. No doubt a delight I'd be shown soon enough.

Our surroundings were no longer quiet and deserted. My eyes followed the masses of people, to-ing and fro-ing, swaddled in travelling clothes. The colours danced and changed and rippled in the sunlight. Jenny would have been mesmerised. They moved to the side to allow the cart to pass, stopping to gawk at the prisoners on the wagon. Thomas slowed down to a stop while Broch made his way ahead to the Tolbooth.

'I'm sorry, Besse, but it'll be me fir the noose if I take you in there without irons,' he said, smiling awkwardly. A smile I hadn't seen in almost twelve years.

'I understand,' I croaked, holding out my hands.

He pulled up the wagon to the front of the prison, where we were met by a scruffy young lad. 'Yer early. They weren't expecting you until tomorrow,' he shouted.

Broch swung down from his horse. 'Aye, well we had a bit o' bad luck on the road and thought we'd better make good time.'

The Tolbooth's huge gables, blunt and solid – with smoking chimney pots adding to the mist that flowed around the fortified building – loomed menacingly in the middle of the High Street. The sickness crashed like a wave against my ribs.

I could see the prick of the highest stone, where the

head of James Douglas, 4th Earl of Morton and last of the four regeants of Scotland, had stayed on top of the north gable, for almost two years, looking down on St Giles' Cathedral. Now, there were the scattered bodies of those that proceeded me. I began to shake.

'Try not tae worry.' Thomas placed a hand on my knee. 'I'm sure it's something and nothing. You'll be home to yer bairn before you know it.'

I swallowed hard. If Rupert wasn't coming for me, the only way I was going to leave the Tolbooth was to be fed to the ravens. My feet were as though they had been melded to the floor with wax.

'I cannae . . . my legs.' I looked down at my useless legs, urging them to move. I tried to take a step but teetered and fell. Thomas plucked me from the ground and put me back on my feet.

Broch went ahead with the rest of the prisoners and beckoned for us to follow. The stench hit my stomach like a blow. A gaoler swilled the stairs as we passed, but the drain was choked. It smelled as though it held all the waste from the Luckenbooths.

'Christ, man!' Thomas coughed. 'What in God's name?' He covered his mouth with his injured arm. 'The last time I smelled something like that was when I found one of my father's goats; it had been dead a week.'

'These degenerates swim in their own piss,' said the gaoler.

'By the smell of it, dead rats as well.' Thomas pulled out a slip of paper from his inside pocket and handed it over.

'Is this the one from over in Haddingtonshire?' He

looked me up and down like he was inspecting a sow. 'She's tae go wi' the rest of the bastard bearers. Last cell.' He motioned towards a corridor. 'You'll need these.' He threw Thomas a ring of keys.

Bastard bearers. I was to be a bastard bearer. I could barely hear my thoughts for the rushing of my heart in my ears. Thomas's steady hand steered me on through the archway.

Inside, my eyes adjusted. I followed him down a labyrinth of passageways, past huge doors with tiny, barred windows. As we moved along the walkway, an eye appeared between the thin pieces of twisted metal in one of the windows.

'What's a pretty little thing like you doin' getting herself locked up in here?' the voice from inside, like molten tallow, dripped through the gap.

Instinctively, I slowed to take a better look. The eye swapped to a mouth.

'Skewerin' my captain like that . . . I hopes the gaolers are keepin' an eye on you, sweet lady.'

'Enough of that!' Thomas rapped the keys across the metal. 'Settle down, Cullan.'

I felt the colour drain from my face and stop somewhere about my toes.

'Besse, you must keep yer heid,' Thomas said without so much as a sideways glance. 'The monsters behind these doors aren't the ones you have tae worry about.'

No, the monster I lived with was far more frightening. I tried to steady my nerves. ''Tis as black as the Earl o' Hell's waistcoat down here,' my voice quivered.

'Aye, it is,' he said, swinging his ring of keys. 'You'll no sooner get used tae it and they'll have you back out in the yard poundin' hemp.'

We halted abruptly at a cell door, with a peek-hole so small you couldn't tell what lay behind it.

'Here we are.'

I was greeted by the smell of warm piss and overly ripe bodies as I peered into what would be my living quarters. The floor was littered with the bodies of seven women, each encrusted in an accumulation of blood, sweat and filth.

When I sent Thomas away, it had always been my biggest fear that I'd spend every waking minute we were parted wondering if he had been confined to somewhere like this, some cell in a distant part of the world, waiting to be set free; or in an abbey somewhere, being healed by monks. The truth of it was, the bastard I'd chosen had done exactly that and much worse and now he was abandoning us.

Thomas hung his head, not wanting to meet my eyes as he removed the irons. He squeezed my hand softly. 'Dinnae weep, lass. It'll be alright.'

The door closed, leaving me standing in the middle of the bodies like an orphaned child. I listened to the sound of his footsteps as he left. He had brought me almost certainly to my death.

Two men I had known in my life and both of them bastards.

An ice-cold hand startled me as it brushed my leg. I glanced down to be greeted by a watery-eyed expression of hopelessness. Her hair was slick with grease and debris, tied neatly in a plait that ran down her back. She gave a faint smile of recognition.

'Alanis Napier,' I whispered.

'The very same.' She got awkwardly to her knees. 'How'd you end up in here, Besse?'

Faint murmurs rippled through the bodies on the floor.

'Same reason as you, I'd expect?' I sniffed, drying my face on the tattered fold of my skirt. 'I heard you were taken after ye'd tended auld Malcolm?'

'Aye, you heard right. He was havin' trouble . . . performing his husbandly duties. He asked me for a salve tae help wi' it.' She looked at the ground thoughtfully. 'It musnae have worked, because that animal Rivet showed up and I was taken.'

'Aye, twas the same wee bastard that had me arrested,' I said.

'What of yer husband and child?'

'Rupert is . . . Rupert is . . . looking after her at home. He tried to stop them, but they were taken with bloodlust.'

Why did I lie for him? Even now, after all he'd done. I would still defend him. It was like a sickness. If I admitted what he was to them, I would have to admit it to myself and I was not ready, not with a baby on the way and my only hope of rescue sitting firmly on Rupert's shoulders.

'Aye, half of Scotland is aflame.'

'What of the rest of you?'

'I . . . I gave birth to a bastard. He was taken from me but I'll have him back in no time.'

My heart belted against my ribs. They'd allowed her to have her child. I'd be allowed to keep mine.

'Aye, well, at least you'll only be going in the stocks fir

yer philanderin'.' Alanis put her hands on her hips, looking scornfully at the poor woman. 'I get you miss yer bairn, but the rest of us, our pyres will be keeping you warm all winter.'

My hopes were dashed: she hadn't been accused of witchcraft, as I had; she was only an adulterer. I squatted and listened intently to each of their stories in turn. They had been mothers, daughters, sisters and wives. Now, they were the forgotten: bastard bearers, the cunning folk and the wicked. From what I could tell, there were only two of us who had been marked as witches; the rest would be given their punishments and released.

'They'll be here fir us soon. We pound hemp from sunrise to sunset.' Alanis indicated the small, barred window near the ceiling of the west wall where a slither of light seeped in.

Alanis Napier had always been angry and worrisome, and the children of Humbie were fearful of her. After she'd been taken, they'd thrown stones at her poor cat until it fled. They'd delighted in digging up her beautiful herb garden and burning her old cot-house to the ground. No one had gone near the ruins since.

Deserted by my husband, even if I managed to get back to Jenny, we'd have no home left to go back to. Just a pile of smoking ruins. We'd have to return to Agnes.

We were disturbed by the pounding of footsteps along the corridor. Keys rattled like coins in a sporran. I leaned my head against the doorframe to peer through the cracks.

As the door opened, all those around me got to their feet, like flowers moving towards the sun. They filed in line, like a herd of sheep. I followed reluctantly.

Mind's Eye

Jenny followed him at a safe distance; the trail twisted to and fro before it headed downhill and away from Mill House. The light was changing so slowly that she barely noticed the darkness creep closer. No fluttering. No scratching. Suddenly, the woods had become quiet.

She stopped listening. She wasn't sure how far she'd come. Her heart pounded and her muscles ached from running; even though the sweat stood on her brow, her body hadn't become acclimatised to the chill of the winter air. Rushes of breath hung like tiny clouds.

Fear stopped her in her tracks. The tears that she had been holding back for days tumbled down her cheeks, which burned with the cold. She rubbed them with the heal of her palm, smearing them in dirt. She hadn't expected to see her father in that clearing. To hear the terrible things he had done to her mother. Without evidence, who would believe her?

Her mother had always been frightened of her father, as far back as she could remember. He only ever brought her bruises and babies. His blackness would descend over the house when he returned, reeking of whisky and sea fret. Jenny would wish him away, balled up, tight as anything on the pallet beneath her parents' bed. Soon enough, he'd be away again, like the high tide.

The air felt heavy with a wetness that would soon bring snow. A shiver rippled across her body. She had no time to waste and would have to make it back before it began to fall. She fastened her coat and braced herself against the biting wind.

Through a break in the trees, Jenny spotted her father's mare, tethered to a post outside a cot-house that was neither big nor small. *Not a bad place to hole up*, she thought to herself. Only the ravens would make it this far, and they would keep her father's secrets. Moving as quietly as she could, she began to follow the ditch which curved away from the trees, leading down towards the cot-house.

A warm glow burned from a room near the east side.

Her stomach clenched. She moved silently towards the house and was almost at the corner when she whirled at a faint sound behind her and stumbled. A wolf stood not twenty feet away, under the bow of a tree. Yellow eyes stared at her through the darkness as the beast drew nearer.

Jenny scrambled to her feet, backing away slowly until she could feel the corner of the house against her hands. Fleeing was useless. In the summer she had watched as they'd hunted down wild boar with ease, she would be no match for it.

Her hands were so numb with the cold she could barely move her fingers. She bent down, scrambling around in the earth for a stone, a branch, anything she could use as a weapon. Her fingers brushed a rock – she scooped it up and hurled it, skimming the wolf and stopping it in its tracks.

She began to fling anything she could get her hands on, more rocks, more twigs, even her shoes, but all missed. The wolf flattened its ears and let out a rumbling growl.

It happened in an instant. She didn't see the wolf leave the ground. It leapt towards her, closing the gap. She let out a high-pitched squeal and turned to run when she heard something whistle past her ear. There followed the narrow blur of a second arrow and then a third, which thumped into the wolf's chest. It fell to the floor.

'Behind me.'

Jenny spun. At the edge of the cot-house was a woman, her bow fixed on the heaving wolf. Younger than her mother by a few years, with fair hair and fine clothes – the likes of which Jenny had never seen – the woman stood with her cloak hung open, displaying a stomach that was as round as her mother's had been before they'd had to say goodbye to her dead brother.

Jenny stumbled behind the woman, only to be met by an enormous, slobbering mass of dog. It sniffed at her before returning its attention back to the grey lump of wolf on the floor. Its mistress walked over and nudged the carcass with her foot.

'What are you doing out here, boy?' The woman spoke with a French accent.

'I . . . I . . .' The words caught in the back of Jenny's throat. A memory murmured like a harp; it was the woman they'd seen in the apothecary, wealthy and spoilt.

'You will catch your death out here. Please come in.' She turned, and the dog began to follow. 'We must try and be quiet; my husband is sleeping.'

It was dark inside the cot-house. As Jenny staggered

towards the glow of the fire, she could make out a bed in the corner of the room; beneath a bearskin, with his back to them, a man lay sleeping soundly.

'Are you hurt? Scratched? Freezing, no doubt, and a bit shaken. Sit by the fire and I'll bring you something to drink.'

The place had an unfamiliar chill and, although the peat fire was wonderfully hot, it gave off very little light. Jenny's skin burned as the blood rushed back to the cold parts. She tried to flex her fingers.

'I am Cecille.' Her eyes flickered over Jenny's filthy clothes and bare feet. 'Please?' She handed her a cup filled with warm milk.

Jenny took it gratefully, rolling it between her hands to help with the thaw. Cecille's expression was one of pity, the way her mother looked at the pigs when they were due for slaughter.

'What is such a young boy doing out alone in the woods?'

'I just got lost, is all.' She was too exhausted to come up with a better lie.

The man on the bed began to stir. A flurry of black curls rested on the nape of his neck. Jenny glanced about the cot-house; it was like Cecille's hair, neat, tidy and well kept.

'We must be careful not to wake him. We leave for France in a few months, and he's exhausted. I've been of no help.' She rubbed the pear shape of her taught stomach. 'He is working all hours, trying to pack all of his belongings. We were meant to leave much sooner but now we will have to wait out the winter.'

'My father told me France is the most beautiful place he's ever seen, and the richest.' Jenny thought of Cecille's fine clothes and the money she'd offered at the apothecary; her father was right. 'My mam says he's an eejit with a head of feathers and there's none as bonny as Scotland.'

'Well, I think your father is a wise man.' She smiled and even in the dim light, Jenny could see the twinkle in her eye. 'I have the most beautiful home there. My late husband used to make wine and he turned quite a profit.'

'Pardon, mistress, but why are you in Scotland?'

'Women are not allowed to own such things. I met my new husband in France; he is also a widow.' She turned and gave a smile to the slumbering lump in the corner. Cecille bent close to Jenny's ear. 'His wife was burnt as a witch. She had bewitched him and their child. He waits for his estate to be settled and he has been unable to find his daughter, poor creature was lost after her mother was taken. Once she she is back in his care, and the weather has turned we will all return to Fran—'

She was interrupted by movement from the bed. The blood thundered in Jenny's ears as she stared at the face of her father, fast asleep in another woman's bed.

'I'll no' keep you any longer, mistress.' Jenny rose to her feet, stumbling over a stool. 'My mistress will be worried.' She seemed to have lost control of her legs, as well as her tongue. Then she ran towards the door and flung it open, Cecille trailing after her.

'But you've no shoes.'

'I'll be fine.' Jenny thrust the cup towards her. 'Thank you.' She felt like a hen on a hot baked stone.

'Please, take these.' Cecille passed her a small pair of

lady's shoes; they were creased and worn and much too big for Jenny, but she took them gratefully. She needed to tell her nan. Her mother. Someone, anyone.

'However will you find your way home at such a late hour?' Cecille said. 'There's not a patch of daylight left.'

Without another word, Jenny bolted from the door and disappeared into the darkness. She intended to stay lost.

Hard Labour

Agnes felt like she had been travelling, half-frozen in the darkness of the wagon, for days. Now, from the flogging post of the Tolbooth yard, she watched as the women were herded outside in an awful parade, blinking against the sunlight. She could hear the distant caw of the crows; cruel, dark shapes circling like a hungry omen across the sky.

At the same time, a man descended the hand-hewn stairs, with the coil of a whip tucked under one arm.

'Only one fir flogging, captain,' said a voice from behind her. 'Caught tryin' to escape.'

'A serious offence.' He regarded her coolly. 'Look at the poor wretch . . . how could a one-legged cripple manage to escape my men?' He circled Agnes while a line of quarrelling crows watched on from the top of the wall.

'The men entered the church and found her while looking fir Dr Fian. Inconspicuous as she was in her travelling cloak and missing of leg, none thought tae keep an eye on her. She escaped through the refectory door, but they soon brought the cripple to heal.'

Agnes had known all too well that they would catch

her. She wasn't trying to escape but while all those men hunted her like a dog, their attentions were not on the doctor. She'd take the lashing if it bought him and the baby more time.

'I'll not have an old cripple make a mockery of my men. Lay her back bare.'

The coldness of the dirk chilled her skin as it slipped through the fabric of her clothes. She set her forehead against the flagging post and waited. The first lash drew blood. She flinched with the second swing, crying out. By the third she could feel the trickle of blood in the small of her back and her face was drenched in sweat and tears. By the final stroke, she was screaming. She closed her eyes and let the rope take her weight.

A shout from overhead was followed by a grating noise, causing the crows to cover the sky in a sudden blanket of night. Agnes stirred, barely in time to see a shower of filth cascading down into the yard from the stairwell.

'How long do you mean tae keep me here?' she said, shaking from the shock and cold. 'What are you accusin' me of?'

When Agnes was younger, she was a sizeable woman. Never as attractive as she might have been if she'd taken more care in her appearance, she was still pretty enough to get away with anything. Now, she commanded the same respect, but out of fear rather than beauty. But not in the Tolbooth. Ignoring her, they cut her down and shoved her roughly across the yard, in a tirade of cursing. Her eyes searched the milling crowd for any sign of Besse or Dr Fian. She hit the ground with a thump, at the feet of gawping strangers.

'Agnes?'

From the corner of her eye, she saw a woman surge forward, parting the gathering crowd.

'Agnes, is that you?'

'Besse!' Agnes threw her arms wide. 'I thought I'd never see you again.' She touched a hand to Besse's cheek, wiping away tears.

'Are you here because of me?'

Agnes squeezed her hands. 'Ach, of course not. It was Dr Fian they came fer. Came upon St Andrew's, not long after they'd taken you. I managed to get him out through the north door and took my chances as a cripple. Turns out my good name proceeds me.'

Besse plucked Agnes from the floor, handing her the crutch.

'Jean Gray told me you'd been taken. Where is Jenny? Do they have Jenny?' she asked with urgency. The last she'd seen of Besse, she had gone to fetch Jenny. The thoughts of her granddaughter in such a place were too much to bear.

'Before we left for Acheson's, I hid her at Mistress Cochran's,' Besse whispered. 'No one would think to look for her there.'

'Why would you think tae leave her there?' Agnes drew a sharp breath; she hated Mistress Cochran, almost as much as she hated Rupert. 'What are you saying tae me, that my grandchild will be safe with that woman?'

'Where would you have liked me to leave her, Mother?' Besse said, jabbing her finger. 'Rupert is missing. Would you have had me bring her to Acheson's to witness the whooring? Mind you, it might have benefitted the child; she's going tae need an honest living when she's left an orphan.'

'You could have left her with Jonet.'

'Jonet? The woman whose husband I'm accused of killing? That Jonet?' She laughed. 'I'd wager she wouldnae have taken kindly tae minding my child. Or, worse, handed her over tae the witch pricker. She'd no more mind my child than dance wi' the Devil himself!'

Agnes held her hands up in defeat. 'I know. I know. You did right.'

'I dinnae ken if it's right, but Mistress Cochran's was all I had.'

'Have they charged you with anything?' Agnes said, settling herself down to rest. Her face as white as a pearl, with a glisten to it like thawed frost.

'No, they didnae get the chance. No sooner was I arrested than I was brought here by order of the king,' said Besse.

By now a small crowd of women began to gather, inspecting Agnes's wounds. One of them gasped.

'Hush now. It'll heal, I have skin like an ox,' Agnes said as she tried to pull the fabric around her, but she flinched. 'Will no one will tell me how long they mean to keep us here?'

'Not too long, I shouldn't expect. At the rate the witch pricker is collecting us, they're soon going to run out of room.' Alanis laughed a little shakily. 'I've heard whispers, of rapes and such. Them that's with child are spared, at least until the bairn is born.'

Agnes looked sharply at Besse.

'Aye, they'll strip you and prick you, looking fir yer witch's mark,' said another woman, Barbara. 'They'll no' always be truthful about it, neither. Why would they, when they get paid so handsomely for doin' it? I've even heard stories of false pricks and testimonies so false it puts my grandmother's hearth stories tae shame.'

'Charlatans, the lot of them!' said Alanis. 'Not even the children are safe. They arrested the Kintor twins not two days since, the—'

Agnes caught the look of horror that spread across Besse's fine features. 'She's safe.' She placed a hand on hers. 'They won't think to look there.'

'What of these Kintor twins? What have they done with them?' Besse said, her words barbed.

'Here, no doubt,' Barbara said with a flick of her hand. 'Holed up behind a wall of stone, somewhere no one will see them again.'

Agnes breathed hard. The same fate could not befall her granddaughter.

Besse helped Agnes to her feet, covering her back with the plaid she'd retrieved from the whipping post.

Agnes pulled Besse close, squeezing her hand tighter. 'How in God's name are we getting out of here?'

FEBRUARY 1590

'Hell is empty and all the devils are here'
THE TEMPEST

Thou Shalt Not Suffer a Witch

There was nothing but time between the walls of the Tolbooth. We had no way to measure it. Too much of it allowed us to think, and thinking could be lethal. In the quiet, my thoughts turned to Jenny, hidden away as though some kind of hideous creature. It had been months since I'd seen her, *hadn't it?* Time blurred and smudged itself between the stone. *Was it longer? How long would she be safe?* I placed a hand against my stomach. I had not one child but two. *No one will take my children.*

We would play a game, each of us watching as the shards of sunlight stayed longer against the east wall, bringing with it the hope of spring. We used it like a sundial. What month it was, we could only guess. We had no way of knowing. All we could be sure of was that the lives of those outside the walls kept moving, just as the seasons changed and the sun set while we festered, stuck frozen in our misery.

Every day I waited for news of Rupert. Some shred of gossip that would let me know he was safe, that all I'd heard had been a lie, but it never came. When word reached him that my mother and I had been taken, he would come looking. He would find Jenny. Just one look at me and he'd know I was with child, his child.

Agnes lay propped on one arm in swaddles of fabric, whispering. 'They wanted to know all manner of things about Dr Fian. Why we met at the Auld Kirk. Why I was helping. Why I was no' getting sick.'

I rubbed a hand against my temples where the rope burns were beginning to heal. 'Now 'tis a crime tae help the sick?' I shook my head. 'Was it the witch pricker?'

'Ach, no, he was a wee slip of a boy, still wet behind the ears. Didnae have the sense the good Lord graced him wi', so I had a bit o' fun wi' him.'

My mother could drive a coach and horses through anything.

'Mother of God, what did you do?' I asked.

'Well, put it this way, the laddie is going tae have a very restless night's sleep, wondering which of my familiars are going tae pay him a visit and suckle at his teats.' She chuckled.

'Mother!'

'Well, when you get to my age, you canna—'

The door crashed open. My skin prickled like gooseflesh as I peered awkwardly into the darkness. A silhouette of a man blocked the way.

'Elizabeth Craw.'

A shocked gasp rang out from the other women.

'Aye.' I took a step forward and patted the damp hand clutching my elbow. 'It'll be alright, Ma.'

'Put out yer hands.'

I could barely keep them from shaking as I held them

out, fear rubbing at me like an open sore. What little food we had been given meant that the child growing beneath my clothes looked like no more than a slight curve of my skirts.

Thomas stepped forward, the dusty light creating a halo about him. He looked straight through me.

'I've tanned yer arse when you were a laddie, Thomas Reed!' Agnes shouted after us. 'Don't think I'll no' do the same if you hurt my child, you hear me!'

I was taken – in irons again – passing doors six inches thick with eyes behind them full of pity and relief. I placed my manacled hands protectively over the curve of my belly. Smoky tendrils ebbed and flowed from the torches that dimly lit the corridor as it rounded into the gloom of a stairwell. I could barely see my footing. We plunged deeper, to the bowels of the prison no longer in use, apart from by the witch prickers.

'Where is it that you mean tae take me?' I said, in almost a whisper.

My question echoed against the sound of his footsteps, unanswered.

Tell him you're with child.

The thought thundered in my mind. Would it stop him? Would he turn on his heel and return me to my cell? He was no longer the man I remembered. The man that came to mind when I thought of Thomas Reed couldn't have raised his hand against a living creature.

Tell him.

We hit the bottom and came upon a door that was slightly ajar. I peered cautiously in. The room was small but well lit; it smelled strongly of grease and filth. It was sparsely furnished with two chairs and a table, covered in instruments of torture.

'I'm with child.' I breathed the words so quietly that they almost dissolved.

He shot me a look, but it was too late, we were already inside.

'Take her to the wall,' said a voice near the fireplace.

He took a long breath, as though agonising over what to do next. I felt him falter before he took my hands in his and dragged me the length of the room and chained me to the wall. I tried to swallow against the choking sensation, closing my eyes and swaying while subduing the sudden urge to vomit.

'Thank you, Thomas,' said the voice.

I peered in its direction. A man of some forty years, standing still and quiet, propped against the wall by the fire. He was almost six feet tall with hair the colour of pepper, and he had a fine, trimmed beard to match. Holding the holy Bible, he resembled a priest. It looked so tiny in his enormous hands.

'Can you read, witch?' The reflection of the fire flickered in his eyes.

'Aye, I can,' I said, straightening myself. If it was reading he wanted, Agnes had taught me my words; I knew enough.

'I hear you are no longer of innocence and good virtue?'

I felt the rage boil inside me, as it did when Rupert raised his fists, but this man was not my husband. He did not get to speak to me that way.

'Oh aye, I'm of good virtue. Now, I couldnae say the same about the wee bastard that tried tae rape me.'

He took the back of his hand, the one holding the Bible, across my face. I buckled at the knee. I made no noise. No intake of breath. I would not give him the satisfaction. I got back to my feet, my eyes not leaving his.

'You'll learn to keep a civil tongue in yer head,' he said. 'Thomas, do you know why twenty women have given themselves over to the craft, but only one man?'

Thomas's eyes flickered over me for a second longer than he'd meant to before he shook his head.

'The reason is easy: their sex is frailer than the man is, so it is easier to be entrapped in these gross snares with the Devil, as was proved to be true by the Serpent's deceiving of Eve at the beginning. He has been more familiar with the female sex since then.'

The one man could only be Dr Fian. Fear and disgust churned inside me. Twenty of us accused of witchcraft, damned because of our womanhood. What of Dr Fian?

'Have you read the Bible?' He slid his hands across its leather. I nodded. 'Then you must know what an abomination you are?'

I could hold my temper no longer. It spilled out of me hot and sharp, like Master Rivet's poker.

'An abomination, am I?' He was closer now, close enough that I could feel his breath against my skin. I saw my chance and struck hard with my free leg; my skirts slowed the swing, but it connected right where I intended. It's what comes of being Agnes Sampson's child. He let out a roar and folded on himself. I spat.

He rose again, bolt upright and breathless. 'I see you are a woman of spirit. Thomas, hold her down.'

I shrieked and thrashed – if they were going to do it, I wasn't going to make it easy for them. That was until the priest struck me in the side of the head with a bone-crunching thump.

I came to, swilled with water and propped on one of the chairs, clothes soaked through and no longer manacled but my wrists bound with rope to the arms of a chair. I wound my ankles around its legs like snakes and braced myself, trying to suppress the shivering as it rippled across my freezing body.

I tried to collect my thoughts, but they were fragmented like a broken pot. What was it that I was being accused of?

'It's good to have you back with us.' He rolled the screws between his fingers.

'Good fir who?' My tongue probed my swollen lip. 'It certainly isnae me.'

'At least you haven't lost yer voice, succubus.'

'Pity you hadnae lost yers.' I laughed a little shakily. 'How's yer bollocks?'

'You are accused before the Church's court of the crime of witchcraft.'

'I was accused of being a harlot as well – doesnae mean I'm one of those either.'

'All witchcraft comes from carnal lust, which in you is insatiable,' he snarled. 'You are tainted with the heresy of witchcraft, are you not?'

'I am no such thing.'

'You and yer kind conduct yer Sabbats at St Andrew's Auld Kirk in Berwick.'

I leaned across the table. 'Those are fir witches. I'm no' a witch.'

'Father Buchane,' Thomas began, 'I know this woman. She isn—'

Maybe the Thomas I'd known was still in there, after all.

'Are you questioning the authority of the Almighty, Thomas? Are you a sympathiser of witches? Perhaps it is you I should be pricking?'

'No, father.'

'Then do as I've bid.'

Thomas came behind me then. He took my hands in his, pinning them to the table. I could have fled in those woods, taken my daughter and ran. *I should have left him to die.*

My fingers wriggled like spiders as the priest struggled to force the little one between the metal screws. With each turn, the metal came closer together.

'I'll ask again, where do you conduct your Sabbats?'

I contorted with a hiss. I looked him dead in the eye and spat.

He grabbed at my cheeks with his free hand, pressing them until blood trickled where my teeth punctured the soft flesh. I gasped at their release.

His eyes fixed on mine. 'The Sabbats, where?' he said, twisting again.

'Ask yer wife!'

Time stood still. The pain was slow at first and then intensifying. His face never betrayed him. With a soft *pop*, I felt the bones splintering. I let out a scream like the keening of a banshee. I closed my eyes against the sensation until it made me weep. I could see Jenny. Her homespun skirts flecked with mud and her hair, wild and windswept. I held her close and breathed her in.

With a final twist, she was gone.

He jerked me to my feet, dragging me towards the fire. Why could I not hold my tongue? Why did I keep fighting? *The injustice of it*. I had helped a friend. It wasn't right what they'd said about me, what Master Rivet had said about me. I was guilty of birthing a baby, and that was all.

He wrenched the rope through the manacle on the wall, pulling my arms above my head and pressing my face against the granite. It should not have been like this. My heart pounded and I could feel my whole body tense in readiness.

It's not fair. It's not right. My baby.

'I'll have no more of your lies.'

I could feel my wrath inwardly blazing. These men had no right. No right at all.

His knife slid through the back of what little was left of my dress as if it were butter, leaving the back agape and my flesh on show. A shudder rippled through the beads of sweat standing on my skin. First, he filled my face with violence, now he stripped me. This was not a man of God. He was taking pleasure from it. He was as monstrous as the Devil.

The *clink* of metal in the fireplace filled me with dread.

'Where's your Satan now?'

'Heating a poker by the sound o' it,' I slurred.

When it connected to my skin, I heard it before I felt it. Seconds passed. Finally, I cried out, a sound so guttural, so wild, that I almost buckled at the knee. My head slipped forward, jolting me awake. I was beginning to lose consciousness.

'How did you call upon your storm to try and sink the king's ships?'

My eyes flew open. 'What in the name of Christ are you talking about?!'

'You know very well, witch.'

'Do I?' I could feel the line of the burn across my back. 'I can control the weather now, can I?'

The truth of it twisted suddenly in my stomach. Not only was I a witch but I was an attempted murderess and a traitor to the crown. *There was no hope.* Even if they could find Rupert, how could he prove my innocence?

'Your coven conjured the storm that almost sank *The Grace of God* carrying the king's new bride.'

'If I had a coven that could control the weather, I'd hope to God they wouldn't think it fit tae leave me trapped here with a bastard witch pricker!' I exploded, writhing around on the end of the rope like a fish on a hook. 'You hear me? I am NO witch! I have NO coven!'

'A witch if ever I saw one!' he said. 'Listen to that wicked, poisonous tongue spilling its filth. We have witnesses. You and your coven were at the harbour, drinking and feasting and cavorting with the Devil!'

Acheson's Haven. That's all it could be. The night we went looking for Rupert.

'*Drùisear*!' I spat.

'She speaks with the Devil's tongue.'

He lashed me again and again across my ribs. I closed my eyes against the sound. Jenny and I were back in the kitchen, preparing the pheasant, its limp body thumping against the wood of the table. Jenny giggled and grimaced with every feather we plucked and plucked. Then, darkness.

* * *

I was being shaken gently awake. My head felt full of sawdust as it lolled between my knees. A wave of nausea rolled through me, through both of us, but the movement was unmistakeable. *I'm here, Mother. I'm here.*

Greased torches flickered against the breeze as it moved through the barely lit corridor, chilling my burnt skin as it swirled between my body and the granite at the bottom of the stairwell. The breath from my lungs hitched with every inhale against the pain in my ribs. They felt as though they'd crumble to ash beneath my scorched skin.

Thomas held my hand in his, tracing the lines of my fingers, whispering softly. When he caught the movement of my head, he pressed a flask against my lips; the bitter smell of the liquor made my stomach heave, but I drank it greedily.

'I'm sorry, Besse,' Thomas whispered, fastening the lid on the flask.

My head swam. I shoved his hands away, nausea replaced by repulsion. *I told him I was pregnant.* I began to inwardly seethe. *He may as well have hit me himself.*

'How could y—' I vomited mid-sentence.

'I didnae want tae hurt ye.' He touched my shoulder, making me flinch. 'I woulna—'

'No?' I said forcefully, shaking it off. 'But you did.'

He took a step back. 'When you fainted, I begged him

tae let me take you back to yer cell. I said he'd get no more from you in such a state.'

'I didnae ken you needed a map tae find yer way?' I heaved again, but there was nothing left. 'Where are we?'

'The other stairwell. I thought I'd better see you right first. Didnae fancy taking you back to Agnes as you were. I still remember havin' my heid clouted by her; that woman has hands like broad shovels.' His hand shot to his head at the memory.

It was so easy to remember. To slip back to how we were all those years ago. His eyes settled on my stomach.

'Are you . . . Is it alright?'

'Aye, no thanks tae you.'

'There was nought more I could do.' His voice cracked, pleading.

You could have stopped him.

I cradled my right hand and tentatively moved my fingers. Blood oozed from the open wound around my little finger, which hung limply from the socket. I tore at my filthy underskirt, pulling a length of material and wrapping it shakily around my hand.

'I dinnae think I'll be knitting any socks fir a wee while.' I could feel the sting of old tears on my cheeks, my voice about to crack.

'Never mind socks, someone needs tae be mendin' yer dress,' he said, assessing the back, which gaped open. He tried his best to tuck it in, being mindful of my painful burns.

'A man that can mend a dress. Yer wife must be proud.'

Thomas knitted his brows together. 'Ach, no wife, but a man who cannae darn his own socks ends up wi' very wet feet.' He stepped back and took in my appearance. 'I'm sorry, Besse, but I'll have tae take you back before anyone starts askin' questions.' He held me by the elbow and helped me to my feet.

I could barely put one foot in front of the other as he guided me slowly back up the spiral staircase. We walked in silence. I couldn't bring myself to look at him and his betrayal. *One. Two. Three.* I kept my gaze to the floor and counted the gaps between the stones. I had told him my deepest secret, and he had taken it and discarded it as though it was nothing.

We arrived back at the cell that it felt like I'd left only moments ago.

'Besse, I willnae let anything happen tae ye,' he croaked. 'You have my word.'

I stepped over the threshold, eyes to the floor. *Thomas Francis Reed can rot in Hell.*

'What have they done to ye?' Agnes pulled herself to her feet.

I couldn't see her face in the darkness. I shook my head, but the words tripped on my tongue. She didn't say another word and just took me in her arms, as the door closed with a bang.

A Girl

Over the next few months, Jenny found tending the horses to be a welcome distraction and thankfully, Ian left her to it. During the hours in the stables, she picked out the pony she would take and managed to stow away enough food for a few days' journey. She spent her days shovelling and sweeping from dawn until dusk, collapsing into her bed as the dark crept back in, with a full stomach, and prayed she'd be too exhausted to dream.

Tonight was different. Sleep did not come. The silence of the slumbering house penetrated the walls. Jenny lay on her back, staring at the ceiling, listening to the sound of cracking ice outside her window. She could not – dare not – think of her father, Cecille and her swollen belly. He had allowed the whole town to think her mother was a witch. Her father had been missing for months now, and she knew that many folk believed him to be dead. Secretly, she wished he was.

She lay there, heart hammering in her chest at the thought of what she was about to do. She hadn't the courage to mention her plan to Willy; he knew nothing. He was scairt of everything and would tell Mistress Cochran, and it would be all over. It was going to be a risky journey. The roads were few and snaked through woods full of wild beasts. Jenny only had a vague idea of the direction of the Tolbooth and she was scarcely more than twelve.

It didn't matter how frightened she was, she could only think of her mother and Agnes. She missed her mother's smell of lavender when she buried her face into her hair. She missed being told off for getting home too late, thick of mud. It had been more than a month since she'd last seen her. There was no one else she could trust to help her.

Maybe if she asked Master Rivet? He knew his letters. He'd always loved her mother, even if he had struck her for the rents; but that was her father's fault, because he'd stolen them. She was sure when he heard of the awful things her father had done, he would write to Edinburgh and tell them the truth of it. He'd have her mother freed and they'd be home before the week's end.

Scrambling out of bed as quietly as she could, she crept to the chair and pulled on her clothes. They were as cold as they'd been when she'd taken them off. The peat fire was almost burnt to nothing and she hadn't bothered to light it again. She shivered.

Jenny eased open the door onto the passage. She stopped and listened. At the far end, the door to Mistress Cochran's room was ajar; shadows moved around in the dim light of a candle.

The rustling of skirts made her jump. Ducking out of sight, she watched as the cook emerged from the room, frowning. The room slipped back into darkness as she rustled past Jenny with the yellow orb following her down the stairs and towards the kitchen.

Jenny sagged with relief. She slipped down the remaining stairs, avoiding the creaking one and eased open the door at the bottom. She stepped out into the bone-coloured moonlight and took a deep breath of the clutching winter air. The slanting rain had turned to sleet. She hated February.

A lantern had been left perched on the stone ledge above the entrance to the stable. She approached the doorway and listened. Nothing. It seemed as though everyone was asleep in their beds. She ducked beneath the arch and tried not to make a sound, but her feet clicked against the cobbles. She felt bad for abusing Mistress Cochran's hospitality but there was nothing else she could do. She had no time to make them understand; her mother's life was at stake.

She scrabbled around in the dark until she found the edge of the stall belonging to Mistress Cochran's grey mare. Whispering, she edged the mare outside, and the hooves clopped loudly against the cobbles. She tethered the horse to the iron ring hammered into the stone wall of the stable.

She needed to make water before she left. The stable sheltered her from the sleet, and she edged around it in complete blackness, feeling her way. She closed her eyes and tried to be comfortable, squatting with her breeches about her ankles in the slippery mud. She couldn't dismiss the feeling she was being watched.

Just as she finished, a noise stirred behind her. She turned slowly, her eyes straining in the darkness, and was met by the figure of a man looming over her. Hands grabbed her roughly and she was jerked from the floor. She struggled wildly.

'What's yer business here?' said Ian.

'I could ask you the same!' she hissed.

'Mibbe you shouldn't be doin' that around here, Rob.' He relaxed his grip and placed her back on the floor.

'Eh . . . aye.' She stumbled to her feet, fastening herself. 'Do you need me fir something?'

'No, I need tae know what yer sneakin' about in the dark fir. Do you no' have a bed tae go to?'

'I couldnae sleep.' She fumbled for an answer. 'So, I came down here, is all.'

'Just how far d'you think you'd get on that old beast, in the dead of night?'

He grabbed her firmly by the arm and strode back around to the front of the coach house where she'd tethered the mare. In the light of the lantern, she could see the gangling shape of Willy, propped against the wall, with arms like knots in cotton and his chin upturned as he checked the windows for signs of life.

'Even a good horseman wouldn't attempt it in such weather,' Ian said.

Willy caught the noise and turned.

'I would've been fine.'

'I dare say you would have been, at least fir the first few miles,' he went on, clearly angered. 'But the dark roads are no place fir a young girl.'

Her heart almost stopped. Willy's mouth hung open; he put her in mind of a gasping fish.

'Now, are you going tae tell me what it is you think yer doing? I want the truth of it.'

It was over. Ian stared, his eyes boring into her, waiting for the truth. Could she trust him? Here, all the laddies looked up to him, even Willy, but did that mean he would keep her secret? Would he be so understanding of a witch's child? Or would he be fearful? She glanced from Ian to Willy and back again, biting her bottom lip, before the strain of it all caught up with her.

'My mother left me here, right before she was taken.' The words began to tumble. 'I was there, you see, when Rivet struck her, demanding the rents my father had stolen. Then we fled, and Mistress Cochran took me in.' She took a deep breath; she felt as though she might be sick. 'When they started looking fir the witch's child, she cut off all my hair and gave me her nephew's clothes and hid me here. I wasnae supposed tae tell a soul.'

Ian's attention settled on Willy, who chewed nervously at the dry skin that flaked around his thumb. 'Did you ken about this, laddie?'

Willy's eyes darted around, desperately seeking an answer.

'Aye, he did. But I made him swear, swear on his ma's grave.' She shot Willy a look, to warn him to play along. 'Willy's all I told, and he would ne'er betray me on account o' my ma.'

Willy's mother wasn't dead. She had been a whoor and left him at Mistress Cochran's when the sight of him began scaring away her clients. Jenny had promised she'd help find her, one day, but today she needed her to be dead.

'That true, aye?'

'Aye,' they both said.

'Who is yer mother?'

'My ma is Besse, Besse Craw. And my nan, well, she's Black Agnes.'

Ian nodded sagely. Everyone in Tranent knew her grandmother.

Jenny pulled at her coat nervously and carried on. 'Then, over at the rocks, when ye'd asked me tae go and empty the barrow, I saw my father. He was telling them to look fir me. I thought, mibbe, he had come to find me after hearing what had befallen my mother, and that he'd pay what he owed. But no! He wanted to make sure he had got rid of my mother and sent her away.'

Ian listened intently, as did Willy. She told them of her father's new wife, Cecille, and their baby and the run-in with the wolf.

'He wanted rid of us! All so that he could sneak another woman into his bed! He only wants to steal what she has, like he did from my mother. The only thing we have worth anything is this rosary.' She was shouting now, pulling it from her pocket. 'Now Cecille has a child in her belly and a fine estate in France that my father will inherit, and they are already making preparations to leave.'

She looked at Ian through a haze of tears. From the look on his face, she could see he didn't believe her. Why would he? If she couldn't get him to believe her, no one else would. She sat down again, curling her knees into her chest and sobbing. If her mother died, her father would get away with what he'd done. All would be lost.

'Please say you believe me,' she said.

Willy ran to her, crouching into the mud, his eyes

brimming with tears. 'We'll tell someone. Couldn't we?' He looked up at Iain. 'We can tell the truth and then they'll let her mother go.'

Besse and Agnes had been the only real family he'd really known, other than Ian.

'It isnae as simple as that,' Ian said. 'My mother died in the Tolbooth, God rest her soul, fir a crime she didnae commit, leaving me and my younger sister. Mistress Cochran's mother took us in.'

'Where is she now? Yer sister.' She sniffed, rubbing her eyes with the heel of her palm.

Ian's face softened. 'I lost Annie when she was not much older than you are now, to the pox. Very well, I'll help you, Rob— You havenae told me yer name, lassie?'

'Jenny. Jenny Craw.' She rubbed at her nose with the back of her sleeve, sniffing loudly.

'Well, Jenny, you're of no use to yer mother dead.' He patted the mare, leading it back to the stall. 'Could you take me to Cecille's house again?'

She nodded.

'Then we'll leave tomorrow.'

The Hanged Man

Months since I'd been taken. Since I'd seen my daughter. Months of my belly stretching and contorting to fit my growing child. It would not be long before he'd arrive – in a hail of accusation and suspicion – and be taken from me still wet.

I no longer dreamed. I drifted in and out of nightmares.

I was out in the orchard, not quite our orchard as it was lined with trees twisted and gnarled. The wind clutched at me, buffeting my skin. Jenny and Willy were playing around the hollow trunk of an apple tree. She was wearing the travelling clothes I'd left her in.

Shadowy figures screeched above them. Twisted fingers reaching out, clutching at them like a furious storm. I tried to call out, but there was only skin where my mouth should have been. I broke into a run, but the shadows dissolved and spilled to the floor, grabbing at my ankles and dragging me further to the ground.

When I awoke, I was sweating. It felt as though I had never been to sleep. The sun dripped in streaks of pink and gold across the sky. I couldn't tell if the bitter stink was coming from our foul breath or the human waste that seemed to be frozen in the fissures of the stone. A wave of nausea crept up my throat, trying to force its way out from behind my teeth. When I had carried Jenny, I'd hated the feeling and wished it to be over. To not have the sudden, constant urge to vomit. Now, the feeling brought comfort: for as long as I could feel it, my boy was alive.

I rolled over, bracing myself to rise, and came face to face with a pair of green eyes. Blue veins whispered in the marble of her face, framed by sunken sockets. She was as cold and as stiff as the granite we lay upon.

The shock hit me like a punch to the stomach. I could hardly breathe. I stumbled to my feet, gasping, cradling my broken hand. I hadn't even known her name and now she lay dead.

Agnes came and stood next to me. 'We havenae a coin to give her fir the ferryman to carry her soul,' she said.

It made no matter; the woman's spirit had fled from her body and the suffering had gone from her face.

'I dinnae think she'll be needin' coins where she'll be going,' Euphame, another prisoner, grunted from the floor. 'You dinnae need them in Hell.'

'Don't you speak ill of the dead. There but fir the grace of God goes you, Euphame Cullane,' I said. 'Could've been any one of us.'

The scorched skin on my back oozed where the blisters had burst, causing the cloth to stick. I flinched at every movement as it tore away from the skin.

'I'm no' gonna die in here like that, and neither are you. We'll get back to Jenny.' Agnes blew the words softly in my ear. 'Here . . .' She pushed a handful of white willow bark into my good hand.

It awed me to think of what my mother had stuffed in

the lining of her skirts; it was no wonder she swayed like the bow of a ship. I put it in my mouth and chewed. 'How do you propose we make our escape?'

'Aye, well, I havenae worked out the finer points of it. They still havenae told us what it is we're accused of doing.'

The memory of the torture yesterday swarmed like a nest of angry bees, stinging with such ferocity that that I gasped for air. We were accused of attempting to kill the king's new bride. I shuddered and pressed myself hard against the wall, trying to stop the roll of nausea.

'I ken why we've been arrested,' I said at last, my head swimming. 'That night, up at Acheson's Haven, you remember? The king's fleet almost sank on the crossing; it was carrying his new bride.' I breathed heavy, gulp after gulp of air. 'The king believes a coven of witches called upon the storm. We are those witches.'

'No,' Agnes choked. 'It cannae be? I don't believe it.'

'Believe it, because that is exactly what they think we are. He broke my fingers wanting to know where our coven met, wanting to know how we called upon the storm.' I shook my head. 'They will stop at nothing to prove our guilt.'

Just as they did with the woman whose burning I witnessed. *Was she guilty of nothing more than fending off the advances of men?*

Agnes stared at me, bewildered. 'We cannae be burned for stoppin' at a tavern?'

'I dinnae ken what else they have, but they are damn sure it was us to blame.'

Euphame snorted and shook her head, then gave my

hand a disparaging look. I wiggled my fingers, in an attempt to show they still worked. Agnes had forced the little finger back into its socket and now it was black as pudding and just as swollen. I doubted very much that I'd ever have full use of it again.

We all stood around awkwardly as the conversation turned to the poor stiff body on the floor. From the look of her, she must have been dead a wee while. Euphame whistled softly while the rest of us paid our last respects. I didn't care to imagine how crude her disposal would be. A pitiful shroud and then thrown out to be food for the worms. Whatever they decided, the poor woman deserved better than what they would offer. *We all deserved better.*

We were mothers. Sisters. Grandmothers. Until we were witches. We were the many. Damned because we knew too much. Condemned by the men we loved. The people we worked for or the neighbours we saved. They did not care what they did to us, as long as we confessed to what they thought we were. Broken legs. Broken fingers. Our limbs did not matter to them. They were no longer our own. We were no longer human. Before, we were alive. We lived. We breathed. Now, we were the forgotten. The bearers of bastards. The wicked. The damned. The Devil's handmaids.

* * *

I was grateful when the gaolers came to take us to the yard. The curve of the steps down didn't seem so sinister in the daylight. I placed my manacled hands on the swelling bulge beneath my skirts. We had almost rounded the final corner when I heard the soft thump of Agnes hitting the floor.

I bent down to help her up, tangled in my chains.

'I cannae see us end our days like this, hen,' she said, her hands shaking in mine. 'My body may be failin', but as God is my witness, this will no' be it.'

'Enough! Get to work!' a gaoler shouted.

We scurried across the floor, like the rats that shared our food, and began our daily ritual of pounding hemp. Agnes gave them a glare that, had I not known different, should have shrivelled their manhoods. Her reputation definitely proceeded her, but she was no witch.

'D'you hear that?' said Agnes. The others stopped to look. 'The crows have come a callin'.'

Shapes swirled as the sky blackened above us. My eyes came upon the silhouette of the gallows up on the north wall. A stark reminder of what was to come. A man swayed limply in the breeze. The noise from the expectant crows changed to soft rattles and clicks as they settled to roost, waiting for the body to go cold, when they would pick the meat.

Agnes crossed herself in the centre of her chest, so small it went completely unnoticed by the gaolers.

'Mother!' I hissed. 'We're in enough trouble already without you adding to it.'

'What are they goin' tae do about it? Put me tae the stake again?' She settled her skirts.

'I heard there's a pirate in here.'

'A pirate, you say?' Andrew Barton, I thought. 'And how'd you come tae that?' I said.

'When you were taken last night,' she said in a whisper,

so as not to draw attention, 'I was earwiggin' and I heard 'em talkin' about what he did. Stolen something from the king's ship, by all accounts. When they arrested him, he hadnae' – she mouthed the last words – 'any o' the jewels on him.'

'If I were him, I would have eaten the buggers,' I said quietly. 'The night I was brought here,' I began – remembering every detail: the smell of the storm; its heaviness against my skin – 'there was such an almighty scuffle and he got loose from the wagon. I was so scairt, Ma. So scairt, and I hid behind some rocks, but he found me.'

Agnes's eyes widened. 'Please tell me he didnae—'

'No.' I placed my good hand on hers. 'No, but he tried to drag me back to his ship. He said I'd be safe, that he'd left the jewels near a crossroads and that there was safe passage on a waiting ship.'

'He told you that?' Agnes glanced nervously over her shoulder. 'The pirate?'

I nodded. 'He wore Rupert's ring about his neck.' I leant forward, our faces almost touching. 'Andrew Barton has the rents, and my husband has arranged passage on that ship to France in May.'

We watched each other anxiously, in grim silence. A gaoler walked by, eavesdropping like a washerwoman. When he was a good safe distance, Agnes spoke again.

'Surely Rupert wouldn't leave you and Jenny? I ken there is no blood lost between us, but I didnae think he'd be capable of such a thing. Are you sure?'

'The ring around Andrew Barton's neck says different.'

'Are you telling me that swinging from that pirates

neck is yer husband's wedding rin—' Agnes stopped, her face concentrating on the comings and goings about us. The beginnings of a quarrel drifted through the air, bitter words were spat to and fro between a small group of men in the northern corner of the yard.

A crowd began to gather around the commotion.

'Halt' and 'Put a stop to it!' rang out as gaolers hurried to douse the mass of arms and legs with a pale of seawater. The men scattered like hornets from a smoking nest.

'Did you no' see that?' Agnes whispered in my ear.

We could hear the sound of flesh tearing as the men received their lashes.

'I dinnae want tae bear witness to such a spectacle.'

'No' the lashes.' She gave a sideways glance and carried on. 'I meant the gaolers. With all the commotion, we were left unattended. Did you no' ken?'

'No.'

'We need tae get yer husband's ring back.' I could almost hear her thoughts. 'And then we need tae find a way to—'

'Aye, well, you just keep those thoughts to yerself, Mother,' I interrupted. 'We are innocent. When we're brought tae trial, it'll be proven, and they'll find the witches that did it.' Not that I believed my own words.

It's all been a mistake. We should never have gone to Acheson's.

The chill of the darkness soon arrived to bring an end to our work. The clouds parted to reveal a backdrop of glittering stars. As we approached the third stair, a lantern was thrust in our faces. Agnes caught my elbow.

'You two,' said the gaoler. 'You're fir trial in the morning.'

A Rat Without a Tail

The burn was a thin, green ribbon that widened as they crossed the moor. Even in winter it was rich with green ferns and a splash of purple heather, all dusted in a powder of frost.

They had left at cockcrow, on the grey mare and gelding. Ian warned that the woods would draw too much attention, so they had taken the track past the loch. In the dawn light, it looked like a piece of beaten silver.

'I bet yer not afraid of anything?' Jenny said to Ian. She sat almost on the grey mare's withers, back pressed against Willy, who clung to her. He had insisted he accompany them, even though he hated horses.

'Ach, I'm afraid of lots of things.' Ian reached over and ruffled her hair, placing one of his hats on her head. 'But dinnae fash, lassie, I'm no' afraid of men like yer father, and I willnae see any harm come tae ya, or Willy. He willnae ken it's you, just dinnae say a word and, fir God's sake, Willy, keep yer head down.'

She reined her horse downhill, through a gap in the tree-line. Wisps of smoke curled into the air from the chimney of the cot-house, which was larger than the one she shared with her mother. Her mother had always told her that all plants and herbs wanted to do was live, *we only have to give them a helping hand.* Beneath the open shutters were barren flower-beds where only weeds would grow.

In the daylight, it looked peaceful and inviting although she couldn't seem to shake the feeling she was being watched.

'Willy, you need tae stay here. You ken my da will know it's you.'

'I'll only be over there.' He pointed to a thin wall of trees, bare as sticks.

She watched him disappear behind them. Fear knotted in her stomach. What if she had been wrong? It had been so dark . . . maybe he just looked like her father?

'Is this it?' Ian brought the gelding to a halt.

'Aye, it is.' She held her breath.

Ian swung himself down from the saddle and rapped on the door. It felt like an eternity before it opened. There he was, her father, just as she'd remembered him but a little softer around the edges, ruddier in the cheeks. He looked like a pig being fattened up for Christmas.

'Master Craw, is it?' said Ian. 'I'm here about yer daughter and wife.'

Rupert glanced at Jenny and then back to Ian.

'I suppose you're here fir the reward? You'd better come in,' he muttered and disappeared through the door.

Inside, the air was as warm as July, with a fire burning fiercely in the hearth. Ian took the seat nearest the window; Jenny took the one next to him. Her father, hunched over the stool, churned the ashes with a poker, like he always did when he was home.

'News travels. You must ken the Leiths?' Rupert said.

'Aye, I ken the Leiths very well.' Ian cleared his throat and reset his jacket. 'What of the reward?'

'I willnae pay a penny until my daughter is returned to me. Where is it you said you were from?'

'I didn't. Yer wife is in a great deal of trouble, and I know of a house where yer daughter has stayed since yer wife's arrest.'

Rupert ambled over to the table and sat not a hair's breadth from Jenny and drained the contents of a tankard. She could feel her cheeks redden. She chewed on her bottom lip to quell the urge to call his name and kick his leg for all he had done.

'That creature is no concern of mine. She's tae be burned at the stake. My daughter on the other hand . . . I'll pay handsomely fir her safe return.' He skipped a small velvet pouch into the middle of the table. 'Call it a down-payment, and I'll arrange the rest once I have her.'

Creature? How could he say such things about her mother? If he thought for one second that she'd go willingly . . . She would rather live with Mistress Cochran forever than return to her father. He was a monster.

Ian tipped the contents of the pouch into his palm. 'Why is it yer daughter commands such a high price?'

'She's my own flesh and blood. Isn't that enough?'

'From what I understand, yer not a man who values family as much as some.'

'You wound me, sir.' Rupert placed a hand over his chest. 'Can a man not love his child?'

'Aye, a man can.' Ian tipped the coins into the pouch and slid it back across the table. 'You, I'm not so sure. Where were you when yer wife was taken? Did you no want to look for your daughter then?'

'I had fled, terrified fir my life after seeing the monster my wife was. Just like her own mother.'

Jenny could feel her fury boil. He had no right to talk of her mother or her grandmother like that. He was a liar and a thief. She wished Black Agnes would curse his face with pustules. She balled up her fists in her lap. She felt a rush of heat to her cheeks, so hot she was sure her father would see.

'Knowing what yer wife was, how could you not take yer child?'

'What can I say?' Rupert threw his hands up in defeat. 'I'm a coward.'

He is worse than a coward.

'And I'm expected tae believe in yer new-found courage?'

'Nothing gets past you, does it?' Rupert said with a hint of a smile. 'Are you sure you dinnae work fir the bailiff?'

'No, but I do ken you owe him a lot of money. So, what is it you really want yer daughter fer?'

'Well now, if my wife is tae be hanged fir her crimes, then they are going tae need witnesses, and who better than her husband and daughter?'

Ian didn't let his face betray him. Jenny could feel her outrage seething inside her. He hadn't been able to rid himself of her mother so now he would make them testify, to see her to her death. She would not. He could not make her. Never.

'When my wife was taken, she had something of mine – a necklace – and she would have given it to our daughter. It's worth a pretty penny. A man could do a lot with that sort of coin, and she won't be needing it where she's going.'

Jenny stiffened. It had to be the black onyx rosary. She'd hidden it inside her bag before they'd left. He was going to take the very last thing she had left of her mother.

'Yer wife could be burned and your daughter is missing, but you've no interest in helping them?'

'What I do have an interest in . . . sir, is where the money is coming from tae pay my debt to the Laird Ruthven before he has my head. It certainly isnae coming from a wife and child that I'd have tae provide fer.'

Jenny realised now: it was all for money. All of it. The money he'd stolen from Master Rivet to pay his debts to Lord Ruthven. She had no doubt that the poor woman he had his claws into now, would be seeing him as a true gentleman, a rich man who could give her everything her heart desired. She wouldn't know him like Jenny and her mother did, for the monster he truly was. She hated him. She hated him and she wished he would drop down dead.

'If it means that much tae you, I'd be willin' tae fetch the necklace and yer daughter, fir a price.'

'I like a bargain, sir. Now, what is it that you have in mind?' His eyes were alight with interest.

'Give me a week and I'll bring you the necklace and child,' said Ian.

'That willnae do. My new bride waits in North Berwick fir safe passage to France which I need to pay fir. You have until the end of the week if you want the other half of the money, or you'll find that I am not a patient man.'

Ian said nothing, simply nodded.

Rupert's eyes fixed on Jenny now. 'Does he not speak?'

Jenny lowered her gaze, concentrating on the wood grain of the table. *Please don't notice. Please don't notice.* She held her breath.

'No, not since he was a child. Come now, Rob.' Ian held out his free arm and ushered her to the door.

'I'll be seeing you again.' Rupert cast them one last look before Ian and Jenny mounted the horses.

The saddle creaked as Jenny settled herself into it, letting her breath out slowly.

'Dinnae fash, *caileag*. I told you, I willnae let any harm come tae ye.' Ian pushed the gelding on, trying to put as much distance as possible between them and Rupert. 'Do you ken what it is he wants from ye?'

'Aye, it's this.' Jenny fished around inside her saddle bag and brought out the rosary. 'It's the only thing me mother ever owned that was worth anything. She used to say if it wasnae nailed down, he'd have it away. I have tae keep it safe.'

'Let's fetch Willy, and we'll head back. We need tae speak wi' Master Rivet.'

'Do you think he can hel—'

Jenny jumped as Rupert came out of the shadows, armed with a pistol. They hadn't heard him above the noise of the horses brushing through the undergrowth.

'Jenny' – Rupert smiled the same reptilian smile he kept for her mother – 'so nice of you tae come and visit yer poor auld father.' Then he looked squarely at Ian, the pistol resting on his forearm, aimed at the stable hand's torso.

For a few seconds, no one moved.

'You best hand her over,' said Rupert. 'I might even let you leave, if you do.'

'We'll be leaving, with or without yer permission.'

'Jenny, get off that horse now.' Rupert swung the pistol in her direction.

There was nowhere to hide. Her eyes darted from her father to the clearing where they'd left Willy. Jenny began to tremble, and the rosary in her hand was slippery with sweat. Her heart kicked against her ribs. She had seen that look on his face more times than she cared to count, usually before he used his fists. There was no stopping it now.

'Stay where you are,' Ian barked as he struggled to hold the gelding.

The rain drummed against her. Jenny glanced around, trying to find a way out, a way to charge her mare at him and batter him to the ground. How could she scoop Willy up on the way? She was sure he was there, just behind the tree-line. But what if charging her father caused him to fire the pistol? There was no room. He was too close. She stared at him with loathing.

'You've got until the count of three.'

Eyes wide, she carried on staring at her father. If she gave in now, she would have no choice but to testify against her mother. He would see to it. She could feel herself shaking.

'I'll no' let you have that child.' Ian brought his gelding in front, blocking Rupert's advances.

Rupert now levelled the pistol at Ian. 'One.'

He cocked the pistol.

'Two. I've told you, I'm not a patient man.' His eyes

flickered to Jenny, watching her face. Ian didn't move.

Jenny told herself to breathe. Her legs fizzed with the urge to flee.

'Three.'

The noise rang out, echoing through the trees and sending clouds of crows scattering.

Jenny's head hit the floor with a thud as the horse threw her backwards and bolted. Then came a thump and a loud grunt. Ian lay to her left, groaning.

Then came fingers, pulling her over. She was too stunned to put up a fight. A noise rang in her ears like the chalice in church clattering against a candlestick. She sat up dizzily. Her mother's rosary was gone. It must have flown out of her hand in the fall.

'Quick!' Willy was urging her to her feet, 'You have tae get up, Jenny.'

Jenny could hear nothing but her own breath and her own heart as she got to her feet. They took off running. She could barely see anything past a foot in front of her, but she could hear Willy running in the direction of the trees, pulling her forwards through the ruts and tall grass.

She didn't see him coming. But she felt him grab at a handful of her overcoat.

'Run!' she screamed 'Run!' And Willy ran.

She'd almost reached the trees when the bulk of her father hit her, sending her spinning onto the ground. She looked up to see Willy running and making it through the trees.

'Hand it over, I know you have it!' Her father's face contorted with rage as he turned her over. 'Or you'll be headed the same place as yer mother.'

Rupert hauled her to her feet, twisting her arm painfully behind her. She glanced over at Ian. For a second she could have sworn his fingers twitched, but now he was still. Tears pricked her cheeks.

'I don't have it,' she said as her eyes caught the pearls of the rosary in the long tufts of grass.

He followed her gaze. 'You always were a foolish child,' he said, smiling. 'Just what I was looking for.' He scooped up the rosary, letting the beads roll between dry hands.

Jenny squirmed but it only made him grip her arm tighter.

'You'll be coming with us to France, but not before yer testimony. Yer going tae make sure that yer mother burns.' His eyes swivelled towards the body. 'I dinnae suppose he'll cause us any more trouble.'

'I want my mother! I hate you!' She kicked at him wildly.

'You'll see yer mother soon enough at court,' he said, pulling her back to his waiting horse. 'Either you behave, or I soon see to it that I'm a childless widow. I have a good friend over in the Tolbooth who's going tae make sure yer mother and that interfering grandmother of yours will be dead before we board the ship fir France.'

He slipped the rosary into his pocket and pulled out a thin piece of twine.

'Now, hold still and this willnae hurt.' He bound her wrists. 'I cannae have you riding all over the countryside shouting and upsetting my new wife. Court is set fir tomorrow's first light. We'll be there by noon today tae make sure we give oor testimony.'

He thrust her over the front of the saddle before settling in behind her. *No. No. No.* She couldn't say anything against her mother. She wouldn't. *Think!* There had to be something he wanted. Something that would change his mind.

'I promise, Da, I willnae tell anyone. If you let me go, it can be our secret. You can keep Ma's rosary: sell it, like you said.'

'Enough!'

He pushed the horse on and up the track. Through the rain Jenny could see the still figure of Ian. His right arm was in tatters; she had never seen so much blood. With the last of his strength, he'd tried to protect her and Willy.

She closed her eyes against the sight, trying to stem the steady flow of tears. Her father didn't like it when she cried. She sniffed quietly. If Willy had made it, he wouldn't stop until he found her.

She would need to bide her time and wait for him.

Trial

I clung to my mother as we were led down the stairs. Looking around, I could see half of Edinburgh had gathered. At first, I couldn't understand why they all stood about, staring at us in silence. A sea of faces, men and women alike. Realisation crept up my throat, clawing at it and forcing my breath from my lungs. They were here for the Tranent Witches.

I couldn't stop my hands from shaking. I didn't know what to do in front of such a crowd. As we drew nearer, I could see the faces of neighbours, of people who had visited me in desperation, in sickness and in death.

It was then that I saw Jonet Muir, at the front of the crowd, wrapped in a new pale-yellow shawl. It should have brought comfort to see someone I recognised, but fear seized my heart. Agnes glanced up briefly, her eyes meeting Jonet's. I watched as the colour drained from her face. We both knew what it meant. Her testimony alone could see us meet our end, even without charges brought by the Crown.

The session was to be held on the ground floor, with the doors left open to accommodate the ever-growing crowd. We were jostled into the stand, facing two men who had been sent by the Dalkeith Presbytery, Adam Johnson and George Ramsay, to assist in the investigation.

As the dittay was read, I kept my eyes to the floor, my hands covering the smooth curve of my ever larger belly. *Tap. Tap. Tap. I'm here,* he said. I could see the vague outline of my mother next to me, but I dared not look. Our fear, like a fine silver cord, stretched between us.

'The accused, one Elizabeth Craw and one Agnes Sampson' – George Ramsay's voice rang out, steady across the silence of the court room – 'did use witchcraft to attempt to cause the death of King James VI and his new bride, whereby raising a tempest to sink the king's ship, *The Grace of God.* Elizabeth Craw and Agnes Sampson, you have been charged under the Scottish Witchcraft Act of 1563. Anyone who should use, practise or exercise witchcraft, enchantment, charm or sorcery, whereby any person is killed or destroyed, shall be put tae death without benefit of clergy.'

'Call the first witness,' said Adam Johnson.

A small woman, fine and wiry, with a face like a rodent, took the stand. She bobbed her head nervously to both the examiners and began by stating her name, Katherine Meldrum. She hailed from a croft not far from Tranent, apparently. What could she be witness of? I'd never set eyes on the woman in my life, nor the husband she spoke of.

'That daughter of Sampson's was always wayward,' Katherine said, nodding in my direction. 'Trouble followed her wherever she went. Hair like fire and heart like a stone, that's what my poor husband used to say, God rest his soul. I'll tell you exactly why it happened: I made the mistake of knocking on her mother's door. Those Sampson women hold a grudge. I only asked that she not have strangers knocking at all hours of the night. Keep mistaking her door fir mine, you see, wanting all manner of conjurations and love spells. Next thing we know, our herd of cows is all giving milk runny with blood.'

The crowd gave an audible gasp.

'Did yer late-night callers cease?'

'No such luck . . .'

Nonsense. She must have thought to chance her luck, paid by one of the presbytery. I looked at my mother, who stared fixedly at the crowd, breathing steadily.

'That will be all. Call the next witness.'

'You swim her, and you just see what happens,' Katherine Meldrum shouted as she was taken down. 'Those vessels never stood a chance against their blackness.'

When he came forward, my heart almost stopped. I was too afraid to raise my eyes and look at the judges. *Breathe. Breathe.* Dressed in black gown, roped about the middle, he surveyed the crowd subduing them to silence, as though he were preaching one of his sermons.

Father Cowper.

''Tis right that you call her a witch!' He pointed at us, finger shaking. 'Wi my own eyes, I saw this woman call her familiar upon me. A great, fearsome creature, black as night, chased me down with its thundering hooves and cast me to the earth in mortal peril!'

My rage bubbled up. 'My mare bolted, you old fool!'

The crowd jeered. My mother shot me a look that I hadn't seen since I was a child.

'Silence in the dock!' shouted George Ramsay.

Father Cowper carried on, alive with malice. 'You shall not suffir a witch to live, fir a man or woman who is a medium or spiritist amongst you must be put to death and suffir the judgement of the Almighty! Let the court hear, those who practise the magic arts – the idolaters and all the liars – they will be consigned to the fiery lake of burning sulphur!'

'Can you please give the court the date of this offence?'

'Aye, if it pleases the court. Twas twixt one and two, All Hallows' Eve.'

Poisonous wretched toad. All Hallows' Eve my arse. He hadn't even got the time right. He would not let the truth get in the way of the crowd hanging on his every word.

'And did you hear the conjuration?'

'I'm sorry, no. I couldnae understand the incoherent babble she whispered to the beast before it flew at me.'

The crowd looked on in awe at his testimony, lapping up every word. I chewed at the inside of my cheek until I tasted the metallic tang of blood. I rifled through the memory of that morning, riddled with such fear, but I could think of nothing. Nothing. My mare had taken off into the gloom, startled by half the village baying with bloodlust. If my mare ran him down, it could have only been an accident, an accident caused by my accusers.

How many more could they parade through? Paid or pressured for their testimony. So far, all had named only me – that was until Isobel Gowdie took the stand.

'It is no secret that half the village is terrified of Agnes Sampson. But not Goodwife Cuthbert. No, you ask the farrier, John Pigg, he'll tell you, over there to examine their sick mare. As Agnes stoops over it, Cuthbert lunges at her somethin' fierce, clawing and gauging at her face; blamin' her, she was, fir the poor animal's affliction. Agnes stood bolt upright – it was before she lost her leg, you understand? – and I listened to her spitting vengeful, threatening curses before she walked away from the scene of the crime as though nothing had gone on.'

I could remember that day clearly. Agnes had called upon a favour from John Pigg. She'd seen that horse prone in the field, unable to get to its feet, poor beast. Goodwife Cuthbert had a fiery temper and had been none too pleased when my mother appeared with him, thinking she'd be saddled with the cost. They had cross words about it, nothing more. Isobel Gowdie had been as close to that conversation as I was to finding Rupert.

'If there is nothing further?'

'No, yer honour.' Isobel Gowdie bobbed her head and descended in three steps from the dock. It was almost noon when she slipped away into the crowd of people all milling about, waiting their turn.

'The evidence presented to the court only goes to confirm that the accused both dabble in witchcraft and the black arts. When we reconvene this afternoon, we are to hear more testament from those who witnessed these women on the night in question.'

* * *

When everyone returned, blood-hunger still upon them, they settled themselves in for the afternoon's proceedings. We listened to the testimony of neighbours, of people I'd thought friends. With every testimony, the tightness in my muscles eased and the nausea ebbed away. There was no substance to their accusations. It reeked of the court's desperation to prove our guilt.

Marion: As the moon was rising, I pounded her door. I called out but she wouldn't answer! Look at what she did to me! Just look at my head, as bald as a bollock! All I wanted was for her to reverse her magic, but she wouldn't take it back, no matter how I begged.

Gilbert: Oh aye, I heard them at their witches' feast talkin' and chantin' with that sodomite, Fian. Next thing I know, the procession, led by Craw herself, follows the Dutchman and they all boarded The Grace of God. *I could hear the festivities from my own door! An unholy din, with Craw on that Jew's harp!*

Widow Clarke: I've seen that familiar of theirs. Cat black as coal and such an impish name. Roams all over Tranent, worrying the hens. He does their bidding. Just look at them! Dirty, ragged and hunched! Witches, if ever I saw them!

Neighbour: Every week at church I am reminded that God can look into my soul and judge me against the commandments painted on the nave. My child has been sick since I've fallen out with Agnes. Night after night my child lay shrieking and clawing and menaced by buzzing insects until the day she died. I accused her then, to her face. The words had no sooner left my lips than I collapsed to the ground, my poor husband having to carry me home. I heard that her own mother had been hanged as a witch, that bad blood runs through their veins.

Mary Hoggard: My husband apprenticed as a cooper. All his life he worked hard. My first child was born quiet, but we was compensated with eight strong 'uns. We'd been neighbours to Agnes all our married life, but you ken you can only be charitable for so long. A huge fallin'-out like that was only going tae brew trouble. Then his father went and threatened to have Agnes searched for her witch's mark . . . well, you can only imagine.

Robert Bernard: Nothing will give me greater pleasure than to see these wretches launched into eternity. In the autumn of 1567, I reported Sampson as a common scold. Normally the humiliation of the douking stool would make disorderly women repent, but not Agnes Sampson – it only made her worse.

Then came the Dutchman, Coel Egbert, who'd mistaken us for whores.

'Flickering in lustrous light I watched Craw put the Jew's harp to her lips with Napier and Sampson, pished as newts, they were, singin' "The Witches Reel". Such an unholy sound; to make the imps dance and the Devil call. I watched as the drunkards followed me aboard *The Grace of God*, dancing and swaying about the quarterdeck with the women of Copenhagen. Devil's handmaids, the lot of 'em!'

The chill of his smile. My mouth hung open. I could feel myself shaking, nausea crashing into me. How could we defend against such lies? Against monsters wanting nothing more than revenge for their hurt pride.

He carried on. 'I watched them throw a monstrous creature into the sea, legs of a cat and the body of a man, and I watched the sea boil and ooze, bringing about a tempest.'

I urged myself to breathe and my legs to hold fast as they buckled beneath me. My heart beat a tattoo. The room began to spin. And then, just as I thought the ground would take me, swallow me whole, I was flooded with relief. Across the room, I watched Rupert weave his way through the crowd to stand beside the examiners; and next to him, holding his hand tightly, Jenny.

My family. I knew he wouldn't leave me. As soon as he'd heard, he must have tried to find Jenny, and now he was going to tell them the truth. To put a stop to it. He was here. He would save us. I pressed myself forwards, trying desperately to catch his eye. He would be able to see from the bulge beneath my skirts that I was with child. For the first time in a long time, I felt the thrill of excitement.

Jenny kept her eyes to the floor and her hand firmly in her father's. Her hair was shorn almost to her head, but I'd know my own child anywhere. The Dutchman rambled on but I heard not one word of it, for whatever he said, Rupert would prove that I wasn't a witch and take me home. Take us home.

Then he raised his head and looked straight through me. *Why would he look straight through me?* I glanced behind me, to see what else could have caught his eye, but there was nothing. He mustn't have seen me. That could be the only explanation.

'Jenny,' I croaked.

Agnes looked up in the direction I was calling. I heard her gasp.

Jenny raised her gaze to meet ours across the room. She was pale and trembling, with a wisp of a bruise across her cheek. *What had they done to her?* It felt like I'd taken a beating to the chest. What unspeakable things had they done to my child before her father found her? My broken finger throbbed.

'Call the next witness, Master Rupert William Craw.'

I had been so taken with the sight of her, that I hadn't noticed the Dutchman conclude his testimony.

This was it. This was it. I could feel my legs begin to shake. We would be free before sundown. Rupert would finally know about our second child. *Home.* My mouth watered at the thought of it. I could taste salted gannet and roasted mutton. The image of the table, the crackle of the fire and, most of all, my arms around my child.

'What evidence is it you have fir the court?'

'The woman you accuse of witchcraft, Elizabeth Craw, has been my wife for nigh on twelve years. It's not right what they say about her . . . What me and my daughter suffered at her and her mother's hands was much, much worse.'

'Rupert?' His name escaped my lips as a scream.

He didn't look in my direction. I could feel my chest tighten as the panic crept over me. I swallowed hard against the lump in my throat. What was he doing?

'I feared for my very soul, so I fled, leaving my poor daughter behind.' He cleared his throat, and the crowd gawped in silence, hanging on his every word. 'When I heard the good news that you'd arrested the monster, I knew it was safe to return.'

'What is it that you feared?'

'Not long before I left, I was taken with a terrible sickness. Convulsions and the like.' He glanced at me fearfully, 'At the sight of the new moon, she gave me a draught to drink – supplied by her mother, no doubt – and told me it would make it stop. Afraid of her as I was, I could do nothing but drink it. I sank into delirium and watched her diabolical imp of a cat devouring everything in its wake. It would have killed for her, had she asked it. I was fearful fir my life under the spell of her poisonous draught. When I came to, I was healed.'

My mind reeled. My own husband accusing me of witchcraft? All the while, Jenny stood at his side, unable to raise her eyes to even look at me briefly.

He carried on. 'I ask the court, why would someone take so much trouble, at risk of death to themselves, to alleviate the sufferin' of others? I tell you now, because my wife, Besse Craw, is in league with the Devil himself! He spared her! How else could my wife know such extraordinary cures? I dinnae care who her mother is; a humble maidservant is no doctor. How else could she acquire the knowledge of leechcraft if it weren't from conjuration!'

I buckled at the knee. Chest heaving. Gasping for a snatch of breath. I knew he had hated my work with herbs, but I never thought he could be so cruel, ruthless. My vision began to blur.

'We thank you, Master Craw, fir yer testimony. And yer daughter? Has yer daughter a charge to level against these women?'

'Aye, she does. Don't you, Jenny?'

Through the bars, I watched her eyes swivel wildly between me and her father. She shook her head violently, tears streaming down her cheeks. The familiar ache of despair gripped my heart. Surely he would not make her testify?

He ushered her forward, trembling, before the court. I had never felt hate like it. Rage stirred in every muscle, every sinew of my being. I looked at Rupert with such malice that, had I been a witch, he would have dropped dead on the spot. And I wished it so. Right then and there. I wished I had given him that draught. That I had poisoned him, and he was dead in the ground. *Dead*.

'What is it you have to say, child?' Adam Johnson said kindly.

Tears stained her cheeks and she rubbed at them with the heel of her hand. She swallowed hard and shook her head. I dug my nails into my palm.

'Speak up, girl.'

'I . . . I . . .' She looked again at Rupert, who glowered back at her.

I watched as she straightened herself and clenched her fists. The same way she did when she was about to defy me.

'I havenae anything tae say about my ma or my nan.'

'That isnae what you told me, Jenny.' Rupert stepped menacingly close to her.

'Aye, it is.' She looked straight at him, jaw clenched. Unblinking. My child to her boots.

He didn't look angry. He never did. 'Apologies, my daughter seems to have forgotten herself.' He grabbed her by the arm and escorted her from the dock.

Not for the first time in my married life, I feared for my daughter. Rupert didn't take well to being embarrassed in public, a lesson I had learned not soon enough. I watched as they snaked back through the crowd and through the doorway and from my view. I wanted nothing more than to follow them, to take her from him and denounce him for the bastard he was. Our relationship had always been fraught and charged with rage. There were times that I had thought I loved him and hated him in equal measure. Now, as I watched him disappear with my only daughter, knowing what he'd done . . . now, *I hated him more.*

After the testimony, the judges talked amongst themselves for several minutes, each looking between Agnes and me. There was no one left to save us now. No gallant hero to stop proceedings. We were to be burned, and our ashes scattered into the wind.

Adam Johnson and George Ramsay got to their feet and commanded their audience to listen.

'We find ourselves unable to determine guilt solely on the evidence provided.' He looked around at the expectant crowd. 'Therefore, under the circumstances, these women are to be conducted to Holyrood House and brought before King James VI on his return to confess their guilt.'

Holyrood House

We found ourselves on our knees again, in some kind of holding room, no bigger than a pigsty and strewn with straw. The only opening was a metal slot in the wood, too high for me to reach. I pressed my face against the stone and eyed the gap beneath. I could see nothing in the darkness but listened to the creaking of their shoes and the rattling of keys dwindling as they disappeared further into the prison.

I whipped around to face my mother. 'Did you see him? That bastard! I cannae believe he would do that! Poor Jenny, looked scairt half tae death! He may as well have killed me himself!'

'I saw, Besse, I saw.' She grabbed at my hand to steady me. 'Shhhh . . . You have tae calm, no good can come of it. We must keep our heads.'

I melted into her arms and sobbed like a child. My life had crumbled before my very eyes. The man I'd once loved wanted me dead and would go to any lengths to make it happen. He had taken my child. He had taken my freedom, and he intended to take my life.

'Did you see his wee mouth when Jenny refused to do as he bid? Looked like a cat's arsehole,' she said and laughed as she stroked my hair. 'They cannae find us guilty of a crime we didnae commit, and if they do, God will know the truth of it.'

'You heard them all: half the village has turned against us. Even my own husband!' I sniffed and wiped my eyes with the hem of my skirt. 'Why would he do such a thing?'

'That I cannae say, he always was a bedswerver.'

'Mother!'

'Mark Acheson said as much, up at the tavern' – she dismissed me with her hand – 'Rupert's been frequenting the place almost six months with another woman on his arm.'

That was it. Within me, I felt courage begin to grow inside me. Or rage. Or strength. Whatever it was, he would no longer get the better of me. Agnes had been keeping my husband's secret from me all this time. My husband had a mistress. But I had my own secret. I was with child. A child he would not take from me. At last I knew what it meant to hate.

'Do you ken who she is?' I said, pulling myself up into a sitting position, hands balling into fists.

'Ach no, nobody did. All Mark could tell me was that she had a French tongue in her head.'

'We cannae let him get away with this. His son sits in my belly. He will never know his father. My heart is free, and my son is free; as long as there is breath in my body Rupert will never take either. I swear it.'

* * *

They came before sunlight. Three months they had held us waiting for the king.

'Craw. Sampson,' the gaoler said.

I was jolted awake. Fear gripped at my throat, causing me to gasp. I clutched at Agnes, who lay sleeping like the dead at my feet. She sat bolt upright, and I pulled her from the floor, to be bound and shackled for transport.

Dawn slashed the sky with red as we stumbled into the narrow walkway, only to be herded into the back of a waiting cart.

'Where are you taking us?'

He thrust us through the door. The only light in our snicket came from the broken shards that filtered in. The space was so small that neither one of us could sit comfortably. Agnes lay awkwardly propped on her left arm, breathing heavily, while I stood on tiptoes to catch a glimpse through the barred hole.

'Can you see anythin'?'

I pushed my eye harder against the wood, angling my head just so. The cart moved off at a steady rattle. Above, the bell rang in the high tower, signalling market day. I could feel the press of the crowd. Hear their shouts and the clicking tongues of fishwives that infiltrated our wooden box, like insects. All scurrying about their business. Not one of them riddled with guilt about the women they'd sent to burn.

'Only auld Widow Clarke . . . I'll give her dirty, ragged and hunched.' I tried to shout the last bit through the bars.

'Where are we headed?' Agnes rasped. I could barely hear her over the din.

'North, towards the Canongate.'

'The way to Holyrood?'

'Aye' – I craned my neck – 'looks that way.'

I clattered to the floor as the cart lurched, sending a hot shock of pain through my crippled finger. It was pale and no longer delicate, the knuckle now twisted into a shape I no longer recognised. I clambered on to my knees in an attempt to steady myself, but I must have looked more like a new-born calf.

'You have a good look about ye,' Agnes said, eyeing the curve of my belly. 'Going tae be a strong wee one.'

'He's going tae need to be.' I glanced down. 'He willnae keep me from the pyre much longer.'

We stared at each other for a moment, in silence, as if hoping for the answer to a question we were both either too wary, or too afraid, to ask.

* * *

We thundered through the archway of the gatehouse without as much as a second glance. The private gardens that lined our approach were littered with archery butts. Even at a distance, the vastness of Holyrood's quadrangle jutted impressively from the landscape, marked by four turrets. The northwestern tower had once housed Queen Mary.

'Looks like we're here,' Agnes said as she peered through the same gap that I had.

My stomach quivered with sickness. We were to be taken before the king. To be tortured – or worse. *Agnes.* My eyes settled on the woman who had taken me in as a child. Had been my only mother. She looked bone-tired and weary. She was only here because of me, because of Rupert. I felt riddled with guilt.

The horse slowed to a walk and made a long arc before coming to a stop. Fresh spring air flooded in with the light. On all fours, I swallowed it greedily, until my lungs ached. Agnes did the same, like tasting freedom. We had been so long in the foul stench of the Tolbooth, I felt alive.

'Besse,' Agnes whispered and took my hand in hers.

Manacled together, we were dragged from the cart and met by the palace men.

'On yer feet, witches!'

One of them encouraged us to stand with a boot to my mother's ribs. She hissed. My anger flared, but there was nothing I could do. She was afraid, just as I was. Where would another beating get us? They may have taken everything else from me, but I would not lose another child. We clumsily got to our feet, each using the other as a ballast.

The palace had been designed to overawe; the lavishness of it was almost grotesque. Agnes gawped. It was like nothing I'd ever seen. Ever the trips with Rupert to Dirleton Castle paled in comparison.

The only noise was the crunch of my feet against the gravel and Agnes's intermittent wheezing. I prayed that she wasn't sickening. We had no herbs. No tinctures. Nothing. We were led not through the open doors of the palace but past the ornate carvings of the abbey doors and to the heretics' entrance.

We shuffled past the vestry, my bare feet slapping against the stone floor and the clack of Agnes's crutch reverberating around the abbey's vaulted ceiling. The air inside was stale and damp. We clung to each other, as much as we could in chains. It was little comfort as we gazed about its luxury, at the throne and the king sat upon it.

Agnes's breath hitched.

I felt as though I was floating above the scene, blood thundering in my ears. King James VI of Scotland sat before us beneath a latticed web of lead and stained glass, framed by velvet which bled from the walls in slashes.

He was never without his favourites. To his right stood Alexander Lindsay, Sir William Keith, the Laird of Barnbarroch and a selection of the most handsome gentlemen from the king's chamber. He set his jaw at the sight of us.

Alexander Lindsay stepped forward and read aloud the indictment: 'The accused, together with their coven, did attempt to cause the death of Anne of Denmark, Queen Consort and wife of King James VI, by means of witchcraft and invocations of spirits of the Devil to raise a tempest to cause their fleet to sink. What do you say?'

What was there to say? I had pleaded innocence until my throat was hoarse and the breath had fled my body. Guilt would bring death. Innocence would bring death, slowly. When we said nothing, the man to my left kicked me in the back of the knees, sending me to the ground and taking Agnes with me. We knelt there, in front of the court.

'Are these the detestable enchanters that tried tae sink the queen's ship?' The king's accent was thick like Scotch broth.

'Keep them in their fetters,' said the Laird of Barnbarroch.

'I understand we have been unable to extract a confession from either of them? And yet, it's been said, Satan himself appeared to them' – King James thrust a hand towards us – 'and promised to raise a mist, casting mysel' and my new bride into the North Sea?'

'It is Your Majesty, from the mouth of the County Bailiff, David Rivet, in Tranent. He named them as witches, and that that was where the storm began.'

The king nodded.

Panic rose in my chest and my breath caught. This wasn't the baying mob filled with bloodlust. This was the Cradle King. His reputation preceded him. I had heard the stories, of his hatred for women, and of the men of his bedchamber. Here we were, accused of heresy and attempting to kill his queen.

'We are but lowly howdies. Skills passed down through generations.' Agnes stumbled, resting on her crutch, and gave an awkward curtsey. She would have done well at a playhouse. 'We only deliver bairns. We dinnae hold wi' witchcraft and Devil worship.'

'To make women learned and foxes tame has the same effect – both become more cunning. And I find cunning women insufferable,' said the king.

'I can assure you, we are no cunning women. Only healers.'

It was no use. We were to be damned either way. As soon as they could cut my baby from me, I'd be put on the pyre, just like all the others.

'Have you not reason to be ashamed of this filthy novelty of healing?' he said, appearing even-tempered, although I could hear the anger in his burr. 'Witchcraft is hateful to the eyes, harmful to the mind and dangerous to the Church, is it not?' All about him nodded. 'I have listened in great length to the testimony of witnesses. You have both been named, by John Fian amongst others, as the witches who tried to sink my new bride's ship. But yer storm was no match for yer king.'

'Your Highness, my mother speaks the truth. We have no coven, we are—'

He cut me off. 'I understand that you are the one who plays the Jew's harp for the Devil. I want to hear it. You will play it for me now, or I will see you hanged.'

I watched my mother's eyes widen. I had not played the Jew's harp since I was a wee girl. Agnes had taught me. A woman would knock at the door and Agnes would draw down the shutters, always cautious, never conducting her business by the window. She'd set me away playing and would hum while she worked. Out of their pockets they'd often throw me shillings, or else, too poor for shillings, they'd nod and clap, accompanying me. It was never a dull day with us.

'Come on then, stir yerself.' The gaoler grabbed at my arm and hauled me to my feet, pushing the harp into my hand.

I did not say anything but simply stretched out my palm. At first, I thought I might not do it. That I would refuse, walk out and never return. That was if I believed that the decision was mine to make. But, of course, I was a fool, for there was no choice.

I muttered and lowered my head, turning the tiny metal object over and over before placing it gently to my lips.

The sound reverberated, flowing and echoing about the stone. My heart ached at the sadness of the sound and the words as my mother chose to sing them:

> Cummer go ye before, Cummer go ye
> If you willna go before, Cummer let me
> Ring-a-ring-a-widdershins
> Linkin lithley widdershins,
> Cummer Carlin Crone and Queyn
> Round go we
>
> Cummer go ye before, Cummer go ye
> If you willna go before, Cummer let me
> Ring-a-ring-a-widdershins
> Loopin' lightly widdershins
> Kilted coats and fleein' hair
> Three times three.
>
> Cummer go ye before, Cummer go ye
> If ye willna go before, Cummer let me
> Ring-a-ring-a-widdershins
> Whirlin' skirlin' widdershins
> De'il tak the hindmost
> Wha'er she be.

'So, it is true? Just as the witness said.' The king sat forward, placing his hands on his knees. 'An unholy din to make the imps dance and the Devil sing: the words of "The Witches Reel".' He cleared his throat. 'Now, I want yer confessions.'

What had I done?

'You will be brought to justice. First, the crone. Guards, remove her hair. I want to see her witch's mark.'

I scrambled for her, but I was too late. Rough hands grabbed Agnes and dragged her before the king. They held her down while one of them fetched the sheers. I couldn't imagine how Agnes was feeling. Relief and shame coursed through my body, because this time it wasn't me.

'What of yer coven?' He watched in great delight as they removed every tuft of hair from her head.

'I cannae say, exactly. I've never seen a meeting of a coven, though I've heard of them,' she said.

I could barely understand the words as she forced them from her lips, her right cheek pressed against the stone with a knee. Cumbersome as I was, I pushed against the hands that held me still, trying desperately to get to her.

'What of yer rituals? The witnesses say you rose a tempest in the sea, the likes of which has never been seen. How do you explain that?'

'They saw nothing of the sort. It has never been seen because it didnae happen.' She kept her voice even. Rage for her, for our situation bubbled beneath my skin. 'It's been said you have the Great Witch of Balwearie, you bring her here, have her confirm my guilt!'

'I have no need of her, yet.' He waved a hand dismissively. 'Men, I want her wrenched until she confesses.'

It felt as though they'd poured gunpowder on to the spark of fear in my belly. It was a pain I'd known only too well, after Master Rivet had ordered the same punishment for me in the town square. I couldn't stop myself from trembling as they dragged my mother to her feet.

The echoing chamber came alive with the bustle of

commotion. One of the guards brought ropes and began binding her temples. Two twists before they each took an end and pulled.

'Mother!'

She made a noise like screaming lambs as the rope pulled. The minutes ticked slowly by. I tried to meet her eyes through the confusion, but she kept them firmly closed.

'Don't worry, you'll get yer turn,' said the guard, pressing a boot down menacingly into the soft flesh of my calf.

When they finally stopped, she wilted.

I fought and kicked with everything I had, throwing my weight left and right then left again. Finally, I wriggled free and, ignoring their pawing and shouts, I crawled to her.

I caught her by the elbow and held her upright, my eyes red with tears. 'Mother, I'm here, I'm here.'

She groped for my hand and squeezed. 'Besse!'

Her voice was shrill, distant. The force of them was immense as they hit me, sending me sidelong, crashing to the ground, cracking my head against the stone with a bone-crunching thump. White-hot pain shot through my neck. I floundered and tried to get back to my feet, cradling my unborn child.

The king's gaze fell upon me. 'Take the other foul creature, chain her to the cell wall and remove her fingernails.'

Agnes went to speak, but hesitated.

They seized my arm with nauseating accuracy. I was dragged, kicking and screaming, towards the rear of the abbey.

'Let go of me! Bastards! You let go!' I kicked again, leg flailing with nothing to push against, no foothold to brace against.

'I am the witch you seek,' Agnes said finally, turning her eyes from me and back to the king. 'Leave her be.'

It was as if time stood still. Silence rang out about the abbey, as it waited with bated breath to hear what the witch had to say. No one moved. I could barely hear the sound of my own breathing as my heart thundered in my chest.

'I was called tae the Auld Kirk, on All Hallows' Eve, by my master,' Agnes said. 'I'd taken my seat among the men and women when demons shaped like dogs and kittens appeared, jumping upon everyone's laps, all except mine. I was asked if I wanted to join the witches' society. I said yes and was made tae swear upon a book.'

My mind raced. *Why would she say such a thing?* 'What are you doing? Mother, you take that back! Stop it! Stop saying it!'

'Fairytales and conjecture.' The king rested his head upon his hands, bored with the charade.

'Once I had given my word, a demon climbed upon my lap and told me it would do my bidding.' She cleared her throat and spoke louder. 'The Devil spoke tae us. He had us dig up corpses about the kirkyard and remove their limbs. We were to sew them to the body of a dead cat.'

'Ma! You did no such thing!' My voice was hoarse from my screams. She wouldn't look in my direction. 'Stop that this instant!'

She inclined her head to King James. 'We threw that

wee beastie, of our own making, into the North Sea and watched the water boil. The clouds swirled and thunder cracked, bringing a storm to rival Satan himself.'

'These are just lies, to protect the real culprit.' He looked at me in disgust.

'I tell ye,' she was shouting now, '*I* called upon the storm, me! I tried to sink the Devil's greatest enemy. You dinnae believe me?'

'Silence.' He held up a hand. 'There is no truth in yer words.'

'I can prove it.'

'Is that so?' said Alexander Lindsay. 'I would not believe a word of what she says. She's just trying to save her daughter.'

'Mibbe. Mibbe not. But my master tells me things. Things that no one else would ken. Like what you said to yer wife, the first night in yer marital bed.'

'Tell me, witch, what did I say?' King James said.

'Your Majesty, there may be things that would make their toes curl.' She nodded her head towards the men behind him. 'I wouldnae like tae make these fellows blush. May I whisper it?'

All about the king glanced at each other.

'Very well, I'll entertain it. Guards, is she still bound?'

One of them rattled her chains. 'Yes, Your Majesty.'

'Very well. Leave her be.'

He rose to his feet and made his way towards her, the guards receded into the cloisters. I could hear the grin in his voice. 'Go on then, witch, tell me the words that passed between me and my wife.'

She spoke so quietly that if I hadn't held my breath, I may not have heard her.

'You asked me if I was a witch and I tell you, *I am.*' She stopped for dramatic effect and looked him dead in the eye. She wanted him to remember her. 'My master told me that you couldnae perform that night, limp and wet as a newt, yer poor wife left wanting.'

King James stopped so suddenly that he looked as though he was frozen.

'Hell is empty and all the Devils are here,' he said finally.

'You snuck out in the dead of night, leavin' yer lovely wife alone in the marital bed.' The words oozed from her tongue. 'Seeking the cock of another man. My master has eyes everywhere.' She clenched her jaw in triumph.

Everything Dr Fian had told us . . . with a little bit of my mother's flair for drama.

'You'll pay fir that,' he said simply.

'And my master will make you pay if you touch my daughter. She is under my protection.'

I gasped, my body betraying me. He would never let my mother live. Not now.

'Take them back to the Tolbooth and send the witch prickers – I want their confessions before they're burned at the stake. You have until the week's end.'

'No . . . no . . . no . . .' I gasped.

King James turned on his heel and disappeared in a flurry of fabric. My mother had signed her own execution warrant.

* * *

It had been three days since we'd returned from Holyrood. Three days until the week's end. I stared at the curve of my belly, swelling with each passing day. Soon, the day would be upon me and they'd take my child away before sending me to the stake. Every twinge, every flutter, filled me with terror, for although I had come to terms with it, of what would happen, I knew what it was to lose a child. I could not bring myself to say goodbye.

The wind moaned against the cracks and fissures of the stone. I had been glad to have my mother with me. Although had I known the kind of terror it would lead us to, I would never have given Jonet Muir the belladonna, and I would never have trusted my husband.

The long silence of the night was broken by the rattle of keys and the crashing of doors on broken hinges. *Were they coming for me?* I backed away from the door. They'd taken my mother two days ago. Two days and there had been nothing. I'd looked for Thomas, sure that he would tell me if . . . I could not bear to think of it. A pool of yellow light crept through a fracture in the wood. I held my breath, my eyes fixed on the door, frightened to blink.

The door crashed open and Agnes was thrown over the threshold.

'Mother!'

She clambered to her feet, resting against the wall, breathing hard.

The clouds parted, causing a beam of moonlight to filter through the bars, catching her shape. Tufts of fine stubble were scattered about her head like moss on a boulder. She shook visibly underneath the swathes of fabric. I went to her.

'Besse . . .' Her voice sounded like a fiddle spring about to snap.

'What have they done to ye?' I whispered, frightened that the others would hear. 'Have they hurt ye?'

Agnes didn't speak. She gave a shake of her head; tears stained her cheeks. Words lost in her torment.

We lay down on the floor, and I tried to press myself against her. To take away her pain. Like I would with Jenny when she was fearful or sad. She looked as fragile as a child. I was jealous of the others, able to close their eyes and sleep. I tried but couldn't. Every time I opened my eyes, I'd see Agnes staring at the wall, lips pressed in a sharp line. She pulled her shawl around her, covering her baldness. Yawning, I placed a hand on her knee. She flinched and pulled herself away.

'Ma, what have they done tae ye?'

She didn't respond and kept her eyes fixed to the wall. Tiny droplets of dried tears glinted on her cheeks. I had never seen my mother so broken.

The sun didn't rise that morning; a sea of clouds rolled across the sky lazily. *Ne'er cast a clout til May be out*. Thick and heavy as they were, they still brought a chill. We muttered amongst ourselves nervously as we waited to be taken to the yard. My mother's gaze had not faltered from the wall.

'Ma.' I waited for a reply but there was nothing. 'Can I help you up?'

She gazed up at me, surprised, as though she was seeing me for the first time. She grasped my hand and pulled herself up. I tried my best to shuffle her crutch underneath her, allowing it to take her weight.

'There you are,' I said, being mindful to be gentle.

A slight smile tugged at the corner of her mouth, though she still seemed slightly bewildered. In the morning light, her hair was all but gone. The bruises that had covered her face when she arrived were angrier now, deep purple welts that masked both her eyes from the bridge of her nose, which looked painfully broken. My heart ached for her.

'Ma, feel . . .' I placed her hand against my stomach, mine over hers. 'This is hope. You must tell them that you did none of those awful things. That you are not what they say you are. We will get out of here.'

She smiled, but it was fragmented, stretched across her face as though it had been painted on. 'They will not stop. It will not end until we confess, or we are dead.' She groped for my hands. 'It was the only way. You must promise me, promise me that when they take you, you say you had nothing to do with it, that it was all me. Swear it to me.'

I shook my head, tears scattering against my cheeks. 'Ma, please . . . There has to be another way . . . Please.' I squeezed her hand.

'Swear it, Besse. If you don't, we'll all be dead, you and that wee bairn, and then were will Jenny be? You have to get back to her, to get her away from that monster.'

I couldn't bring myself to say the words. Through tears, I nodded, grief gripping my heart. We didn't speak again, only sat with our arms around each other. I breathed in her smell, every last memory of her.

I couldn't think of my mother gone. Food for the worms. I felt a shiver of fear. There had to be another way.

Outside the clouds rolled thick with the threat of another spring storm. We took up our places under the watchful eye of the gallows, where Andrew Barton's carcass was still swaying. The women clicked their tongues and busied themselves in their work, something I wished I could do. To forget what was to come. But I couldn't.

My mother shifted uneasily, glancing over her shoulder, eyeing the gaoler with angular features too large for his face. He idled against the wall, flintlock pistol hanging untidily from his waistband and talking lazily to a bald man who was as fat as a Christmas goose and just as ugly.

'He's a wicked bastard.' Agnes spat bitterly across the table. 'Satan himself will be keeping him a special place in Hell.'

She didn't take her eyes off them. My temper boiled. I clenched my fists. They must have been the monsters that had taken her. Once they were at a good safe distance, she hurried from her seat to the part of the wall the men had propped up and dropped awkwardly to the floor.

'Mother,' I hissed, 'what in God's name? Mother!' I glanced around; the men were on the other side of the yard, harassing some of the other cunning folk.

She ignored me, scrambling around on her hands and knees in the dirt, frantically stuffing something inside her skirts.

'For Christ's sake, Mother, will you come on! They're almost upon us.'

She jumped then, pulling herself to her feet and hurrying back to the table before they returned. She picked up her tools and carried on as if she had never left.

'What was all that?' I whispered.

'A bit of gunpowder. Shhh . . .' she hissed.

'What's it for?'

The murmuring of their voices passed our ears as they returned to rest against the wall. She carried on fiddling with the top of her skirts, ignoring them. *What on earth was she doing, risking her neck for unspent gunpowder?* It wasn't like we had a gun.

Andrew Barton had been hanged that very morning. After they'd cut down what was left him, they came to collect Alanis to swill the gallows clean of piss.

'You two,' shouted a gaoler, 'get yer arses up there and get some work done!'

I hesitated, unsure if he meant us.

'Are you deaf? Off wi' you then. It'll do you good to get accustomed to the gallows.'

We scurried after Alanis and on to the top of the gable. The ghoulish offerings marked the turrets and guarded the streets below from atop their spikes. The stiffened body of Andrew Barton lay face down on the floor. Everything above the rope was swollen and black, and the space where his eyes had been was empty. Regardless of his crimes, no man deserved that end.

'Look, it's the pirate.' Agnes scurried over to body, hands roving ghoulishly about its neck.

'Mother, please . . .' I grabbed at her. She was like some kind of half wild animal.

'There!' She dangled a grotesque piece of jewellery in front of me. 'You never ken when you might need it, and it could always be exchanged fir something. It's of little use as a wedding band.'

'Rupert's ring . . .' I gasped as she lowered it into my open palm.

She was right, of course. I stuffed it into the tear in the top of my skirt, not wanting to think too long on it. When I'd first seen it about Andrew Barton's neck, my imagination had taken hold, believing my poor husband to be in some sort of trouble. Searching for him led me here. Now, when I looked at it, I could see only lies and torment and a marriage in tatters.

I caught sight of Alanis, who was swilling the roof with water. It bubbled and oozed, sucking debris into its vortex. Agnes clattered to her knees and slipped her fingers in and out of the water, as though she were looking for the blue men of the Minch.

'Foolish woman,' Agnes said bitterly.

'What is it? Yer startin' tae have me worried.'

'I wanted some smithy's nails.' She fiddled with the folds of her skirts. 'I thought . . . well, I thought this would be the best place to find them.'

I picked up the broom with my good hand and chased what was left of the spill over the edge. 'I didnae ken you had a horse wanted shoeing?' I said.

'Nosey couldnae come, so they sent Besse?'

I folded my arms. 'You should have said. Here was me only hangin' around fir the want of transport.'

'Do you see a horse?' she carried on. 'No, but it doesnae mean I don't have use of them.'

'What use do you have fir smithy nails?' Alanis said, deliberately sweeping near our conversation.

'This is where we will end our days, disgraced like murderers and heretics. Displayed for all to see. Seems as though there's nothing better tae domesticate yer women then the rotting heads of them that's crossed you. I intend to make sure that them who're about to wrong me will regret it, so I need as many smithy nails as you can get yer hands on.'

'Get back to work!' a gaoler shouted.

For the rest of the day, we scuttled around like the skittering, hard-shelled beetles we shared our cell with. By the time we'd finished, the sky was darker than the thieves' hole. As we were being rounded up to be led back to our cell, Alanis stuffed something into the top of Agnes's apron.

'A gift from the smithy,' she whispered.

The Innkeeper's Daughter

Jenny knew her da was going to make her pay for not telling the lies he had told her to say about her ma – it was only a matter of when. They were no more than a few hours outside of North Berwick when the first bout of sickness came over her. Maybe it was God, thanking her for being truthful? What kind of da would he be to raise a belt to her when she was sick? God would have been watching the trial, and God didn't let liars get away with it. She hoped he'd be struck down with those lumps under the skin in his neck and a terrible fever, like the one that had taken Goodwife Rivet.

Her father hastily stopped near a small stream when her face and chest started burning up. Her face became slick with sweat as the illness took hold, and she vomited, again and again. She didn't think it would ever stop. She wished she could be at home in her bed, with her ma making a fuss, instead of on the riverbank, in the rain.

She felt weak and her skin burned fiercely but they pressed on, as long as she was able to ride. It was dark by the time they reached the inn. Rupert threw down his reins and headed inside. Jenny followed feebly.

There was a low ceiling and a musty smell that stung her nose. The innkeeper behind the bar shouted after

Rupert, but he wasn't listening. He had already pushed his way through the bustling crowd, skirted the bar and made his way up the stairs two at a time, dragging Jenny behind him. He pushed her against the wall of the landing, and Jenny braced herself as the shivering began to take hold again.

'Don't you even think about breathing a word of this to Cecille,' Rupert said. 'Not about the trial. None of it. David Rivet could always be persuaded to say he saw you with yer mother up at St Andrew's, and then you'd be on Gallows Hill with a noose around yer neck faster than yer mother. And as fir yer little performance in the Tolbooth, you'll be payin' fir that tomorrow.'

He rapped on the last door of the landing. The door opened softly. Cecille stood in the doorway, dressed outlandishly, in a dress of cream and gold, her wheat-coloured hair in ringlets and ribbons.

'You've finally returned, I was starting to worry. Where have you been?' She took Rupert by the hand, as though he was a child, and walked him inside.

'Getting my affairs in order. We can finally make preparations to leave,' He followed her into the bedchamber. 'I just have one more errand.'

Jenny hesitated in the doorway, looking as pale as a lamb. Inside, the air was warm and thick from the peat fire. It made her feel dizzy.

'Who is this?' Cecille crossed back to the doorway. 'Oh, this is the boy I told you about . . . the one with the wolf. Come in, come in. How did you—'

Her father interrupted. 'Cecille, this is my daughter, Jenny.'

Jenny couldn't tell if it was alarm or shock as Cecille's gaze fluttered from Rupert to her and back again. Then her face split into a huge smile.

'I finally get to meet you.' Cecille looked her up and down, wrinkling her nose at the less than pleasant smell. 'You look terrible.'

Jenny couldn't answer. She was limp with exhaustion. She eased herself on to the bed. She couldn't make out Cecille's muffled French words; she didn't need to. She lay back into the softness and fell fast asleep.

* * *

She sat up with a jerk, to the feel of hands pulling at the sleeves of her shirt. The sunlight streamed into the bedchamber and she was met with the round, smiling faces of Cecille and a lanky young woman. Her da was nowhere to be seen.

'Good morning. It is finally time to start the preparations for our travel.' Cecille asked. 'Annie, should I send for the dressmaker?'

The innkeeper's daughter, Annie, took one look at Jenny. 'Aye, I think we should.'

'No.' Jenny cleared her throat. 'No, I have enough clothes . . . A drink, please.'

Annie held the cup to Jenny's cracked lips and she sipped. She had spent the night in a fitful sleep, dreaming of the baby that was due any day and her wicked father. She wished for her mother or grandmother; she wouldn't have even minded her withered stump of a leg. Just the sight of them would have made her feel better

Jenny managed a smile and sank back into the bed. She decided she might stay put, that it might be better to lie there and let the bed hold her. But that wouldn't help her mother. She swung her legs over the edge of the bed, she didn't have much time.

'How do you feel?' Annie asked. 'You were bleatin' like a goat in yer sleep.'

'A bit more mysel'.' Jenny sat forward, wriggling in her sweat-soaked shirt. 'Just bad dreams is all.' Mibbe if she got some fresh air, away from the stuffy fire, she might feel a little better.

'I dare say you could do with a wash and some clean clothes.'

Cecille armed herself with dresses and underskirts while Annie washed her hair and cleaned her with a basin of water. The navy dress Cecille had picked out for her reminded Jenny of a stained-glass window in church. *Garish.* Her mother would never have picked out anything blue; she would have known Jenny would hate it.

'*Tu es belle!*' Cecille beamed at Jenny, who stood in only her shift, her hair flat against her head. It had grown since the months she had last been with Cecille. 'You can wear the dress tomorrow. Annie has kindly agreed to take us into town to visit with a friend of hers who is a seamstress, and I must speak with the apothecary before we make the long journey to France, Monday week.'

She put a hand on Jenny.

Jenny nodded. Today was Saturday, so that gave her a week to slip away. She had to get back to Master Rivet, to tell him what her father had done. He was the town bailiff, so he could go to the court and tell them that it was all her father. She should have gone sooner but ever since the trial her father kept eyes on her, now, even if she got caught, she was her mother's only hope.

'You will love your new home.' Cecille rubbed her stomach, which was as tight as a drum, and busied herself placing the dress in her trunk.

New home? Her home was here in Scotland with her mother and nan and Ratbag the cat. Not in France. Cecille's sing-song voice irritated her ears and the thought of leaving for France made her feel as though she might be sick again.

'Och, get some rest.' Annie smiled at the corner of her eyes and helped Jenny back under the covers. 'I promise, I'll show you all of North Berwick before you board the ship. Yer ma says that she'd like tae get you some new dresses.'

'She's not my ma,' Jenny said hotly.

'Aye, well, you dinnae want to go to yer new home in France in clothes fit fir a laddie.'

'Yes, I do. And she's not my ma; my ma is in the Tolbooth.'

'Hush now,' said Annie, no doubt wishing she'd never said anything. 'I'll here no more of it.' She tucked the bedclothes in around Jenny. 'You cannae go about upsetting Mistress Craw, not in her condition. Get some sleep and I'll be back in the morning.'

Jenny watched the innkeeper's daughter bid farewell and slip back downstairs. She settled herself back, stared at the ceiling and tried to think.

Down the Hole

It must have been gone midnight when I was taken down into the pits of the prison. Silence amplified the eeriness. Monstrous creatures danced across walls. My irons were tighter now, pinching at my wrists. The moonlight cast shadows across the uneven granite steps, and even without fetters I stumbled. We were so deep now that the corridors no longer held torches, a gauntlet forgotten to the rest of the prison.

A pool of light flickered into the gloom of the corridor from a crack in the last door. My heart thumped in my throat. *Not another flogging.* My feet felt as heavy as the granite they stood upon. If they beat me until I was black and blue, it would not change the fact. I was not a witch.

I was shoved over the threshold. The room was warm and filled with the scents of woodsmoke and potage and lamb, making my mouth water and stomach contract with hunger. I was so famished that I was letting my imagination run away with me.

'Leave her be.' It was an order, not a request.

I flinched as the weight of the door closed behind me. The flames weaved against the crackling of the burning wood. Two small chairs were near the fire, one filled with the shape of Thomas Reed and the other empty, with a small wooden cot pressed against the far wall.

He waited until the sound of footsteps had died out before he spoke.

'Sit down, Besse,' he said. 'You ken me well enough tae know I willnae hurt you.' He looked almost sorrowful, spreading his hands across his knees, keeping his eyes on the fire.

Sorrowful. After what he'd let them do. He had no right to be sorrowful.

'You willnae hurt me? You held me down and let that monster beat me. Don't you dare, Thomas Reed.' My whole body rattled with anger. 'Don't you dare!'

'Besse, what else could I do?' His shoulders sagged. 'I cannae keep you safe if I'm dead.'

He turned to me for the first time, taking in the curve of me. He couldn't disguise the look of shock on his face.

'Why would you keep me safe? Out of some misplaced loyalty? It was twelve years ago. Twelve.'

'I didnae ken . . . I . . . Will you sit down? I need tae speak with you.'

I set my jaw and took a deep breath. No man would ever tell me what to do again. I made the decision; I wanted to hear what he had to say. I took the seat next to him. The heat from the flames made my cheeks sting. Fear rattled up my spine, but I pushed it down. I would not let him see it.

He took my hands in his and rubbed them gently. 'I have a confession,' he said before I could speak. 'You were to be brought here fir one of the priests, a great zealot of a man.'

'Mibbe they think if they beat me enough, it will make it so?'

'Oh, he doesnae like tae beat them. It's more an exorcism, of sorts. I couldnae see him "rape the Devil out of ye", as he puts it. Besse, I couldnae let him near you.'

I stood up and stumbled back, sending the chair clattering to the floor. *There was no one I could trust.* '"Rapin' the Devil out of me"? What in the name of Christ!' I exploded. 'You couldnae see him doing it? So, what? You've decided tae wriggle yer maggot at me, hopin' tae rid me of the Devil?'

'Will you calm down.' He lifted the chair to its narrow feet, tried to grab me by the elbow. 'Someone will hear you.'

'Calm down! Don't you touch me Thomas Francis Reed!' I hissed, trying desperately to brush his arms away but, with the weight of my irons, they fell limply at my sides.

He held me there. I waited for it. Waited for the back of his hand. His belt. His fist. He watched me intently, taking in my tattered dress and braid, which reached almost to my waist. Chivalrous, to the very end. He made me sick.

I lifted my face to meet his and whispered, 'Get on wi' it, then. I haven't got all night.'

'That mouth of yers.' He pushed me down into the seat. 'It always was what got you into the most trouble.'

I held up my bound wrists, littered with welts and my finger broken and twisted like a rabbit's leg. 'My mouth, is it? That's what caused all this? Why you held me down?'

'You ken very well what I meant.'

Agnes had tanned my backside on more than one occasion for it, but he had no right to have an opinion on it. He was not my husband.

'I asked that I be the one tae bring you here. I want nothing from you, you understand?'

'Then why?' I sounded shrill. 'Why, Thomas?'

'You would have been brought here, regardless, just like Agnes.'

Agnes. It felt as though I had been punched in the stomach. The grief of it. My mother had been brought here. I inspected the room more critically. The table held a fine cup, filled with wine. From the Communion, no doubt. The cot lined with heavy blankets. The heady smell of melting beeswax hung thick in the air, mingled with hints of woodsmoke and ash. My heart ached for her, brought here to be brutalised by men of the cloth.

'I was there, at the trial,' he said. In all of the commotion, I hadn't noticed him. 'There's talk amongst the men of her confessions, that she has confessed to her involvement. You have to make her ask for forgiveness for what she's done.'

'But she hasnae done anything.' I had to tell him everything. 'We were only at Acheson's because of me. Rupert had disappeared again with Master Rivet's rents, and you ken what the auld bailiff is like: you cannae owe him a tuppence. Agnes thought that Rupert might have been up at Acheson's gambling, so we went up there to find him.' I was shaking now, words spilling faster as I finally allowed mysel' to think about it. 'We were there – Agnes, Dr Fian and I – but we did nothing of what they are saying and then at the trial.'

'I saw Rupert. And was that yer wee girl?'

I nodded, tears streaming, which I wiped away with the heel of my palm. 'I still cannae fathom why he did it, why he would say those things.' It felt as though my heart might break. 'Now that my mother . . .' I stopped, barely able to say the words. 'Now she's . . . confessed tae things she didnae do, so she can save me. I have to put it right. I have to stop her.'

'She's signed her confession. There is nothing more can be done.'

'No . . . No . . . Please tell me she didn't.'

'The kindest thing you can do for Agnes now is to make her repent. They will ask her at the execution, and you have to tell her, make her see sense. If she doesn't they will show her no mercy. She will be burned alive.'

Burned alive. Damn them all to Hell. Every last one of them.

'If it comes to it, promise me you will do something, that you'll no' leave her to suffer? You've known her since you were a child. If you are truthful in what you say then you wouldn't see my mother suffer.'

He rested his hands wearily on the back of the chair. 'You have my word.'

'And you, Thomas Reed, what are yer intentions?'

Experience told me that men were not kind for nothing.

'I've no desire to hurt you, Besse. I want nothing from you. This room is to do with as you will, and I'll stand guard until you're taken back to yer cell, come sun-up. All I ask is that you make them believe I've had my way with ye,' he said shyly. 'If we were to be found out, I'd be joining you in that noose.'

I didn't believe a word of it.

* * *

The dawn slipped in lazily, filling the deep fissures and cracks in the stone. I yawned and swung my feet to the floor and rubbed at the stiffness of my back, the heaviness of my child becoming more cumbersome with each day. For the first time in a long time, my dreams had only been visited by sleep. Thomas, who had kept his word, sat sleepily in the chair by the hearth. The black crust of the fire oozed a deep red, slowly dying. I felt a spring hill and hugged the blanket from the cot around my shoulders.

From across the room, I could see pieces of parchment scattered across the table. Jenny loved to play with ink and quills, given half the chance. I brushed my fingers through the soft feathers. The luxurious reds and golds glistened in the light of the dawn. Although Agnes had taught me to read the Bible, I always wished she could have shown me how to write. If I was to see out my days within the walls of the Tolbooth, I could have at least written to Jenny, letting her know the truth.

Thomas stirred, splintering my thoughts. He yawned as he uncurled from the chair, causing tiny creases to wrinkle near his eyes.

'Did you manage to sleep?' he said, pushing the tails of his shirt into the top of his breeches.

'Aye, more than I have in a long while.'

'That's a lot less comfortable than it looks.' He kicked the leg of the chair. 'We willnae have much time; it's almost sun-up. I'll have tae put you back in yer irons.'

My heart sank. In this room I had been free. As I lifted my skirts, he brushed the soft skin of my ankle with warm hands as he placed the fetters against my legs.

'For what it's worth, I'm sorry,' he said softly.

'Why are you apologising fir something that wasn't yer fault?'

'If ye'd married me, it would have been different.' He cupped my face in his hands. 'I wouldn't have let this happen tae you.'

I pulled away. 'I married Rupert.'

He went to speak but stopped and listened. My ears picked up the sound of footsteps weaving their way down through the staircases.

He took my hair between his hands and unravelled it. Like strips of greased rope. It cascaded down my back and around my shoulders. It smelled of oil and dirt. He stepped back and assessed me. The footsteps neared, tapping against the stone like flint in a tinder box. Thomas grabbed the blanket from my shoulders and threw it to the floor.

The man who entered was slim, beautiful and sharp. His eyes glanced up and down my body and settled on my breasts.

'I think I should like very much like a go of ridding her of the Devil.' He ran a finger across my collarbone.

'It'll take a braver man 'an you, Seton.' Thomas held me firmly by the elbow, like I was his. 'This one speaks with a forked tongue.'

'Aye, so I've heard.' He slipped a hand across my buttock; it made my skin crawl. 'Like her mother.'

Nausea crept up my throat.

'Take her tae the yard,' said Thomas. 'I'll be seein' you again, witch.'

A Burning in the North

My arrival in the yard was met with furtive glances and knowing looks. It was a secret that no one seemed to talk about, but it became abundantly apparent that I wasn't the only one they had tried to rape the Devil out of.

Soon came the patter of rain, bringing the sweet, musky scent of spring. The clouds seemed endless. The gaolers took refuge beneath arches and walkways. My mother was the first to greet me. She removed her shawl, revealing soft grey patches of hair littered between pink flesh. She clucked around me like a hen. How could she after what they'd done to her?

'Are you alright?' She rubbed a rough hand against mine.

'I think so.' I smiled weakly.

How was I to tell her? *Repent of your sins and they will show you mercy.* If you're lucky, they'll strangle you before they light the pyre? My heart ached in grief, grief for the woman I was about to lose. For the outrage of something we were helpless to stop.

'At least you still have all yer hair.' She rubbed at her crown. 'I look like a sheared bollock.'

I laughed. I laughed until the tears rolled down my cheeks, and so did she. How I wished it could be different.

That we could be home at Leaplish. I could only cling to the hope that she'd be there for the birth.

'Aye,' I said, wiping away a tear. 'It smells so bad I barely want tae touch it.' I wrinkled my nose. 'I can see why they took it all off.'

'Aye, well . . . Look, look at that.'

My eyes followed the direction she pointed. Billowing smoke slithered over the wall from the direction of the Nor' Loch. Faint screams carried on the wind as the smell of burning flesh and singed hair clung to the back of my throat.

I tried to catch my breath. Gulp after gulp of air to try and stop myself from shaking. The screams waned but were punctuated by jeers from the crowd that must have gathered for the burning of the witch. Thomas's words rang in my ears.

Alanis never returned.

It took hours before the smoke cleared and the fire died out. Even with the fresh spring air, the smell still lingered in my nostrils. We all bowed our heads as the small charcoal frame passed towards its final resting place, on the other side of the wall.

As we moved back to our cell, looks of disgust shuddered across their faces. I could hear the tongues clicking my name. They all assumed I had been taken and raped into confessing the names of the women I slept beside, whose confidences I had betrayed. It wasn't long before bitter suspicion turned to spiteful accusations as the sound of footsteps echoed against the granite. They turned on me like rabid dogs.

'Here they come to collect their pet,' Margaret piped

up from somewhere near the far corner.

'Not another word Margaret Baxter, I'm warning ye,' hissed Agnes.

One of them spat. It landed on the floor near my bare foot. In the darkness I couldn't make out which direction it came from.

'Like a dog waiting fir her master.'

'Aye, a dog is loyal. A lot more than can be said for you,' said Agnes. 'Where is it that you got that babe in yer belly? The one that's savin' you from the pyre?'

Margaret stepped forward into the dim light of the torches. She was thin and beautiful. Her name I had heard on the lips of gaolers but I had never caught sight of her. Although it was plain to see beneath her dark blue skirts that a baby was on its way. It would be here soon, and then where would its mother be?

'Aye, they cannae put me to death carrying an innocent child. Not until the wean's born, at least.'

'What do you think is going tae come of a witch's child?' Agnes said.

My mother was right. Who would take on a witch's child? After they'd cut my child from me, would they call upon Rupert? Give both my children to him? He had taken everything from me. Everything.

'He's going to get us out of here. He won't leave us.' Margaret arched her back to relieve the ache. 'He knows I'm innocent.'

I had thought the same foolish things about Rupert.

'Here's me thinkin' that when you eat a bowl of potage, you dinnae ken which o' the meat makes you fat.'

Margaret's mouth opened and closed like a gasping fish.

'What do you mean by that, Agnes!'

'I mean, ye've been ridden more times than the village mule.' Agnes straightened her apron. 'So, as fathers go, I'm guessing there'll be a cart full of 'em turns up once the bairn arrives.'

A fire burned within Agnes that even they hadn't managed to extinguish. Now, whatever wickedness that had been done to her had made her an even greater force to be reckoned with.

Margaret rounded on me. 'Nice to see you still have yer hair.' She reached out with fingers brittle and sharp. 'You must be a favourite of the witch pricker.'

'What exactly are you accusing me of, Margaret?' I could feel the rest of their eyes crawling over me.

'Strange, is all, how you get taken away and the following morning, Alanis is sent to her death? Look at that bulge beneath yer skirts. Which one of 'em gave you his seed?'

'She was with child long before you were, Margaret. What did you get fir them filling you up with a bairn?'

This time when the door opened, it was Thomas waiting for me. 'Besse Craw,' he said, looking as though he was attending a funeral.

There were two figures awaiting our arrival. The first, Father Buchane. Eager to be known as a burner of witches, the ambitious priest had taken it upon himself to track down the very person we feared most: John Fenton.

Even before I came to the Tolbooth, news of Fenton's methods had spread far and wide, reaching our ears all the way over in Tranent. He was the monster we told our children about. His infamy had spread through the countryside like a poison, infiltrating every village.

My mother had told the tale; it had been over the border in Berwick. She had gone to fetch supplies of hemlock and beans from Goodwife Johnstone. Agnes arrived late in the evening and had to beg a room at the inn in the village. She spent the night listening to snatches of conversation and stories of the women who had been taken from their beds, husbands left widowed with children to care for.

She awoke the next morning to the sound of screams. A young woman, a wee slip of a thing, had been nailed to the whipping post. She was pregnant, with her clothes torn from her and clumps of her hair blowing like weeds around her feet.

Agnes said that she was no witch. She had simply fallen in love with a married man and then his wife had found them in the marital bed. He vowed that the young maid had bewitched him, lured him under her spell and between her sheets. He said he had been unable to resist her, powerless. She had been mad with hunger for the touch of his flesh. It was obvious that she had renounced Christ and given her mortal soul to the Devil, giving her the power to make him succumb.

Agnes said he was a bloody liar, and it should have been his poisoned tongue that had been nailed to the heretics' post. The poor woman had been rounded up by the priest and questioned by the kirk. Word soon got around that John Fenton had been visiting nearby. He intervened in proceedings and had her stripped naked and flogged. Then, when she didn't confess her sins, he had her scalp wrenched for good measure.

Her bastard came while she was nailed to that post. The wee bairn was unready for the chill of the air. No one went to help her, no one dared. John Fenton made sure of it. No swaddling. Not so much as a touch of a kind hand. It died on the cold, hard earth at its mother's feet. A mother losing her child like that, loses part of her soul. When they set the flames, she didn't scream. Agnes said she finally looked at peace.

It had taken less than an hour to convict her but eight before John Fenton lit the pyre. He charged the town for his services, requesting payment for the nails hammered through her hands and the ropes to secure her. He even costed for the logs that finally took her life.

Empowered by the Pope and backed up by *The Hammer of Witches*, the righteous figures of John Fenton and Father Buchane sat in chairs in front of me now, the table of implements between them framed by a peat fire whose flames licked and crackled as embers tumbled into the black hearth. Like Devils with their pitchforks.

Thomas and I stood in the doorway, his hand gripping my elbow. He hadn't been expecting our new guest.

'Thomas, this is Master John Fenton,' said Father Buchane.

'Master Fenton' – Thomas nodded – 'your reputation precedes you.' I could hear the anger in his voice.

'Thank you . . . Thomas, was it?' said Fenton. 'This must be the witch I have heard so much about.'

'Aye.' Father Buchane rose to his feet. 'I've been unable to extract a confession and it is of the utmost importance, by order of the king.'

'That is indeed what the letter said, father.' Fenton ran his greedy eyes over my body. 'Turn her. I do not want the sorceress to give me the evil eye.'

I was turned in my chains to face the door, which dwarfed me in comparison. Thomas didn't look in my direction. I had never felt more alone.

'Take the witch's hair,' I heard Fenton say. 'I want it all.'

Taking my hair in his hands, Thomas began cutting it away. Curls fell soundlessly around me in drifts. I closed my eyes tightly and made no sound. A part of who I was, cut away and cast on the floor. It seemed like an eternity before he was finished.

'Now, throw it on the fire. We can't risk an enchantment.'

'Yes, Master Fenton.'

'Now, remove the rest.'

The final insult.

The razor moved slowly across my head, making a soft noise as it took away the last of the stubble. The memory of poor Alanis came flooding back. Now I understood why she had met her end: John Fenton had arrived.

'I want her stripped,' Fenton said. 'They cast spells with the skin of the unbaptised and stitch them into their underskirts.'

'She birthed the Ancrofts' child,' Father Buchane replied. 'They say she stole the bairn's caul. Take them off!'

I didn't struggle. I didn't speak. Thomas untied my homespun skirt, dropping it to the floor in crumpled folds. He shed my clothes like he was skinning a snake.

I stood before them, bare to my soul.

My teardrop breasts, stretched and veined, stood to

attention. The nipples hard and pimpled. My belly ripe as a plum, covered in silver stretch marks from the other children I'd carried. My tethered arms covered the small brown mark below my right breast, the one that I'd had as far back as I could remember, burned like a brand. My only view was of the cracked stone wall. I could feel their eyes crawling over every inch of my body.

'She must be shaved.'

Thomas crept between my legs with the razor, his warm breath grazed my skin. The only man to do so since my husband. The ice-cold razor sliced away any memory I had of my husband. I shuddered with revulsion. When he was finished, I stood before them, vulnerable and completely shorn.

'We must inspect her for the witch's mark.'

I heard Fenton rise from his seat. He glided silently across the room like some kind of daemon. I could feel his closeness behind me. It felt like being near a fire that's too hot, warming your flesh as a warning.

'Lift yer arms, witch,' Fenton barked. 'Turn her.'

Thomas slipped a hand over my ribs as he turned me, bringing them to settle just below my breasts. My breath hitched in my throat.

'Turn her back. I see nothing.'

Sleight of hand. Their arrogance had stopped them seeing it. He turned me again, hands rattling over ribs, leaving me to face the door.

'Tie her to the fetters on the wall.'

I was pulled by my chains to the far wall and strapped to the irons.

Rupert had once brought a sow home from market. We

had fed her and fattened her over the summer ready for slaughter. The task of her dispatch had been left to me. She'd followed me trustingly and I had tied her against the wall of the cot-house, but when I looked into her eyes wide with fear, I couldn't go through with it. We had called her Plum, after Jenny's favourite fruit. That pig was more loyal than my husband.

Fenton motioned to the pail on the floor near the door. As Thomas brought it over, it sloshed violently, splashing over the sides and onto the stone, making it slippery underfoot. The ice-cold water was thrown over me, hitting me like a wall and forcing the breath out of me. Every muscle screamed as the shudder rippled over me. I cried out in pain as much as shock.

'Did you have help?'

'N-n-n . . .' I couldn't form the word. The shaking coursed through my body. I rocked my head from side to side.

During the winter of my seventh year, I had always wanted to prove I was bolder than Thomas. We used to dare each other to walk out over the frozen loch. I watched and waited for it to freeze over. The winter sun was cruel and hard when I worked up enough courage to step onto the frozen water. I inched my way forward and, step by step, my confidence grew. I giggled as I spun and danced across the stillness. Then, I heard it. A deep crack from somewhere far below. I was too far from the loch side. I called out but got no reply. I inched my way back, but the skittering and cracking followed every step. I stopped. That was when the ice broke.

I plunged below the surface like a buttered seal, so

fast I made no noise. The cold of the water forced the air from my lungs. Within seconds they began to burn. Sharp sunlight cut through the broken ice and filtered into the darkness of the water. I clawed at it, fighting against the blackness that tried to swallow me whole.

When the hands came, urgent and grasping, the stillness had taken me. I flopped around on the bank, thick with mud, and gasped, swallowing as much air as my lungs would take.

Now, it was as if I was back on the loch side, a helpless child, shuddering and shivering.

'Another pail,' said Fenton.

'Please,' I pleaded, trying to steady my breath, 'no.'

I was swilled with the next pail like piss under the gallows. It came hard and fast and cold, filling my mouth and eyes, like a rat in the gutter they wished to drown. My flesh no longer burned, and my finger no longer throbbed. I was numb.

'Did you mean to sink the queen consort's ship?'

I coughed and retched, spewing water through my nose. I shook my head, strings of spit hanging from my mouth. There was only one thing I could say.

'It was my mother.'

A long silence stretched out.

'We are done, for now.' Fenton wiped his hands as though he were ridding them of something repulsive. 'Take the Devil's whore back to her cell.'

I was unfastened from the wall and yanked from the floor by my elbow. I tried to take a few steps, but the stones were uneven and wet. I slipped, landing hard with a crack. Thomas caught me and put me back on my feet;

my knee was split and bloodied. I didn't look behind me, but I could hear their sneers.

Shrouded in nothing but gooseflesh, I walked on, my eyes fixed on the door. Thomas fell in by my side. Inside I was angry enough to spit.

Sacrificial Lamb

It should have been Rupert that rescued me. Taken his sword and plunged it into that bastard and saved us. I looked at the bruises on my arm, the ones that had almost faded but felt as though they'd left an imprint on my bones. My husband was an evil man. He had caused this and I would rather die than have him save me.

What had I done? How could I ever look at my mother again? I was as much of a fiend as Rupert.

Thomas was bending over me, wrapping me in a blanket. He perched me on the edge of the wee cot in the raping room. The flickering candles gave off a sickly glow, lighting the chains and fetters that hung from the wall. I had collapsed part of the way down the corridor, so he had lifted me from the ground and carried me the rest of the way.

Now, my so-called saviour bent inside the hearth, lighting a fire. Shirtless and his hair stuck to his head, he was soaked and unkempt. I glanced down and realised I was wearing his shirt.

The cold had chilled my bones and lingered there. I slid an exploratory finger over my scalp, which felt soft and strange, like my mother's.

I walked around the edge of the room, fingers tracing

the uneven surfaces. I tried the door, but it was firmly locked.

'Are you sure you're not scairt fir yer life, being locked in here with a witch?'

He stopped, turning his head to face me, and smiled an easy smile. 'No, I've kent you all my life; my first love. No, I dinnae think that you are a witch. I'm more scairt that Agnes will find out I've been locked away in here with you.'

He pulled the narrow cot-bed to the fire. I sat back down, facing Thomas in the chair. He hung a pan of milk on the fire to boil.

'I'm sorry I've no more tae offer ye,' he said, filling two cups.

I took it and clasped my cold hands around it. Despite myself, I thought about how he might smell, his damp skin pressed against my own.

'Is that why you help me?' I asked. 'Because of what was between us?'

'Aye, I suppose that's part of it.' He spread his hands across his knees, unsure of how to go on. 'Why would you not come away with me?'

'I kent what sort of man you were, Thomas Reed; you were bound fir war in France and believed you could change the world. It broke my heart to do it, but I promised myself I would sooner lose you than bury you.' I turned towards the fire.

'So, you married a man you didnae love?'

'Who said I didn't love him?'

'You never told me you did.'

'He was kind and came from good kin. A fair match. He

worked fir the Rivets and he had that wee cot-house. Not that it matters now.'

'You didnae answer my question.'

'He's the father of my child. Of both my children,' I said simply. 'I loved him.'

'What kind of man could do that to his wife, tae let her rot in prison?'

'Mibbe this is my punishment fir not loving him the way a wife should. For always loving the ghost of another man.'

'I love you, Besse, I would never risk yer happiness like Rupert.' He turned to face me.

'He's my husband. Our time is gone.' I pulled away.

'Say it isnae true? I cannae bear the thought of losin' you all over again.' He cupped my face in his hands.

'What do you want from me, Thomas? I will be put to death like the rest of them.'

For the first time it struck me how much I had come to rely on him. How him being with me brought me some small comfort, however flimsy our friendship. How I felt a rush of relief at the very sight of him.

I closed my eyes and imagined the path of my fingers across his chest, tracing the line of his neck. Him taking my hands in his, pressing me softly against the broadness of him, bending his face towards mine.

'I want you. I always have.' He held me with his eyes for the longest time.

Ripe as a Plum, Soft as a Peach

Every night grew quieter than the last.

Agnes watched as Besse returned, shorn, barefoot and naked, with only a rough blanket to cover her shoulders. Agnes relieved herself of some of her own layers and wrapped her daughter crudely. It wasn't much but it would keep out the chill.

'Those vile bastards make me sick,' said Agnes.

'Aye, well, I can tell you John Fenton doesnae do a lot fir me,' said Besse.

'While he's about, there isnae one of us safe.'

'Ma, we need tae talk.'

Agnes could hear the hitch in her voice, the worry of it whatever it was that weighed heavy on her. 'Spit it out, lass.'

'I want you to promise me . . . promise me that when the time comes, when they ask you, that you will repent. Or they'll show you no mercy.'

Besse should have known better than to think she would beg. Agnes had signed her confession, and that was all they were getting. 'I'll not repent fir something I didnae do, that is between me and God.

They'll be judged fir what they do.'

Besse pulled the plaid a bit tighter and sat on the ground. 'De you remember when you found old Master Wrycht beating his mule bloody?'

'Aye, I ken it well. The poor creature had collapsed under the weight of what he was forcin' it tae carry.' Agnes remembered it only too well. Her temper had taken over.

'Aye, and I also remember that you strapped that basket tae old Wrycht's back and whipped his legs with yer cane until he walked those stones home.'

'And he kent very well that I will no' abide cruelty to them that has no means of defendin' themselves. Do you think someone will look after our old mule? They willnae have forgotten him?'

'Of course not, and the pigs and hens.' Besse creased her brow and tears pricked her eyes. 'Jenny won't have; she wouldn't allow it.'

Agnes thought warmly of her granddaughter, her curls, her freckles and how much she reminded her of Besse as a child. Sometimes, if she thought hard enough, it could make this awful place a little more tolerable.

* * *

Outside, the sun thawed the Maytime frost. Margaret, her enormous belly stretched out in front of her, deposited herself near Besse and Agnes.

'I see ye've finally lost yer hair, Besse. What's wrong? Have they run out of women to have burnt?'

Agnes ignored the question. 'Not long before that

bairn's here,' she said. 'Still hangin' on fir the father? Is yer pardon comin' by pigeon?'

Margaret looked at her indignantly. 'Don't you worry, Agnes Sampson, I'll be on the outside tae watch you burn. You mark my words.'

Just then, there was a noise like a bucket spilling water. Warm liquid sloshed about the floor, steaming between Margaret's legs. She let out a scream and bent doubled, laying a hand on her belly as the bulge beneath her skirts tightened.

Agnes began to examine Margaret and the floor beneath her.

'Don't you touch me!'

'Margaret' – Besse held her hand, herself as round as a plum close to splitting its skin – 'you ken she's a howdie, and the only one we have. Yer going tae have to let her take a look.'

She nodded frantically.

'This bairn is coming swift as anything.' Agnes had no water and no clean linen. Nothing to help a child into the world. This would probably be the last child she ever birthed.

Margaret let out another scream; this time her face was soaked with sweat.

'Besse, do you still have some of that willow bark I gave ye?' Agnes asked.

She fidgeted in the tear in her skirt. 'Here.'

'Margaret, I need you tae chew this fir me. It'll help with the pain.'

She took the willow bark and leant forwards, began rocking back and forth as the pain took hold once more.

A trickle of blood stained her leg as she let out another cry. The noise was beginning to attract the attention of the gaolers.

'Besse,' she rasped.

'It's going to be alright,' Besse soothed, rubbing Margaret's back. 'Not long now.'

Agnes worked quickly, trying to move Margaret to the floor, but the gaolers had other ideas.

'Don't touch her, witch!' a thin gaoler shouted.

'The woman's about to birth a child. You leave her alone!' Agnes shouted back.

Rough hands grabbed at Margaret pulling her away. Agnes held on, trying in vain to stop them. She felt the full force of a boot against her shin, and the skin split like a rotting apple.

'They'll be takin' her to David Fryer, the prison physic,' said a young woman.

'A man to birth a child? I've never heard of such nonsense!' Agnes said.

'We'd be better keepin' out of it and stayin' alive,' Besse said as she tightened a piece of cloth around Agnes's leg.

'Besse, I didnae raise you to stand by and watch. If you ken what's right from wrong, you can never choose wrong. It means doing what should be done, even when it—'

'Ma . . .'

A huge hand landed on Agnes's shoulder, startling her.

'Yer coming with me,' said the gaoler.

Agnes rose to her feet without question, pushing against her wooden crutch. Her time had been borrowed and now they were coming to collect. She didn't look back as she disappeared beneath the archway flanked by two guards; her heart was too heavy.

Honesty

The last of the day's light danced into the gloom of the moonrise when I was snatched from my sleep. I fell in line behind Thomas. Humble. Obedient. Silent.

The room was already prepared, with flickering torches and a log-filled fire. The irons hanging on the wall gave a clink in response to our entrance. The room was so far beneath the ground that it required no windows, merely an iron grate which filtered in air from above.

Tonight, it smelled of potage and game; two bowls sat steaming on the table at the fireside. I couldn't stop myself. I ran to the table and ate hungrily. Potage dripped from my fingers and chin, and it was so hot that it scalded the roof of my mouth.

'It's alright, I'll not take it from you.'

'I'm sorry,' I said awkwardly as I rubbed my grubby hand across my chin. 'Do you ken where they've taken my mother?'

'No, but John Fenton is still here. The man is like the black death.'

Thomas ate neatly for such a big man. I wasn't quite used to the company of men, other than Rupert. I felt uncomfortable. My eyes darted to the door and back again.

'It's locked,' he said, watching me, the embarrassment stretching between us until he finally broke the silence. 'You dinnae have tae be scairt, I'm no' going to jump on you. Why don't you start by telling me about yer life after I left.'

My stomach knotted with grief for what was and what could have been. I cleared my throat.

'We wed in the May, Rupert and I, without Agnes's approval. You ken she always had a soft spot fir you; there wasn't another man alive going to be good enough fir her daughter.'

He laughed, which relaxed me a bit.

'We moved into the cot-house. Rupert had worked fir Master Rivet fir years, and we settled in, and I fell pregnant with my boy.'

'So, you have a laddie and a lassie? And another on the way?'

I wanted him to reach across the table, take my shaking hands in his and comfort me. 'No, I lost my boy in childbed, after the first time Rupert took his fists to me. Hoping fir another one, aye.' I rubbed at my swollen belly. 'Rupert had come home drunk, after days away playing dice, with pockets full of money. He was always worried that I'd take it and run off looking fir you, so he'd hidden it before he came to bed. Next morning, he couldn't remember where he'd put it. He accused me of stealing it, beat me black and blue. Never my face, he was always mindful of that. He didnae like people to ken when the monster was upon him.'

'What must you think of me, leavin' you like that, all because my pride was hurt. If I'd known, I would have—'

'Stopped him? Taken me away from my horrible husband? I chose tae marry him.' I looked into his eyes. 'You weren't tae ken. No one did.'

'Could you not have told Agnes?'

'What good would have come of it? Marriage is a sacrament; I couldn't leave my husband.'

'But he can leave you and yer child at the mercy of Rivet?'

'What else could he do? He'd stolen the rents.'

'And still you defend him!'

'I am no defending that monster. I have a duty; he is *still* my husband. Whatever he's done. However wicked and vile, I cannae divorce him. I am only a woman. We dinnae have the same rights as men.' I pushed back the chair and went and sat on the cot.

* * *

We sat in silence for a while. Neither one of us wanting to speak. I felt hurt, but, most of all, I felt angry with myself. I had wanted him. I could offer him nothing. A married woman, imprisoned for witchcraft with two children. *Sinful, sinful woman.*

I felt the cot sink under his weight as he came and sat next to me. Close enough that I could feel the heat from his thigh against mine.

'Besse, I'm sorry if it made you feel like that, I truly am, but I cannae be sorry fir wantin' you as I do.'

'You mustn't.' I brushed my hand against his, wanting so desperately to hold it. 'There is no future . . . I have no future.'

He took me in his arms and lifted my face to meet his. He kissed me then. It was gentle and loving, as though he was tasting me for the first time.

We hung there in the moment.

'We have a future. You and I, Agnes and yer wee daughter. I'm going to make sure of it.'

I wasn't so sure.

The Beating of the Drums

There had been no moon and stars, only shadows from branches that cast black spider-webs against the wall. Agnes had stayed awake and watched as the night sky passed into daylight thinking of everything she would be leaving behind. *How will Besse cope without me?*

She'd been grateful that Besse didn't know about the execution. What was she supposed to say to a daughter she would never see again? No, it was better this way. Besse could grieve for her once she was gone, but not while she was still here.

Come sun-up, the king's justice would be done. Seven in all to be burnt alive.

Agnes got up stiffly, letting the wall take her weight. With a wet finger she rubbed at the dried blood still crusted on the front of her frock. If she was going to meet the man upstairs, she was not about to do it slovenly.

She ran a hand over her course scalp. Her right eye was still able to open, but her face was ruined with wine-coloured bruises. She rested on her makeshift crutch and lifted the swathes of fabric from the floor. They had been better to lie on than the straw-covered stone. She wrapped them about herself, leaving her favourite plaid for last.

She thought about her small cot-house and its

emptiness – her possessions sold to pay for her upkeep in the Tolbooth. The dawn would be dripping in streaks across her empty kitchen, over the worn dip in the stone floor where her chair would have been. No fire would be warming the hearth. Dampness would seep from the earth, eating away at her home. Filling it with rot and decay. It would be as dead as its mistress.

The bees would never return.

Agnes looked at how far the sunlight had crept across the cell wall. She didn't have much time. She rested her weariness against the stone. A slow, mournful wail filtered in from the street below. She turned her face towards the barred window. Agnes listened intently, recognising the baleful song of the banshee keening for her soul.

Three days she had been chained to that wall; hanging like a buck about to be skinned. Sleep had come, but it had been met with the force of their fists and swills of their pails. After three days, she would have confessed she was a mule, if it would make them stop.

Her confessions came in torrents. She told them of the Auld Kirk and the Devil appearing to her in the shape of a black dog. Of George Francis being cut down – reaped like barley after being riddled with apoplexy. She said she was the one that had bewitched him.

Agnes made sure she damned herself and only those that had already met their bitter end. Spurred on by the promise of freedom for Besse, she had described, in great detail, the witch pricker's darkest fantasy; the story of the Sabbat on All Hallows' Eve and her intention to sink the queen's ship.

Her story told, they returned her to the holding cell,

but not with the rest of the prisoners. The next day, the order came from Holyrood, sealing her fate. Since, she had thought of nothing but Besse, Jenny, Dr Fian and the grandchild she would never see.

The rattle of keys made her jump. She could feel the colour drain from her face as she listened to the click of their feet against the stone floor. The condemned never knew when the hangman was coming until he coiled his noose.

* * *

Seven women clung to each other as they stumbled up the grassy slope towards Castle Hill. The drummers that preceded them echoed the beating of their hearts. It was a sound to make heads turn as the procession moved closer to its final destination.

Agnes found herself holding the hand of Margaret; it helped with the trembling. They'd taken Margaret's bairn, ripped him from her and given him to her sister. He might never know his mother, but at least he'd stay with his family.

How she wished she had been given the last rites by the priest. She wanted to die a Catholic, the same way she came into the world. Even though the hand of fear gripped her heart, God knew that her heart was pure.

'Why don't we pray?' said Agnes. 'Did you give that wee bairn a name? Keep him in our thoughts, aye?'

'I named him Andrew, after my father.' Margaret turned. 'Don't let go, Agnes.'

'I willnae.' She squeezed her hand. 'Our Father, who art in heaven . . .'

They moved on a few steps before the legs of the woman in front buckled and gave out, sending her sprawling into the mud. Between them, Agnes and Margaret helped set her back on her feet, and the procession carried on to the slow beat of the drum.

There were at least fifty of the king's men standing together at the base of the hill, and all around them, seas of people stretched in every direction, it seemed as though half of Edinburgh had turned out to watch the spectacle. The onlookers parted as the procession came closer.

'Agnes . . . Agnes . . .' someone shouted from the midst of the mob.

She stopped and caught sight of Thomas Reed, snaking and twisting his way through the crowd.

'What is it? Is it Besse?'

'She wanted me tae give you this.' He bent forwards and placed two small parcels around her neck. 'Some more gunpowder,' he whispered in her ear.

'Thany you fir yer mercy.' She groped for his hand and squeezed it. 'You see her right.'

'I promise.'

She wiped away tears, thinking of him as a child. He had always been a thoughtful boy. She always imagined he'd marry Besse. They pair of them had always been inseparable. If God could answer only one prayer, she'd pray that Thomas Reed would marry her daughter and rid her of Rupert forever.

As they climbed further still, seven huge stakes loomed against the snow-laden sky. Agnes watched the shapes of crows twist and swoop, waiting to pick off what they could.

'They cannae!' Margaret said in a panicked voice, stumbling back. 'Please, I'm no' ready.'

'We rarely are.' Agnes pulled her close and gripped her hand tightly. 'We only have a little way to go, and then you'll feel no more pain. God is all around us. He knows that we're not what they say we are.'

They made the final few steps, hands clasped together, neither wanting to let go of the other. Even as they were fastened to the wooden stakes, they never let go.

The drums began to beat a steady roll. The executioner placed the straw bales wrapped with thick twine all around their feet and shins, covering them almost to their knees.

'Lead us not into temptation,' Margaret said, her voice cracking. 'Deliver us from evil.'

The drums stopped.

Agnes closed her eyes and prayed.

* * *

In the seconds after the explosion, Castle Hill was engulfed in the terrified shouts of everyone that had gathered for the burning. Screams echoed as a thick, black cloud ascended like a murder of crows. Men tripped and stumbled over unseen obstacles, blinking at each other in confusion. Bodies lay everywhere, injured and dead.

What had once been a stake, holding the body of the witch Agnes Sampson, was now a crumbled mound of ash in a smoking hole in the ground.

A Good Time to Die

The sound rolled across Castle Hill like thunder. As the sky darkened, the flames could be seen from miles around. Every nerve in my body jumped as the door flew open.

Thomas stood breathing heavily, his gaze darting between me and the corridor. 'Besse, we have tae be quick. They're all up on Castle Hill; Agnes has blown half the gaolers to kingdom come.'

No. No. No. It couldn't be. Hot tears spilled down my cheeks as sobs burst from my parted lips. My mother, gone. I closed my eyes, trying to steady my breathing. In. Out. In. Out.

'I think I can get you out, but yer going tae have to trust me.'

My eyes flew open. 'No, I cannae run. I cannae leave Jenny.' I tried to back away, but I was frozen, paralysed by shock.

'You're as stubborn as you were as a child! The king will never pardon you, not as long as there is breath in his body.' He grabbed me by the arms, urging me. 'It has to be now. We won't have another chance.'

I shook my head. I should have told them it was me. I should have taken the blame. Cowards, the lot of them, none of them able to see the difference between honourable self-sacrifice and murder. Panic rose inside me. I needed time to think. What if they caught me? What would happen to my baby? I couldn't flee prison – I'd be hunted like a dog.

'They'll be sending a cart to collect the bodies of those that have died, to move them outside of the castle. We need tae make sure you're in it.'

I shuddered as a chill ran through me. 'Dead?'

'We need tae make sure they think you are.'

I felt as though I was standing on the edge of a cliff, waiting to fall. It would never work. How could it? Surely they would see? I shook my head harder this time, hands covering my face.

'Besse' – he shook me by the shoulders – 'I'm going to fetch some linen and wrap you, ready fir the cart wi' the rest of the bodies. I'll tell them I've found you dead. The prison physic is too busy tending those on Castle Hill, so he won't check. I'll load you into the cart and they'll take you out back, beyond the wall. Then I'll come to get you.'

The familiar feeling of panic started to rise into my chest, gripping at me. Lying in a cart with the dead? What if Thomas didn't return? I'd die alone with the corpses. The whole room began to spin. *At least it would be a death of my own choosing.*

'What if we're caught? I cannae let you be a part of it. I'll take my chances in court.'

My mother's death had to stand for something. She had taken the blame. Surely they would see me pardoned?

'This isnae a decision that's yers tae make, Besse. I cannae see you die in here like this.' He took my hands in his and pressed them to his lips. 'I made a promise to you, that I would never let anything happen to you. Now, you willnae make a liar out of me?'

I shook my head. 'You must promise me something. Promise me that if we get caught, you'll deny you had anything to do wi' it. I'll take the blame. I willnae see both of us dead.'

'Then it seems we have a deal.'

* * *

Every time I thought of my mother, I became paralysed. Broken in grief. In the shadows, I imagined not my mother, but the prison physic instead, eyeing the cart. Looking over the dead. Watching. Waiting for a movement. Turning each body over, in turn. The smell of the putrefying flesh. Dragging me out. Taking me back before the judge. Punishments much worse than the last. I tried to steady my breathing. *In. Out. In. Out.*

I waited.

The Tolbooth had sprung back to life. The noise filtered through the walls like birds at sunrise. My body jangled with nerves. At every noise, I found myself on the floor again, face pressed hard to the stone, peering through the crack at the bottom of the door into the grimy darkness.

This time, as my eyes adjusted, I thought I could make out Thomas – or at least who I thought was Thomas – closing another door opposite. I scrambled across the floor and forced my back against the wall, into the corner where the light never touched. The noise from the peeling bolt made my breath hitch.

I waited, listening. Footsteps halted no more than two feet away.

'Besse?' His voice was no more than a whisper.

'I'm here.' I saw the flash of Thomas's teeth. I'd never felt such relief.

'Quickly, now.'

I let out a strangled laugh that was more like a sob and went to him. He held out a thin piece of linen, which caught on the breeze from the street below, billowing like some kind of wraith. That was what he intended to wrap me in, like some kind of grotesque gift.

'Put yer arms about yerself.' His voice was hushed and solemn.

He began at my shoulders, weaving this way and that, covering my body in the thin film of fabric. Wrapped around my stomach, bulging as it was, I looked as stuffed as a haggis.

'Once I cover yer head, you'll see no more until you're over the other side of the wall. I'll cradle you and carry you to the cart where we leave the dead. Whatever happens, you must stay limp. You mustn't utter a sound. Do you understand?'

I nodded numbly.

'You must stay where they leave you, and I'll be back fir you before sun-up.'

I took one last look at him and held his eyes. I could read the anguish on his face, just as he could on mine. Neither of us knew if this was the last time we'd see each other. His might be the last face I would ever see. My breath came in stutters.

Without a word more passing between us, he covered

my face with the linen. I felt his hands press against my waist as he bent and took the weight of me across his chest. I could hear his heartbeat pounding in rhythm with my own. *Please be quick.*

I felt a shiver pass through me, in response to the chill outside my cell. It was freezing. He cradled me against his chest. I kept my breathing shallow. Steady. In time with Thomas. Trying desperately to stop it betraying me.

We passed without notice for the most part, until we came upon a door that must have led to where they kept the bodies. I could make out the voices of three gaolers.

'Evening, Reed. What's yer business here?' A lantern was hoisted in his face.

'Got another one.' I felt the shrug of his shoulders as my weight rocked between his arms.

'There's been a few ripe 'uns today. Which one of 'em's that?' I could feel his closeness as he inspected my carcass.

'One of the witches 'at's been brought up from Tranent.'

'You want tae be careful wi' that,' came a voice, his Scots so broad even I struggled to understand him. 'Did you ken what happened on Castle Hill? Men blown halfway to the Highlands by one o' them Tranent witches.' He prowled closer and I heard him unsheathe what I assumed was his dirk.

Thomas drew himself straighter. 'Well, that's two of 'em gone.'

'Aye, two down, but a few more to go. Where d'you say you found this 'un?'

I could hear the beat of his heart quicken. I could feel the sweat pour from his skin.

'Ach, hanged herself in her cell. I've seen more dead than I'd care to this day.'

'You know the rules. Check it,' the gaoler barked.

'What is it you're going tae check?' I could feel Thomas shift beneath me, readying his hand on his own dirk. 'Dead is dead.'

'Set it down.'

Thomas was calm and his hands were steady as he lowered me on to my side, gently placing my head against the granite. A boot began to poke gingerly around. First, pressing hard against my ankle and then up to my thighs. I stayed soft and limp and held my breath.

'See, dead as I told ye,' said Thomas.

A swift boot connected against my back that almost rattled my heart loose, so hard it pushed the air out of me in a hiss.

'Are you finished?'

'Alright.' He dismissed us. 'Get rid of it, Reed.'

Thomas bent carefully to the floor and scooped me back up. The rusted bolt screeched and we passed through, unobstructed, into the darkness of the courtyard. I panted deep, ragged breaths as my lungs rushed with relief.

'Yer safe. No one will find you here.' His words were small, only meant for my ears.

The world was silent but for the rattle of a cart over the cobbles, one wheel making a slow and steady clicking sound.

'I have another one fir you, Alistair,' said Thomas.

The creaking came to a stop just in front of us. 'Ach, Thomas, where've you been hidin'? I havenae seen you fir a wee while.'

'Just keepin' ma head down, Alistair. You ken how it is.'

'What are you waitin' fer? Put it in before it's anymore ripe.' He rubbed calloused hands together, dry as bones. 'Christ, if I stand here much longer, it'll be me yer burying.'

Thomas slipped me from the safety of his chest and into the waiting cart. *He won't leave me. He'll come back for me.* I repeated the promise to myself. Through the linen I could make out the outline of at least a dozen bodies. I could feel the chill from their stiff limbs as they lay beneath me on all sides. *Not long.*

'I'll be seein' you, old man. I'm off fir a wee dram.'

'Lucky fir some.'

The cart moved the length of the yard. *Click. Click. Click.* It turned left and snaked along an uneven track before coming to an abrupt halt. A quick shove and its contents, me included, were sent tumbling into a ditch. I was thrown against the bodies, like logs of wood, before we came to a rolling stop. Gasping, I pulled the linen from my face, the wind well and truly knocked out of me.

As my eyes adjusted to the darkness, I could make out the bodies. Row upon row, like a mound. Far more than I had ever thought possible. *The smell.* I stumbled to my feet, choking and gagging. A mixture of human waste, death and decay. I fought to free myself, staggering around until I found my footing.

Looking up at the vastness of the Tolbooth's wall, I could see each narrow slit filled with a spectral yellow glow, marking each of the cells of the upper floor. *Not much further.* Head down and breathing hard, I started for the side of the ditch.

Glancing over my shoulder, heart pounding, I moved slowly, unbalanced and unsteady. I took each step as gingerly as I could, as a mark of respect. Whatever had brought them here, whatever they had or hadn't done, they deserved dignity in death. I forced myself to look at a pathetic figure on the floor. A poor woman, who had clearly been hanged, lay on her back, blue eyes staring skyward.

Agnes. The thought startled me. She would be here, beneath my feet, in the mounds of bodies. I couldn't stand the thought of her final resting place being a mass grave of thieves and rapists. I had tended many a dead body, but I had never seen so many. I stared out at the sea of distorted faces. Some men, some women and some unrecognisable through the decay of time.

I took a deep breath and got to searching. Then lumps of debris skittered down. I glanced up to the rim of the ditch and spotted the solitary figure of a man. I crouched low and tucked myself flat against the blackened stone of the prison wall.

The broad shoulders and tall silhouette gave Thomas away immediately. 'Besse?' he whispered.

'Aye, ah'm here.'

He eased himself into the ditch, sending more loose earth tumbling. 'Are you alright?' he said, looking me over. 'We need tae be away from here before someone discovers you gone.' He turned, taking me by the arm.

'But Agnes . . .' I pulled away, trying desperately to roll the stiff body at my feet. 'She has to be here.'

'You cannae.' He pulled at me urgently.

'I'm not leaving her here.' Not my mother. She didn't deserve a heretics' grave.

'Besse, she's gone.' He pulled at me again. 'She's gone.'

I broke into shuddering sobs.

He seized me and pressed me to his chest. 'Please, we must be swift. We have no time tae waste.'

I fell into him. Tears streaked my cheeks. He guided me slowly, his weight pushing me onwards. But no matter how I urged my legs, they didn't want to move. So, Thomas dragged me up the embankment and thrust me on to his waiting horse, sliding in behind me.

Whether out of fear or exhaustion, I couldn't bring myself to speak. We moved together, silently, to the rhythm of the horse. The raw flesh of my back stung as we were pressed, breast to back. I closed my eyes and took deep gulps of sea-salted air as we rode.

When we reached the woods, the Scots pines blocked out every last shard of light. The darkness enveloped us. The horse became skittish, refusing to go forward. It was too treacherous to carry on.

'We'll make camp and leave at sun-up.' He set himself on the floor and lifted me down, letting the horse graze. 'Come.'

He pushed back handfuls of brambles and bracken, allowing me to crawl up a steep slope which opened into a clearing surrounded by birch and rowan, covered in new shoots. Thomas stepped back and assessed our hiding place, rearranging the thicket and twisting branches to create a better camouflage.

'That should do it; they'll no' find us here,' he said finally. 'I'll set a fire and try to find us something to eat.'

My mouth watered at the thought of it, and my belly ached. For weeks I'd eaten potage that had been about as near to meat as I had been to a bath.

Before long he was back in the grove with two small leverets, roasting them over a small fire on a makeshift spit. The gamey smell made my stomach contract. The meat was warm and moist, and I ate it heartily, sucking the bones clean of sinew and gristle. The last time I'd eaten rabbit had been the night he transported me to the Tolbooth. I could feel his eyes upon me as I licked the juice from my filthy fingers.

'I'm sorry there isnae more. It's all I could find,' he said.

'What must you think of me.' I wiped the grease from my mouth with the hem of my skirt. 'Eating like some kind of rabid beast.'

He laughed, a laugh I hadn't heard since we were children.

'I've seen you do worse, Lizzie.'

'I haven't been called that since I was a wee girl.'

'Aye, it was probably me as called you it.'

'I could always tell the proportion of trouble I was in by whether Agnes called me, Besse, Lizzie or Elizabeth.'

He crouched on his hunkers at the fire, and I sat next to him on the damp earth. 'We must find you safe passage on a ship. I know a good friend who might help us. Then we'll head to find yer daughter.'

'It feels like a lifetime since I've seen her.' I wrapped my arms around myself, resting them against the curve of my belly. 'I havenae seen her since the day of the trial. I don't know where Rupert will have taken her. It won't be home. Master Rivet would like to see him beheaded and scattered about the four corners of Scotland.'

'Aye, you could well be right about Rivet.' He filled the fire with dried bracken and broken branches. 'I've arranged to meet Richard Anderson tomorrow at sundown, to talk about a possible ship. He's to come alone, but you must stay hidden. We dinnae ken who will be out looking fir you – it could be half of the Tolbooth.'

'Do you trust him?' I asked, curling myself near the dying fire. I felt uneasy at the idea of leaving mine and Jenny's lives in the hands of a stranger.

'Oh aye, I've known him fir years. We fought together, him and I.' The light from the fire caught the whisper of a smile. 'He saved my life on more than one occasion. He's like an uncle tae me.'

'What is it he does?'

'He has a business transporting beer and he owns a couple of ships. He owes me a favour.'

He settled down next to me.

'Get some rest,' he said, placing a hand on my shoulder. I flinched.

'I . . . Besse . . . I dinnae mean tae imply anything other than friendship. If that's still what you want?'

'I ken you didn't.' *Guilt. Embarrassment. Shame. Misplaced loyalty.* Whatever it was I was feeling, there was nothing I could do about it. 'But I still have a husband. What was between us all those years ago can never happen again. Not while my husband lives and breathes.'

We spoke no more of it. I huddled next to Thomas, but he seemed restless. Sleep felt as though it would never come. My body ached and the skin on my wrists was still raw from the bindings, and my pride hurt more than I cared to admit. Worn out and exhausted, I fell asleep almost immediately.

* * *

When I woke, a grey mist had seeped between the trees, obscuring my view. It might have been near morning, but the veil of grey made it difficult to tell.

Moving off, the horse carried us with ease. Behind us, trees dissolved into the mist, leaving only the tops visible. In front, the mists cleared, revealing vast open moors and glorious feathers of red and gold creeping across the dawn. I delighted in it, closing my eyes and upturning my face to feel it against my skin.

The shock of happiness unnerved me. To feel it again after so long. The fresh spring sun on my skin. The crispness of it. Then came guilt and grief. Creeping up my throat like bile and wrapping their wicked fingers about my heart like a vice.

'What is it that's troubling ye?' Thomas said.

I faltered. Where should I start? My husband's betrayal? My missing daughter? My dead mother? Or attempting to flee, helped by one of the gaolers that tortured me? Flurries of images cascaded in my mind, freezing and flowing like the tide. I squeezed my eyes shut to make them stop. I couldn't let them take me under. *Keep going. So close to getting Jenny back.*

'Why did you do such a thing? Workin' in that awful prison?' I said.

'After I returned, I found out about my mother's passing.

When they couldn't reach me, everything had to be sold. I had no farm and no income. I knew of a man who had been working in the Tolbooth and they needed gaolers.'

'We thought you had died. Agnes and I tried everything to reach you. We sent letter after letter, we tried to stop them but the kirk stepped in and sold it all.'

The memory of it betrayed me. The ache in my heart felt as raw as the day it happened. Week after week I waited for a letter to arrive. Disappointment soon turned to worry and then worry turned to grief. How was I to grieve the man I loved, the man that wasn't my husband.

'Was someone with her? In the end?'

'Aye.' I touched his arm. *I couldn't bear the thought of her alone.* Agnes stayed with her, and I went whenever I could steal away. 'It was peaceful, in the end. She didnae suffer.'

We travelled on in silence, lost in our own thoughts. As the hours ticked by, I became exhausted, leaning back and snatching sleep, my head pressed against his warm chest. How I longed to run my fingers across it. Feel my breath against it.

The ground changed, rising into hills pitched with slabs of granite. Moss sprouted like a carpet around clusters of purple heather. A robin flitted between sparse tangles of leaves. Hopping to the edge of a branch, it peered down, beady eye fixed on us.

'Coverin' with moss the dead's unclosed eyes. The little redbreast teaches charity,' I said, reciting the words Agnes had taught me as a wee girl. 'I hope yer taking good care of her?' It took off, disappearing back into the sanctity of the evergreens.

We stopped at the foot of a rough crag and continued

on foot. Thomas took my hand as we wound our way around a deep track that traced a line of pines before emerging into a clearing.

'See there?' He pointed to a huddled lump of jagged stones, barely big enough to sit. 'I want you to stay amongst them, and don't move a muscle. Not until I say otherwise.'

I didn't think it possible, but I managed to manoeuvre myself behind the small outcrop.

It wasn't long before a man approached, so quietly I almost didn't see him. His face creased into a white-toothed grin and he embraced Thomas.

'Richard, how long has it been?' They patted each other on the back.

'Too long, laddie. Too long.' He stepped back, surveying Thomas. 'Tell me, what is it that made you call upon me in such haste?'

'A very dear friend of mine is in a spot of trouble and needs a quiet escape, and I kent you had a boat.' Thomas glanced about the clearing. 'Have you come alone?'

'Aye, just as you said. Of course, you know it's yers if you need it. I'll ask no questions. I trust you.'

'When are you next leaving?'

'Friday, weeks end.' Richard said. 'He'll have tae earn his keep, and it'll be a fair few weeks until we dock.'

'Well . . . I have a bit of a confession, Richard,' said Thomas, sheepishly. 'You see, it's a woman ye'd be helpin' and a small child.'

'What have you gotten yerself into, lad?'

'It's not how it sounds. She's a widow, simply needing a fresh start far away from here.'

'I hope this isnae going tae bring trouble to my door?' He jabbed a finger at Thomas. 'You ken I'll do ought fir you, but I'm not in the business of smugglin' women and children.'

Thomas turned and motioned towards me. 'Besse, can you come here?'

I didn't really want to, but both men stood waiting for my appearance. 'Aye, alright,' I said, making my way into the clearing.

Richard kept a remarkably still face when he saw my predicament.

'Richard, this is Besse,' Thomas said, thrusting a thumb in my direction.

He smiled broadly and raised his eyebrows. 'This is *the* Besse I've heard so much about?'

Thomas reddened. 'Aye, it is.'

'It's lovely tae finally put a face to the name, and what a lovely face it is, as well.' He took my hand in his. 'You didnae say it was this wee lady that I'd be helpin'. I'd be happy to have you aboard, lass. Do you ken the ship is bound fir the Continent?'

The Continent. The thrill of anticipation took over. Could we really make it? Escape? Start again? Without Rupert? It didn't seem possible but I had to try.

'No, but I'd be pleased with wherever you can take us. I don't have a penny to my name, but I can sew or cook if you need me to.'

What good would I be on a ship, as unbalanced as I was? I'd be a hindrance, not a help, but I had nothing else to offer.

'Not another word. You'll be my guest.' He smiled

again. 'Thomas tells me you have another bairn with you, as well?'

'Aye.' Thomas answered for me. 'She has a wee girl. I'll bring them both, as we agreed.'

I took little part in the rest of the conversation as Thomas and Richard carried on exchanging news, drawing a little closer together to continue their conversation in private. I took myself off. The last of the daylight was coming from the west in strips of grey. I circled around the largest stone, brushing at the grass with my feet. There, just in the cleft of the rock, were tiny shafts of hemlock. It would be perfect for travelling with. My mother never left home without it; she swore it warded off any lecherous advances. I stuffed a piece in the tear inside my skirts.

'We'd best be off,' Thomas said, rising to go. 'Friday, day after next, in the wee port in North Berwick?'

'Aye, I'll be seein' you. We sail at dawn.'

* * *

We travelled until we entered the glen where Mistress Cochran kept her farm, Mill House. It was almost dusk. Even from this distance I could see the yellow glow of candlelight in her inviting kitchen, and I longed for a warm piece of bread and some cheese. *Would she still welcome us if she knew what I'd done to Jonet Muir's husband?*

How had Rupert known to look for her at Mistress Cochran's? He couldn't have known. No one did. *I promise I'll find you, Jenny.*

Thomas reined up the horse near a small clearing edged with bracken and ferns. He dismounted and took me by the waist and lifted me to the ground. He made a small opening in the thicket just big enough for me to slip through.

'Hide yerself in here.'

I peered inside the uncomfortably small space. But, as I crawled in, it was much bigger than I had imagined, with just enough room for me to crouch comfortably. I pulled my skirts in after me. The deep russet colour would disguise me beneath the trunks of oak and birch.

'Make sure to tuck yer feet beneath yer skirts – they show from a long way away.' Don't worry if I'm not back at once; I intend tae speak with Mistress Cochran and I dinnae want to draw attention. I'll have them ready a horse fir you.'

* * *

I laid awake in the dimness of the thicket until it succumbed to the creeping blackness. It felt like I had been in the darkness forever. My back ached but I was thankful that the night was warmer than it had been. Every rider I spotted that was heading in my direction made my heart beat from my chest. I watched their approach, waiting for them to draw near enough for me to see that it wasn't Thomas. I'd watch them go before turning back and settling myself, and waiting once more.

I must have fallen asleep. The sound of the fast approach of more than one horse, urgent and fierce, reached me on the wind. I watched south, my eyes cloudy from sleep, but I could see nothing for the darkness.

One of the riders dismounted. My whole body stiffened.

The thicket obscured my view. I could only make out a pair of black leather boots, cracked and worn, and the black legs of a gelding.

'Besse?' he whispered. 'Besse?'

Thomas. His hair was thick and unruly, as it always had been. His face glistened with sweat, and the horse's black neck was white with foam. He must have ridden hard.

I made my way out of my hiding place on all fours. 'What is it? You rode as though the Devil himself was chasing ye.'

Did my eyes deceive me? There, on a second mount, was Willy, as thin as a whip with shoulders like knots in cotton. I shot him a sharp glance.

'Willy! What are you doin' here? Why did you no' look after Jenny?'

'Mistress Craw' – his face was dreadfully tense – 'I . . . I . . .' He turned away, eyes rimmed with tears.

'Give the laddie a minute,' Thomas said, squeezing my shoulder. 'Here, Mistress Cochran sent you this.' He handed me her plaid and a homespun dress. My fingers numb with cold and nerves, I fumbled to take it.

'I am not a spectacle fir yer eyes,' I said and waited until he turned his back – his eyes lingering a second too long – and then pulled the dress over my tattered shift.

'I think you'd better sit down,' said Thomas.

The grave look on their faces told me that it was too early for celebration. Willy fidgeted uncomfortably in his saddle, not wanting to meet my eyes.

'I'm no' going to sit down, Thomas Reed. I suggest you start talkin'.' I folded my arms.

He heaved a long sigh and paused, scratching at his

beard. 'A while back, auld Ian took Jenny to meet with Rupert. She'd found him in a cot-house not far from Goodwife Muir's.'

What had possessed her to roam the countryside looking for her father?

'It seems that Jenny had somehow convinced herself that Rupert had a new wife. Auld Ian caught Jenny trying to sneak away and confront him, so he went with her.'

'Willy, was this yer idea?'

'No, Mistress Craw. Never. I tried tae stop her but she's as head-strong as a mule.'

Rupert couldn't have a new wife. He could barely look after the one he had. He might have lost Master Rivet's rents, he might even have a mistress, but a new wife? I laughed at the absurdity of it. My husband the bedswerver. My mother was right.

'A new wife? Had away wi' you! Rupert is a lot of things, but a bigamist?' I started to laugh.

'Sure enough, Rupert was there large as life with a new French bride. Pregnant, no less.'

'A pregnant wife? I dinnae believe it!'

I was breathing heavy, my heart kicking against my chest. Another woman. Another child. Another life, and he was taking mine.

'I have no reason tae lie tae you,' Thomas said.

'Aye, it's true, mistress. He shot auld Ian when he tried tae stop him takin' Jenny. Auld Ian only just survived. He's still in his sick bed.'

'Willy tells me he took a necklace of pearls that the lassie had. Left auld Ian fir dead and took wee Jenny.' Thomas's expression was grim. 'Rupert's leaving fir France.'

'It isnae pearls, it's the rosary you gave me.'

In that instant my whole world fell away. *Jenny.* Taken by her own father. The man I thought I'd known. The man I'd bore three children for. The man for whom I'd forsaken all others. Every touch. Every kiss. Every memory. I gripped a rock to steady myself. I didn't care if Rupert fell off the edge of the world, but he wasn't taking my daughter with him.

'France?' I swallowed down the rising nausea.

'That's what auld Ian said. But he'll require a ship.'

Rupert's wedding ring. Andrew Barton was wearing it the night I was taken to the Tolbooth. Rupert had been trying to find safe passage to France for him and his bride.

'They're in North Berwick,' I said.

'What makes you so sure?'

'I might not know much about my husband, but I know this: he's a rotten gambler.' I dangled the chain wedding ring my mother had pulled from Barton's corpse. 'He lost this in a game trying to find passage on a ship to France, in North Berwick. The ship will set sail tomorrow, it leaves the last day of every month.'

'That's almost a day's ride in daylight.'

I walked over to Willy's horse and mounted the saddle, taking the reins in my hand. 'Then we had better make it a night's ride in the darkness, because I am not losing my daughter.'

The Breakwater

Jenny had spent the night listening to the sounds of her father's footsteps up and down the narrow walkway just outside the bedroom door. Cecille had been restless in her advanced confinement and frequent trips to the chamber pot had meant that there had been no opportunity to slip out unnoticed. Where would she go? She wished she had a map, then she would be able to find her way to the Tolbooth and tell them what a liar her father really was.

'Please eat something, child.' Cecille gestured to a dish of cheese, bread and mackerel that sat cooling on the side table beneath the window. The smell made her belly ache for the want of something hot in it. Jenny tiptoed around the foot of the bed, took the dish carefully between two hands and snuck it back to her bed, trying not to wake Cecille's sleeping mass of dog, Bernard.

'Would you like some?' Jenny offered Cecille the dish; her ma would be angry with her for not having good manners. And besides, it wasn't Cecille's fault that her father had turned out to be a good liar; half of Edinburgh had believed him in that dock.

'No.' She smiled and rubbed a hand on her pregnant stomach through her shift. 'We don't seem to like fish.'

The door groaned as her father opened it and leant

on its frame. His outer coat was fitted to the waist and stopped where his breeches met the top of his boots. It was adorned with fine brass buttons and fastenings. He was looking more like a Frenchman than a Scot every day.

'It's time we went for supplies, we have a long journey ahead of us and it's no long afore we will need to board the ship.'

Cecille, as pale as milk, sat propped on a collection of cushions. The great beast of a dog lay on the floor at her feet, snoring soundly. She forced a weak smile at Rupert. 'I'm sorry, my love, but I am too sick to go into town.'

Jenny spotted an opportunity. This was her way out. She could go to town, slip away and no one would notice. She could be back to the Tolbooth by sundown, find Master Rivet and prove her father's lies.

'I can go with the innkeeper's daughter, Annie,' Jenny said, pulling herself from the trundle bed. 'It'll be no trouble. I'll be as quick as anything.'

'I'll go with ye,' her father said from the doorway. 'I must attend another matter in town before we sail.'

He ruined everything. Jenny was cold in her shift, but she'd prefer to be cold than be trussed up in the navy-ness of the monstrous dress. She hated it. When she'd found her father in the woods with his new wife, she thought nothing could be worse, but then came the trial, the prospect of France and all the frilly dresses.

'Am I to wear this?' Jenny wrinkled her nose in disgust, holding the pitiful lump of fabric aloft. She hated it almost as much as she hated her father.

'You look so beautiful in blue. Please' – Cecille gestured – 'when we get to France, I will have a seamstress make you dresses from the best silk, dresses that you have never seen in Scotland. You will look even more magnificent than you do now.'

Just as Jenny was about to protest, Annie arrived, with a basket slung over one arm and a shawl about her shoulders, fastened in place with a silver brooch of a stag. 'Good morning, mistress. I'm here tae take you up into town.'

'I'm sorry, I'm simply too ill to go,' said Cecille. 'But I've written a list of what I need from the apothecary and from the seamstress before we board the ship. If it isn't too much trouble, I've given the list to Jenny.'

'Yes, mistress. When we return, I shall wash all yer things. I don't suppose you want to be returning to yer estate with gowns all spotted with dirt.' She cast an eye over Jenny, and Jenny knew exactly whose dirty clothes she meant.

'That would be wonderful!' exclaimed Cecille. 'Did you hear that, Rupert? Fresh clothes for travelling.'

He laid back against the post and muttered something barely audible. There was the father she knew, Ceceille was just rich enough to make him think before he raised his fists, but the time would come. 'Are you ready tae leave?' he said.

'Aye, I'll only be a minute,' Jenny said.

Jenny raced around the room, throwing herself around as she tied the fastenings on the dress. The shoes were more awkward, and she had to squeeze her feet into them. She tested them on the floor, but they felt clumsy and uneven, not like the shoes her mother gave her. With those, she could run and jump and climb trees.

She assessed the stranger staring back at her from the looking glass. It reminded her of the fish she and Willy once pulled out of the stream, flopping around, mouth gasping, desperate to be back in the water. She looked as uncomfortable in the navy dress as that fish.

'Please, bring me everything on my list.' Cecille reached across the bed, holding a thin scrap of paper between her fine, spindly fingers. 'Can you read it?'

Jenny snatched it. 'Ach no, I cannae, but my da will be coming with us,' she huffed, pulling a shawl around her shoulders. 'He can dae it.'

The innkeeper's daughter bobbed a curtsey. 'Yes, Master Craw.'

Annie was like one of the girls that hung around the boys, all doe eyes and waiting for one of them to marry her. Jenny wondered if Annie had a head full of sand from too much time at the coast. Her father was a gambler, a thief and a liar. A nobody. He deserved no courtesies. Her and Ceceille wanted their heads banging together.

'Come, Jenny,' he said.

He spoke to her like a dog. *Dogs bite.* She stomped after him.

'Don't forget your basket,' Cecille called after her.

She turned, snatched it from the chair and slammed the door behind her.

As they rounded the narrow stair, her father bent and stopped, glowering not an inch from the end of her nose. 'Dinnae even think about making a run fir it, aye? I can get rid o' you quicker than I did yer mother.'

Jenny balled her fists and scowled back, knowing that he meant every last word.

The entrance to the inn was right on the shore overlooking the ocean. There were sailing ships with masts flying sails that were bigger than anything she had even seen. They had been to places she could only dream of. There were the small boats, too, that must have belonged to the fishermen. She could even see the St Andrew's Auld Kirk, jutting out of the small island.

Her mother had never let her come to North Berwick before. It was because she didn't want her father to know that she was helping Agnes up at the Auld Kirk. Jenny would have kept the secret. She would have kept all their secrets.

She'd seen nothing like it in Tranent. The little fishing village hummed with life. Crowded with folk young and old, strapping young men and barefoot women with bairns at their breast. Some drove wagons piled high with wool and hides, while others led horses with little ones on their backs. The whole place smelled like sea and fish; it made her think of her mother's salted gannet.

Jenny trailed far behind, uncomfortable and unsteady under her father's gaze. As they walked, the weight of something small shifted inside the basket. Side to side. She reached beneath the linen and her fingertips grazed something smooth and cold. She pulled it loose and unfurled her hand, revealing a shilling. Cecille must have put it there.

Below a sign that showed three gold balls, her father stopped so suddenly she almost bumped into him. Jenny knew all too well what the sign meant; she'd had to go with her father often enough. The pawnbrokers.

She tried to ignore him and carried on in the direction

that they had been travelling, hoping to put enough distance between them that she could slip into the thrumming crowd.

'We must wait,' Annie said, grabbing her at the elbow and hissing in her ear. 'I promised.'

When he was gone, Jenny went and looked wistfully into shop fronts that lined the walkway. She could hear the shouts of children playing, far off near the sea. She wished she could be there with them, splashing and barefoot, with no worry for her mother and not facing a long journey to France. She could feel Annie's beady eyes boring into her. She couldn't imagine what it would be like, this place that Cecille said was theirs. The places she talked about meant nothing; they were just words, faerie stories. Jenny was just a child the first time her father went to France and her mother had told her the story of the rosary.

Now her father had it, and it was all she had left of her mother.

Annie settled herself against the wall for the long wait. She began plucking and preening at her skirts. It was like when Ian would let Jenny watch the peacocks giving a courting dance to catch a mate. Annie couldn't dance like the peacocks. Her dance was not spectacular, and her face always seemed sour, although pretty enough. She brooded and fawned like a begging dog. All her attention on the young fisherman eager to catch a wife.

It seemed like too good an opportunity to waste. While Annie was otherwise engaged, Jenny slipped away through the bustling throng. That was when she stumbled upon it, the village blacksmith. The smithy didn't raise his head as she walked in; he was too in the forge. Swords, daggers and lances all hung menacingly, and metal hissed as it was plunged into iced water. She wasn't sure what she was looking for, but she would know it when she saw it.

She moved delicately, eyeing pale-blue glass conjured to look like gemstones, that glittered on jewellery. Whatever it was, it would need to catch her father's eye, like a magpie's.

The smithy raised his head, showing a thin slither of crooked teeth. 'Look at you, with your fine dress and' – he stopped at the sight of her cropped hair – 'pretty hair,' he tried. 'You're not from around these parts.' He spoke with an Irish lilt. 'Is there something I can help you with, mistress?'

Jenny knew well enough that if they thought you were rich, they would dance to your every whim. 'I'm looking fir a gift fir my step-mother, a wedding gift, but I'm afraid my father has only given me a little money.' She tried to pronounce every word, just like the rich girls that called for her mother's help.

She watched a smile play around his lips. 'I'm sure I have something that would suit. Maybe yer father will be willing to buy something a little more expensive, fitting fir his new bride?'

'I'm sure he would,' Jenny said, as sweetly as she could, swallowing down the bile. 'for the right piece.' She picked up an intricately inlaid brooch, twisted with thistles and inset with coloured stones, but it wasn't what she really wanted. What she really wanted was already slipped into her sleeve, the cool metal of a ring pressed firmly against her raging pulse. It might be enough to make her father give her back the rosary, or better yet buy her passage to Edinburgh.

'I can see the young lady has good taste.'

Now she had his full attention. The blood roared in her ears, cheeks flushed. 'How much will you take fir it?' She tried to steady her breathing, fast and shallow.

'Six shillings fir that piece, I couldn't take any less.'

She placed it back on the counter. 'My father has only given me a shilling.' She turned, edging her way closer to the door, hand on the latch. 'There he is now. I promised I wouldnae stray far.' She felt the smithy's eyes on her, lingering. *Did he know?* The ring felt as though it was burning into her skin. She swallowed hard, fear stiffening every muscle as she prepared to run.

'Well, you best get after him then. Off you go.'

She was out of the door before he finished.

'Be sure to bring him back. Tell him I look after my customers,' he called after her.

She was off on her toes and away across the market square. She almost thumped into Annie resting against the wall, oblivious and waiting patiently for her father. Annie's homespun dress was neat and dark, fitting her slender frame perfectly. Her black curls and pale skin were offset by freckles that framed her high cheekbones. Jenny followed her gaze. Annie had her eyes fixed firmly on a young laddie carrying a basket of fish.

The first thing to go were Jenny's shoes. She slipped them off, picking up her skirts and watching her toes spread and wriggling them in the dirt. She took a sideways glance at Annie, who still hadn't torn her eyes away from the fish seller. The young fisherman ambled over, transfixed by Annie. He leaned against the wall, smiling, laughing and offering her fresh fish to take home to her father; a good catch for an innkeeper's daughter.

Foolish girl.

Jenny carefully and quietly placed her basket on the floor and disappeared like a ghost into the crowd. Silently weaving between them, unnoticed. All of them headed in the opposite direction to where she was going, and she slipped through them like an upstream salmon. She needed to get as far away as she could. She wished she had Willy or Ian with her; they would have known what to do.

Rushing through the last of the bodies, she began to run, bunching her skirts and pushing her bare feet firmly into the earth. As she rounded the corner of the last building, she glimpsed two women standing talking at the corner of the crossroads. She scrambled over to them.

'Are you lost, lassie?' said the one leaning against the tavern.

A drum roll stirred through the narrow street; men and women were coming out of every alehouse and tavern to see the commotion.

'Aye, miss, I am,' Jenny shouted over the din. 'I need tae get tae Edinburgh, can you tell m—'

Jenny's voice trailed off as her gaze fell to the line of carts that came rumbling up through the crossing. She slunk back in line with the others as they passed. The riders escorting them, on either side of the first cart, spoke in Gaelic, a tongue rarely heard in the south. It was then that she saw the first of the prisoners.

By the proud way she held her head and the beautiful silks she wore, the woman was no thief. Her brown hair tumbled in curls to her shoulders, fastened in place with the exquisite reds and golds of pheasant feathers. At first, Jenny took her for a harlot, but on closer inspection, her dress was too well made; although the crimson silk was crusted with mud and blood, it had been expensive. As she came closer, Jenny recognised her: Lady Glamis. Her wrists were bound tightly with rope, which was tied to the prisoner behind her and the next. Jenny counted five. Four women, but she couldn't see their faces, and one man. She glimpsed at his face and realised who he was: Agnes's friend, Dr Fian. *Were Agnes and her mother on the wagon?*

Her heart thrummed in her ears. She had to follow it. Quiet as a shadow, she slipped through the throng, flitting through the narrow alleyways, never losing sight of the cart. As the procession rounded back past the inn, she glanced up at the deep orange glow that shone through the window and the unmistakable shrill voice of Cecille as she spoke to her brute of a dog. She tried to duck out of sight, hoping that her father still hadn't returned.

Away from the crowd, the village was almost deserted. She crept through a narrow walkway, walled on either side that opened up on to the beach. Winds from the North Sea drove across the beach, making skittering noises through the shale. As she made the sand, she could hear the echoes of their footfall across the cobbles. The dunes opened up onto the breakwater. She knew where they would be going, across the causeway to the kirk of St Andrew's.

Jenny curled her hands into fists and headed straight for it.

Mercy

I put my knees into the horse, galloping fast. The sea-salted air whipped against my face and snatched my breath. The rolling landscape fell away in strips of charcoal, leaving the Tolbooth, Tranent and my old life behind.

We burst into North Berwick, beneath an overcast sky, sometime after dawn. The sea stretched as far as the eye could see with no hint of another shore. We slowed to a trot as we moved through the village, passing large, ramshackle buildings and streets that bustled with life. Approaching the harbour, to the left the stark shape of St Andrew's loomed over the causeway. To the right, long wooden piers reached out into the sea like tentacles. Small boats and sailing ships lolled at intervals, casting shadows into the ripples.

'He'll be at the tavern.' I knew it was true; we would find him wherever the ale flowed as freely as the shillings. I needed time to compose myself. I got off my horse and went and knelt by the water's edge, dipping my hands into the shallow waves and splashing my face, cooling my burning skin.

'There's three.' Thomas stood, filthy and damp from the rain. His hair was slicked to his head. Trickles of rain dripped from the hem of his coat and on to his leather boots, leaving specks.

'Can you take me to them?'

'Aye, but I dinnae think you should be running around North Berwick as you are. Someone will recognise you. Everyone here knew Agnes.'

The words felt strange to my ears. I hadn't thought of her as past. Gone. No longer. She couldn't be. She had always been there. For every skinned knee. Every broken heart. Thinking of her made me remember everything. The meeting of the kirk. My crushed, weeping fingers. My husband, the liar and cheat. And, finally, having to watch Agnes slowly losing her dignity and then her life. *I had been a sheep. I could do nothing but hide away like a mouse, trying to fit in. Denying the only mother I had known. No longer.*

I covered my baldness with my borrowed plaid and wrapped it about my shoulders. 'I'll take my chances.'

His face grew still. 'You ken you may only go in tae the tavern with a gentleman?'

'Aye,' I lied. Mark Acheson had always allowed my mother and I into his tavern. 'You'll be my husband, no?'

He nodded.

'What would you have me do, mistress?' said Willy.

He was tall and thin like knotty wire. He'd grow to be a strapping lad, but right now I couldn't risk any harm coming to anyone else.

'Can you stay here and guard the horses? Once I find Jenny, we're goin' tae need all the help we can get.' I patted his arm.

Finding Rupert and getting my daughter back was the only way forward. There was no going back. I began to flex my injured hand, opening and closing it against the irregular pink scar that now ran the length of my little finger. I couldn't let my hand stiffen and grow clumsy. *A healer needs her hands.*

'Here.' Thomas took the reins and walked the horses over to Willy. 'It'll draw less attention.'

'What about Anderson?' I asked suddenly, remembering the offer of transport on a ship. If I managed to get Jenny free of Rupert, we needed a means of escape.

'Aye. We were tae meet him at sunrise tomorrow, up on the coast, once I had you and Jenny. There's still time, but I dinna think he'll wait fir us.'

'Can you not send him word?'

He shook his head, smoothing the hair behind his ears. 'What am I supposed tae say? I cannae imagine you travelling without yer child . . . So, unless we find Jenny . . .' He glanced at me.

I rested my hand beneath my bust and on my full belly. 'Then we don't have much time.'

Thomas seemed to have a definite idea of where we were going. I followed as he crossed to the other side of the harbour. The track twisted up through the town. The rainwater filled the deeper hollows made by the wheels of carts, and I struggled to keep my footing in the slippery mud. As we moved between the silent houses, gooseflesh crawled up my arms. Its emptiness frightened me more than the bustling. *Where had they all gone?* It had been bustling when we arrived.

We came upon the first tavern when the sun was still low in the east. An old beggar was sitting on the step outside nursing a sore head.

'I'm lookin' fir a man who may be staying here with a young child. A wee girl of no more than twelve.' Thomas stood a little to the side, observing me as I spoke.

'No' here . . . lassie.' He slurred.

'My husband and I' – I gestured for Thomas to come closer, slipping my arm into his – 'are looking fir our daughter. She's with her uncle, and her grandmother is sick.'

A grin spread across his face. 'Witch.' He stumbled sideways trying to get to his feet.

I felt Thomas stiffen and he took a protective step in front of me.

'What did you say?' My heart thumped against my ribs.

He jabbed a crooked finger. 'The witches . . . They burn 'em.' His lips parted, revealing a row of filthy, rotting teeth. 'Burnt offerings.'

Thomas pulled himself straighter and squared his shoulders. 'I'm afraid yer upsetting my wife in her advanced confinement with yer talk of witches. What with our child missing an' all.' He laid a hand on the old man.

'See –' his gaze focussed further up the coastline – 'watch 'em burn!'

My eye followed his. Out in the bay, the morning sky was black with smoke. Flames licked from the outcrop of St Andrew's Auld Kirk. The horror of it hit me with such force that I buckled at the knee. That was where the townsfolk were. I looked around in desperation at Thomas.

'Besse' – he cupped my face in his hands – 'she's going to be alright.'

I tried to speak but the words caught in my throat.

'Thank you.' Thomas waved at the man and took me in his arms, taking my weight and steering me in the direction of the kirk. 'We'll be seein' you.'

Tears slid down my cheeks.

'What if we're too late?' I whispered. 'What if—'

As I said it, he gripped my fingers in his and pressed his forehead to mine. 'It isnae Jenny.' He stepped back. 'You have tae believe it, fir that wee one and fir Jenny.'

He was right. What use was I to anyone? I needed to keep my head.

'Half of North Berwick must be there,' I said.

He lifted his head, looking towards the causeway. 'We need to go to St Andrew's. Can you take us, without being seen?'

I nodded frantically.

* * *

It was near midday when we reached the outskirts of the Auld Kirk. I had never seen so much commotion in all the time I had visited St Andrew's. We were met by a sea of heads, all clamouring and craning for a better view, marking a half-circle around the four stakes in the centre. My blood ran cold. Thick, black smoke billowed, changing direction on the wind from the North Sea as quick as the gulls.

There were children everywhere, running in all directions while their parents chattered absently. With my plaid covering my head, I might have been anyone. I tried to stand on my tiptoes, looking for Jenny's black curls, until I remembered they had been shorn off. The girl nearest me, a slender slip of a thing, head covered with a shawl, was scanning the crowd as anxiously as I was.

'Wait here,' Thomas muttered before disappearing.

At the same moment, a ripple of excitement spread quickly through the crowd. My nerves felt jagged, raw, being surrounded by them all baying with blood lust. I could feel the energy shift and the spectators begin to gawp. I strained to see. Glancing around and searching for Thomas in the crowd.

There were four of them, hands bound in front, and linked together with chains. My pulse quickened. The first was a woman, small and elderly, whose clothes were ragged and torn. She reminded me of Agnes. I watched as she swayed slightly from side to side, unable to keep her balance, riddled with exhaustion.

The crowd jeered.

I felt Thomas behind me before I heard him. He leant in slightly. 'The first pyre is lit, fir a wealthy woman, and three more besides, but I saw no sign of any children.'

It felt as though the vice around my chest had loosened its grip. *No children.* I let out the breath I'd been holding.

I urged myself to leave but could barely tear my gaze away. I watched the elderly woman stumble, slipping and falling into the man with whom she shared chains, almost knocking him from his feet. He plucked her from the ground. He had the stoop, gait and strong features of a tall man. *Dr Fian.*

The horror of what I was about to witness crawled up my throat. I dug my nails into my palm to stop me from calling out.

As they moved him to his pyre, he began to struggle, twisting and trying to free himself from their grasp. He was a shaggy, moth-eaten wreck whose fear-etched face aged him terribly. The last thing I wanted was to watch. But I couldn't let him go to his death alone. I took a few paces forward, moving into a space that had been vacated by more unruly children. I straightened myself, being careful not to remove my plaid fully, but enough so that he could see my face. As a condemned man, the last he should see was the face of a friend.

His eye caught mine and he ceased struggling. Silence drifted over the crowd. Dr Fian straightened himself up and opened his mouth to speak.

'I renounce you, Satan, and all of yer wiles. I am guilty of what they say. I have listened too much to thee. Thou hast undone me and I utterly forsake you.'

The executioner stepped forward and spoke clearly to the expectant crowd. 'Doctor John Fian, you have been found guilty of using sorcery, witchcraft and incantations to preach at St Andrew's Kirk to a number of notorious witches, to encourage them to bewitch and drown His Majesty in the sea, coming from Denmark. You are to be executed, last day of May, in the year of Our Lord, 1590. As you have publicly renounced Satan, mercy shall be shown: you will be strangled until death and then burned.'

I looked at Thomas, tears pricking my eyes. All I could think of was my mother, and I could feel my boy moving and rolling; a foot, then a fist.

There were no drums. No noise to speak of. They simply tied John Fian to the stake and set stacks of hay all around his feet. The executioner stepped behind and guided a noose around the condemned man's neck. I held John's eye until his body twitched and went limp.

'God rest poor John,' Thomas said as we watched them light the pyre beneath him.

From where I stood, the smell of searing flesh filled my nostrils. A smell I would never get used to. No matter how many burnings I witnessed. This time, I was simply grateful that they had finally put an end to his suffering. A mixture of hoarse and grating caws spiralled in the burning sky above us as the executioner motioned for the next to the pyre.

The crowd began to surge forward, people pushing and shoving for a better view as they brought the next one out. At that same moment, I saw a flicker of movement and a flash of black hair as a man snaked between them, heading in the direction of the cobbled lane towards town.

'That's Rupert.' I pointed. 'I'd ken that snake anywhere.'

'Where?' Thomas jerked his head and looked in the direction of the lane.

'Rupert! He's gone!'

I took off after him, pushing my way through the crowd. Thomas struggled to keep up.

'Besse, where did he go?' Thomas shouted, his head and shoulders above the crowd.

'This way,' I said, as I fended off the advancing throng of spectators. 'We cannae lose him'.

I caught another glimpse of Rupert's black hair, disappearing north, behind the kirk wall. My heartbeat thundered in my ears as I started to run.

A Wise Father Knows His Own Daughter

Across the breakwater, the ground still shivered with frost in the shadow of St Andrew's. The wind keened something terrible. It was a strange place. Urgent and hidden, Jenny followed the procession, slipping through the knots of people unnoticed.

The thought hit her like a fist. She was dressed like the rich girls from Edinburgh. No one would look twice at a rich girl. She held her head high, straightened her blue dress and manoeuvred herself front and centre.

Lady Glamis's tear-streaked face gazed out upon her congregation. Jenny listened intently to the gaggle of women gossiping. 'Guilty of poisoning her husband, she is,' said the first. 'Sat up there like a lost cow,' said another. 'Fancy making her poor son watch her burn.' Jenny flinched.

The burnings were the tinder spark that had lit Scotland aflame, sweeping its way through the towns and villages of the Lowlands, and her father had used it to rid himself of her mother. She knew that now. She didn't look away when they set the pyre and the smoke billowed skywards. She had to bear witness. She had to know if her mother and grandmother were there. It was the least she could do.

Next, they ushered up Dr Fian; hands bound in front and chained to an old woman. All skin arranged loosely on bone. Jenny studied all of their faces intently. That one was definitely John Fian; she'd seen him at her grandmother's house.

Jenny moved a pace forward, straining on her tiptoes to make out the face of the last woman.

'There you are, daughter! I've been looking fir you,' came a hiss in her ear. A large hand fastened on to Jenny's elbow and jerked her from the ground. 'What did you think you were doin', leaving like that? Yer mother's no' here. I got word from the Tolbooth, she's already dead, so yer too late.'

'Dead.' It came out in almost a whisper, as if saying it too loud would make it true. 'No.' Tears slid from her eyes, hot and wet. Her chest felt as though he'd punched her in it. The pain gripped her heart like a vice. 'No! It's no true! You let go of me!' It came out in stuttering shouts.

'You'll be quiet if you ken what's good fir you.'

Her foot lashed out and she kicked and kicked, but his grip only tightened.

'You must help me! Please!' Faces turned but they all just assumed she was another wayward child being disciplined by her father.

'Excuse me, may we pass?' His voice was full of authority as he marched her through the crowd, keeping a fierce grip on her arm. 'My poor bairn's been taken over with a case of hysteria. I must get her somewhere quiet.'

They all turned away, anxious parents pulling their

children close. The girl nearest her, about the same age, peered out from behind her mother, eyes wide like silver shillings. Jenny snatched at the sleeves of the gown, pulling her close.

'You must help me! Please! I'm scairt! He's killed my mother! Please!'

'Send fir the priest! Her mother's been burnt a witch and I fear the Devil is taking her,' Rupert shouted. 'Fetch him, now!'

A roar went up from the crowd, and people began rushing in all directions, tripping over one another to get away from her. Rupert seized Jenny and hustled her in the direction of the north wall of the kirk.

Beyond, the wind made a mournful cry through the trees, slipping into the ocean that surrounded it on all sides. The air was thick with a mixture of sea fret and smoke. Cairns marked the dead, casting shadows in the midday sun. It didn't make her shudder. If her mother was dead, she would be here amongst the cairns, watching over her.

'Yer mother's daughter!' His voice was guttural. 'You could have had a life wi' us in France. Instead, you want tae fight me like a feral animal. I'll teach you.'

The grass tussocks edged the steep slope down into the North Sea. Jenny wriggled against the heavy fabric of her loathsome skirts, but he carried her like a peg puppet towards the slope's edge. He let her to the floor, keeping himself between Jenny and any means of escape.

'Da, Da, I'm sorry.' The words stuttered as she clamoured to her feet, back to the sea.

'I can't let you ruin it fir me, Jenny. I have a chance tae make somethin' of myself. I can be a nobleman in France, with a new wife and child.' He was pacing. 'I cannae stay here, a pauper and peasant collecting rents fir Master Rivet. I know that you must think ill of me.' His voice was soft now as he moved gradually closer, crowding her against the top of the slope down. 'You must believe me,' he said, reaching for her. 'I never wanted tae hurt her, but she wouldnae leave me be, hunting all over the countryside, her and her mother.'

She had heard it all before. Seen him after he'd covered her mother in bruises. Full of sorrow. Full of guilt. It never lasted.

'But you killed her, Da.' The words stung her as she forced them from her lips. 'Bound to a stake and lit like a torch, sent tae the Devil fir somethin' you accused her of. You betrayed her. You betrayed me.'

'My sweet Jenny. You're my only child.'

He stepped towards her. She caught the flicker of movement from the direction they'd came. Through the floating mist, she could no longer see the light from the pyres. A dark shadow of a woman sailed between the cairns. The kirkyard was not a place to come without a powerful charm, and Jenny crossed herself. The spirit came closer.

Rupert swung around, aghast at the sight before him.

'You leave my daughter alone!' it said.

Truth

Rupert slipped and stumbled backwards, letting out a cry. Trembling, he reached into his pocket and pulled out a small wooden cross, holding it before his face, praying aloud to the Blessed Virgin.

'Rupert . . .' I came no nearer but pulled down my plaid, exposing my bare head.

'Yer . . . Yer dead! Mary, mother of God!' He crossed himself, moving further away and crowding Jenny ever closer to the slope down. 'Her spirit come back tae haunt me!'

'You'll wish I was, Rupert Craw.'

I saw the lightning-quick flash of rage across his face. 'Besse. My beautiful Besse.' His voice was soft now, and he moved towards me, brushing a hand gently down my arm. I stiffened. 'I didnae think I'd ever see you again, and look at you: what have they done tae ye?' He moved his body gradually closer, slipping his hand to my cheek. 'We must celebrate, finally reunited with my wife and about tae be a father again?' He stroked my swollen belly.

There was a time when that would have worked. When I would have believed it. Now, he repulsed me.

'Which wife would that be?'

While I had his attention, Jenny seized her chance and

edged her way towards the kirk wall, in the direction Thomas was hiding. She would be safe.

'What d'you mean?' His eyebrows raised with surprise. 'You know that there's only ever been you. I'd ride tae Hell fir you and back again.'

There was his first lie. I felt the air change. I couldn't tell if it was the set of his jaw or the look in his eye, but his darkness was boiling beneath the surface.

'You couldn't imagine I'd abandon you and Jenny? My wife and child? And now another babe on the way.'

'I hear ye've two wives now. Mibbe more.'

I saw the blank, dark look in his eyes.

'I dinnae ken what you mean?'

Lie number two.

'You know very well what I mean. I know about the woman who carries yer other child.'

His eyes narrowed, and I knew then that there was no going back. The sea began to rush behind him, spewing sea-salted spray.

'Do you now?'

'Aye,' I said. 'I grew suspicious when I met a privateer who went by the name of Barton. He carried a wedding ring around his neck; said a man had lost it in a game of dice, trying to win passage to France.' Rupert hadn't expected this; I watched his eyes widen. 'I'd ken that ring anywhere.'

He stopped for a moment, the corners of his mouth twitching, I wondered for a second what he might do.

'A man can lose at a game of dice, can he not? It isnae a crime.' He smiled cruelly.

'Aye, a man can bet on a game of dice; lose, even.' I

stared directly into his eyes. What had come over me? He no longer frightened me, after being tortured by true Devils and surviving. There was nothing more Rupert could do. 'You wanted passage to France fir you and yer lovely new bride with a baby in her belly. I'm goin' tae see you hanged fir adultery.'

At that, I could see by the look on his face that I had gone too far. He clamped a hand on my elbow with such force that I cried out. A rush of nausea climbed up my throat.

'You should be dead,' he said menacingly. 'Tied to a stake. Lit like a torch and launched into eternity! Before I left, it cost me ten shillings tae have Rivet name you as a witch. And Jenny almost caught me plantin' the belladonna on the table . . . I couldnae have planned it better.'

He threw me down.

'Rivet? Did you pay that beast tae rape me as well? Why? Because I was in yer way?'

'Not tae rape you, no, but who am I tae begrudge a man his pleasures.' His hazel eyes met mine. 'I have a wealthy woman in Cecille; her late husband had a business selling wine in France and she can give me healthy weans.' His hand grazed my stomach. 'I can have the life I truly deserve.'

'Did you ever love me?'

'I was fond of you, aye, but then again, I was fond of that old sow we had.' He was playing with me now. 'I'd always hoped ye'd inherit the property from Agnes, but frail as she was, she was planning tae outlive the rest o' us.'

The sea fret became heavier, and driving rain howled in

from the North Sea. The corner of his mouth twisted into a lopsided smile. He meant to hurt me.

'So, you did it then? Had Agnes and me arrested so you could inherit what was left? Is there anyone you havenae deceived and betrayed?' I choked on my words.

'Aye, I hadnae anticipated the wee witch's child, kicking and yellin' and roaming all over the countryside screaming fir it's mother.' His head snapped around, looking for Jenny. 'The apple disnae fall far.'

A look of shock spread across his face. He pulled me close to him, wrapping his fist around my arm until I was twisted so close to his chest that I could feel his breath against my lips. It felt as though the arm would break. My eyes filled with tears. 'What witch's tricks are these? Where is she?'

'Somewhere safe, away from you.'

The deep-set hazel eyes, that I'd once loved, blazed at me.

'Fetch her, Besse,' he growled. 'I'll no' be tellin' you again.' I could barely hear him over the crashing of the waves.

Standing as close to the top of the slope as we were, I could have taken us over. The fathomless North Sea, as rough as it was, and they'd never find the bastard again. And I'd go to heaven knowing that my daughter was safe. I suddenly took a step forward, pushing him back.

My baby boy. I felt the movement, just enough to bring me back to my senses. 'You'll never have her or my son!'

I heard the crack of a branch and a flurry of footsteps to my rear. Rupert's head flung round as he realised that I wasn't alone.

'You took yer time,' I said.

'It didnae seem fitting tae interrupt until the Bailiff had heard every word,' said Thomas, advancing with North Berwick County Bailiff David Lowrie and a handful of his men.

Rupert released his grip and stared at the group of men that surrounded us. 'Arrest her!' he demanded, pointing at me. 'She sold her soul tae the Devil himself.'

'I sold my soul the day I married you, Rupert Craw, and now I'm taking it back.'

It was David Lowrie that spoke next. 'I want this vagabond, Rupert Craw, arrested. Wanderers are the chief cause of our problems. Spending twice as much as labourers as they lie idly in taverns day and night, drinking excessively and plotting their crimes.' He turned to a man next to him. 'Send word for the arrest of Master David Rivet for abuse of his position as the County Bailiff of Tranent.'

'Dinnae listen to her poisonous tongue!' Rupert kicked and screamed as they led him away in irons. 'Lies! Every word of it!'

A small crowd had gathered by now. Jenny pushed her way through the gawkers. 'Ma!' She came running and wrapped her arms around me. I pressed my lips to her head. I thought I'd never let go.

'Jenny. My sweet Jenny,' I whispered through hot tears. 'Is it really you?' I held her face in my hands, taking in every freckle and every fleck in her hazel eyes. Her black hair was all but gone. I closed my eyes and held her tighter. She was crying as hard as I was.

'Ma, he . . . he told me you were dead.' She sniffed,

wiping her eyes with the heel of her palm. Looking at me as though I was an apparition. She pushed her face into my chest and clung there.

'Are you alright?' I felt her nod. I stroked the top of her head. 'I promise you, I'll never let him hurt us again.'

'Besse' – I felt Thomas's warm hand against my shoulder – 'the bailiff is lookin' tae pardon you. We must go to the village.'

I turned to him and gave him a weak smile. My whole body trembled with exhaustion. My elbow was still tender, throbbing where he had grabbed it. I imagined the purple finger marks exploding into existence on my pale skin. A final reminder of what he was. Of what he always had been.

Slowly I put one foot in front of the other, never letting go of Jenny. Thomas placed an arm around my shoulders, pulling up my plaid and holding it there.

The sea of spectators parted, allowing us room to pass. The fret had started to lift, revealing the tops of taverns and inns shadowed by a sun that sank lower in the sky. The tails of smoke faded on the wind. One step and then another, the three of us clinging to each other as though one of us might break if we let go.

When we reached the other side of the causeway, I was breathless. Thomas found us a bed for the night at a local inn. My head buzzed and my body ached as we made the last of the stairs. I slowly pushed open the door to the smell of supper. The shutters were closed and a candle flickered in the darkness. Compared to what I had endured, the room was spacious and comfortable. The bed was as heavy with bedclothes as my eyelids.

'Get some sleep, Besse,' Thomas said.

'I'm so sorry . . . I . . . Thank you . . .' was all I could manage.

He put a hand under my chin and turned me to face him. 'Ye've no need. It was the very least I could do. You need not be scairt anymore. I promise.'

I put a hand on his arm and squeezed my thanks. 'Where will you sleep?'

'Just in the next room. I won't be far. Goodnight, you two.' He pulled the door to and was gone.

Jenny took the supper of cheese and bread and sat at the hearth. In all the time we'd been apart, had I forgotten how to talk to my child? I sat on the floor next to her, my skirts bunched around me, full-bellied. She carried on eating and stared into the fire. Neither of us wanted to speak.

'Jenny . . . I . . .' She put her tiny hand in mine and squeezed it. My heart felt as though it might burst. 'I'm so very sorry.'

'Is that my wee brother or sister?'

I had forgotten that she knew nothing of it.

'Aye, it is. A wee boy, I think.'

She scrunched her face. 'Ach, another laddie, I'm surrounded by them. But dinnae be naming him Rupert; give him a good name like Willy or Ian.'

It was something I hadn't even had time to think of. 'We'll give him a fine name. You can help me pick it, if ye'd like?'

'Aye.' I watched her chewing and swallowing ravenously, thinking. 'I was scairt, Ma, really scairt. I thought you were dead and then Da took yer rosary, and he was goin' tae sell it. I dinnae think he did, but yer here now and we're together and that's all that really matters.' She shovelled in another mouthful.

'Dinnae worry yer heid about the rosary; there will always be another.'

She sat quietly for a while, until the candle melted into a puddle of wax and the embers of the fire glowed red.

'Ma, did auld Ian die?'

I could tell by the way she asked it that it must have been eating away at her. 'Ach, no,' I wrapped my arm around her, pulling her tight. 'Have you been worrying about that?' She nodded. 'He was hurt bad, aye, but he got back tae Mistress Cochran's and he told her about what yer da had done.'

I felt her body relax then. 'He was really nice and he helped me, and it made me sad tae think of him dead.'

As she said the words, it made me think of Agnes. 'Jenny, I have something tae tell you.' I kept my voice steady and an arm around her. 'You ken Agnes was arrested?' I felt her nod. 'She died, before we could get her home.'

'Nan was very old, Ma. Mibbe God just wanted her wi' Him? You ken everyone loved her company.'

There was a heavy pain in my chest, like a broken heart, where my mother should have been. I felt tears prick my eyes. To be a bairn again and look at the world through her eyes.

Jenny stood up, already out of her dress and crawling into bed in nothing but her shift and closing her eyes. I curled myself on the bed next to her and fell immediately asleep.

I woke some time before dawn, to faint noises from

outside my door. The creaking of floorboards echoed from the hall; the steps were slow and heavy. I felt uneasy. I still hadn't received my pardon. I sat bolt upright, my hand feeling around in the darkness for the tinderbox and candle. Lighting it, I slid out of bed as quietly as I could, being careful not to wake Jenny, and wrapped my plaid around my shift. Once I peeled open the door, I paused, watching through the small crack.

Thomas paced the corridor. I stepped out and pulled the door to.

'What are you doing, sneakin' about out here?'

'I wasnae "sneaking" about, as you put it,' he said testily. 'I just couldnae sleep, is all; worried that the bailiff might renege on his offer of pardon. Reckless to think otherwise after what ye've been through, until we have sight of it, at least.' He looked down at me, face troubled. 'So, ah thought it best that I stay out here as tae keep you and Jenny safe.'

'Thank ye,' I said. 'It's very kind of you, an' I'm sorry we've caused you so much trouble.'

His face broke into a broad smile then. 'It's been no trouble, and I would do it all again. Go on back tae bed, and I'll be here.'

I looked towards the light that was seeping in around the shutters. 'The sun's almost up, why don't you come in?' I pulled my plaid a little tighter. 'We can have breakfast before we go tae the kirk tae meet the bailiff. I'd appreciate the company.'

Justice

We talked quietly over the remnants of supper until the sun rose. Thomas had been my suitor all those years ago and now I counted him as my only friend. I watched as he knitted his brows together in concentration whilst trying to fasten his dirk to his belt.

'I informed the bailiff that we would attend this morning,' he said, examining the dirk before he placed it down on the table.

'What of Rupert?' I picked the dirk up, fastening it for him.

'He's been imprisoned and held fir trial as a persistent adulterer. He's tae be taken to court this morning and tried.'

'A capital offence.' I flinched, in spite of myself. I didn't know if, in good conscience, I could see my husband go to the gallows.

'Aye, it is.'

Just then, Jenny stirred. I stopped suddenly and shot Thomas a look. 'Are you hungry?' I asked, changing the subject and praying that she hadn't heard any snatches of conversation.

She climbed out from beneath the mound of blankets and stretched. Short curls of hair were scattered about her head. She padded to the small table near the fire and looked about at the offerings that were left. 'Aye, a bit.'

There were three dry oatcakes and a pat of butter between us. 'Only oatcakes,' I said. 'Eat up quickly, Jenny, we must travel to the Barony Court.'

'Who are we going tae see?' Jenny asked.

'We're going tae see the County Bailiff, David Lowrie,' I said.

From what I had heard David Lowrie was a fair man, trying to make a name for himself on the Court Circuit. Not content with sitting idly by, he made sure he always uncovered the truth. From what I had seen of him last night, that appeared to be the case, though I doubted that Rupert would appreciate the gesture.

We had been told to meet him at a tavern in the village before making our way to court. We stopped and tethered our ponies outside. Jenny complained about the uncomfortable navy dress she wore from the moment we stopped and, by the time we were inside, she had turned her attention to her uncomfortable shoes.

My eyes adjusted to the gloom and, although the air was stale, I was pleased of its warmth. I hadn't felt thawed since I left the Tolbooth. There were three or four men sitting round a table, talking to each other in low voices. They stopped and stared at us. My stomach rolled.

'Elizabeth Craw.'

I heard the voice of David Lowrie calling me from the rear of the tavern. I held tightly on to Jenny's hand as I made my way towards the slim, silhouetted figure standing by the open window. He was dressed in a clean saffron shirt, smart breeches and a dark waistcoat.

'Please, Goodwife Craw . . .' He motioned to the seats spread out across from him. 'When Master Reed here called upon me yesterday I couldn't quite believe what I was hearing.' He stopped, gesturing to the owner of the tavern. 'Could I offer you a drink?'

'No, Master Lowrie. Thank you, but no.'

'Very well.' He carried on. 'When we converged at the kirk, I listened to everything that Rupert Craw said. He awaits trial and I will attend later, in the hope of a confession and his reconciliation with God. Would you like to make peace with the accused?'

'Master Lowrie,' I said, smiling as gracefully as I could, 'I really would like tae receive my pardon to allow me to continue with the rest of my journey and—'

'I feel it necessary that you meet with the accused,' he interrupted, strumming his fingers against the table. 'As his victim, it is only just. I'll arrange fir you to attend him in his cell and then I shall have yer pardon ready.' He waved a hand dismissively.

Yet another man telling me what to do.

One of Lowrie's men sidled over to us and waited impatiently. 'Mistress, if ye'd like to follow me?'

He hustled us out of the door and across the street, towards the North Berwick holding cells. Jenny walked between us, so sweet and innocent. I didn't want the last memory of her father to be of him in a cell.

Thomas saw the expression on my face. 'Jenny,' he said softly, bending down to her, 'I need tae tend the horses. Do you think you could help me?'

She looked from Thomas to me and back again. 'No, I dinnae think I want to leave my ma.' She clamped her hand around mine and took a step closer.

'I promise, it will only take a minute,' I said. 'Thomas will take good care of you, just like he has done of me.' I smiled and squeezed her hand. 'He brought me home tae you, didn't he?'

Her brow furrowed as she came to a decision. 'I'll help, but you have tae come straight back.' With that she threw her arms around me, gave me one final squeeze. As they wandered towards the bustle of the market, I watched as she groped for his hand. She looked so tiny in comparison.

* * *

My young escort rattled the keys on his belt, in an attempt to hurry me along. With one final glance, I disappeared beneath the heavy lintel of the court.

I fought off waves of nausea as we moved down the narrow walkway. I followed his step as we passed barred cells filled with thieves, rapists and murderers, all being held for court. I clasped my hands together to stop their shaking. Why did it trouble me? Was it not only days since I had been behind walls just like these?

Rupert was being held in the last cell, overlooking the main crossing. He had his back to me as I approached. I expected him to look barely recognisable, the guilt of his crimes etched about his posture. But he stood there with perfectly combed black hair, gold and navy waistcoat, like he wasn't a monster.

'Rupert Craw, you've a visitor.'

He turned. Surprise turned to realisation. Had he expected his French bride? He glared at me, lips pressed tightly together.

'I'll be here.' The young man took his leave and leaned uneasily against the far wall.

'What is it you want from me?' Rupert said.

I took a deep breath. 'They've said you'll hang.'

'So they say,' he said, eyes resting on me. 'I want none of yer pity.' He moved again, back to the barred window, and peered into the street.

'Pity isnae my intention, Rupert.'

'Then if it's yer rosary ye've come for, yer too late. I sold it to buy passage to France.' He let out a noise like the start of a laugh. 'Though I canna see that I'll be making the voyage.'

'Have you no remorse? You've robbed me of my mother and almost robbed me of my life, leaving my child without a mother.'

'No.' His hazel eyes settled again on my face; a darkness flickered beneath them for a second, and then it was gone. 'My only mistake, if you can call it that, was not seein' you burn.'

I quelled the sudden urge to vomit. The nausea came over me in a wave. How could I expect remorse from a self-serving adulterer? A man who thought me of no consequence and took what he wanted because it felt good.

I opened my mouth to reply but suddenly whatever had tethered us as man and wife was finally severed. I stared at him for a moment, a man I no longer knew. I took a step back.

'You're going to die,' I said. 'May God have mercy on yer soul.'

His face drew into a wicked smile. I had seen something in the depths of his eyes, something that I never wanted to ever see again. I turned back down the darkened corridor and to the doorway, leaving him there to the king's justice, just as he had done with me, but for crimes he was guilty of.

I didn't realise I was crying until I tasted the salt of my tears.

EPILOGUE

Five months later

From my mother's chair at the window, the crows looked like flies as they wheeled and flapped, crooning, just as the sky lightened with the new day. Jenny carried Agnes on her hip, tickling her, making her cackle; such a joyous sound that I never thought I'd hear again at Leaplish.

This was our home now. The home I'd grown up in. Agnes rushed into the world, with a shock of red hair and my green eyes, not three weeks after my pardon, much to my surprise and Jenny's delight.

It was hard to look at my girls and not see Rupert in their faces. I tried not to think of him, but mibbe it was a gesture, a smile, a word, and then I'd see him in there. He'd been buried in the north side of the church with the heretics. Some days, when the wind was just right, I thought I could hear him. But I pushed it aside; his ghost has no hold on me. We have a fresh start.

When I'd been pardoned, they'd pardoned my mother as a gesture of goodwill, for all they had put us through. David Lowrie gave me my mother's land and family hearthstone. Thomas made sure to bring her home for me, and we'd buried her where the land met the forest. Around her, I had planted row upon row of herbs, flowers and plants to bring the bees humming back to life.

The door to our room was ajar to let the fresh air drift in. I poked my head cautiously in to see my new husband sleeping soundly, turned away from the door and slightly worse for wear.

Jenny burst into the dimness of the kitchen, causing the candle to sputter. I still hadn't managed to extract her from the breeches and saffron shirt that Thomas had bought her in North Berwick.

'Thomas, come and see Agnes,' she said, smiling. 'She loves it when I tickle her!'

His lashes fluttered. 'I will, as soon as the room isnae spinning as much.' He propped himself up, holding a hand shakily to his head. He never could handle his drink.

I laughed, leaning on the door frame. 'Dinnae listen. If yer waitin' fir the carpenters in his forehead tae abate, I think you'll be waiting until the week's end.'

She waited, fidgeting in the doorway.

'Go on,' I smiled. 'He'll be out in a wee while.' She scurried back out.

When I looked at Jenny, my mother was all I could see. Even though we shared no blood, she was there, in Jenny's boldness, in her fearlessness and her spirit. She would always be with us, and now we had little Agnes. Tears pricked my eyes.

Thomas wandered over to me at the window, putting a hand on my shoulder. 'Are you alright?'

'Sorry?' I had been so mesmerised with the girls I hadn't heard him.

He looked down at me. 'Are you sure you're alright? You were crying.'

I placed my hand to his cheek. 'I was crying fir the joy you've brought me, and I thank God every day fir the man that you are and that I get tae spend the rest of my life loving you the way you've always loved me.'

He pulled me close and kissed my forehead. We stood entwined, me pressed to his chest and my arms around his back, listening to the beating of his heart. He took a deep breath and nodded.

'God knows I am thankful fir you, Besse, and wee Jenny and Agnes.' He said softly. 'I only wish Agnes was here to see us now.'

The night we'd arrived home, I'd gone to the hive and knocked gently, murmuring the doleful news to the bees that their mistress was dead. I would be as good a mistress as I could be, but I would never be Agnes.

'I think we'd better see what all the fuss is about,' he said.

I sniffed and wiped my face. 'Aye, I think we'd better.'

Clutching my plaid around me, I followed him outside and into the autumn morning. We walked side by side over to where the girls were sitting in the grass. Agnes lay propped on a blanket, gurgling in the cool October sunshine while Jenny flitted up and down the lines of plants, pruning and picking berries and leaves to replenish our stores of apothecary jars. I was delighted that she had been taking such an interest, and now with Thomas allowing me to work as a healer, I'd be able to earn a steady living. He had even been tutoring me with my letters, to allow me to read Dr Fian's notes on leech work.

Thomas scooped Agnes from the floor, cradling her in the crook of his arm, and she squealed with delight. He placed an arm around me, drawing me close. 'Our wee family.'

'Aye, our wee family.'

ACKNOWLEDGMENTS

Where do I start with who I need to thank?

First, my editor, Edward Crossan, and the whole team at Polygon for their incredible insight and support throughout the editing and publication of this book, helping to make it everything I hoped for and more.

To my mentor, Lily Cooper, and everyone at Future Bookshelf for the amazing opportunity and for her incisive advice and support.

To my wonderful beta readers, whose unwavering support got me through. I have to give a special mention to Rebecca Netley, Kate Galley and Julia Kelly, who have listened to me waffle and, at times, stopped me throwing my laptop out of the window.

To the writing sprinters, without you and our nightly sprints, I would not have powered through. Your sympathy and solidarity helped when sometimes I felt like a turtle stampeding through treacle! I can't thank you enough.

I couldn't write the acknowledgments without mentioning the phenomenal #VWG whose advice, support, inspiration, humour and gifs kept me going. Such amazingly talented writers and all-around good eggs!

And finally, to my family.

To my best pal, Sharon Duffy, who read early drafts and supported me and listened to me witter on every day at the stables without question. Thank you!

To my mam, for instilling in me a love of reading from

an early age with our trips to the library and for all your love and support.

And to Molly, for always being interested in my writing adventures. x